WHEN THE MOURNING DOVE CALLS

LEIGH ANDERS

ACKNOWLEDGMENTS

Many thanks to all who helped me bring my story, *When the Mourning Dove Calls*, to life. It was a collaborative effort involving many special people.

Special thanks to my son for sharing his expertise on some of the tools that law enforcement uses to identify and locate bad actors. I admire your patience and appreciate that you didn't ignore my annoying and repeated questions.

Thanks to Brandon for the cover design. As always you created a classy and professional cover that captures the essence of my story. It entices the reader to step inside to meet the characters, and to share the joys and the sorrows in their lives.

Thanks to EC and MJ, my editors. Your insightful directions, comments, and suggestions were always right on target. You helped me flesh out my characters and brought out the best in my story.

And thanks to my amazing family. Your love and support mean more than I have words to describe. Some of the scenes in my book are drawn from a life of knowing all of you. My oldest sister is the one who made me aware of the Appalachian plant called love vine which is depicted in my story.

Lastly, thanks to the people of Appalachia for your courage

and strength during good times and bad. Your colorful legends and beautiful mountains have added flavor to my life as well as to this story.

PROLOGUE

Afghanistan

First Lieutenant Kelsey Barrett shifted her position on the hard ground. The stone grinding into the flesh of her left hip was starting to feel like a boulder. She peered through the darkness at her companion, Captain Jason Wilder. He seemed oblivious to the cold, rocky ground where they had taken position. The only thing that broke the stillness was the sound of his breath moving in and out, in and out, in a soft rhythm. He lay motionless—propped up on his elbows—stone-like. He had hardly moved the whole time they had been lying here on the plateau. *Unlike me,* she thought as she wiggled again to further dislodge the stone.

The night was black, with visibility down to just a few feet. Captain Wilder's profile was barely visible in the darkness. From his stillness, one might assume he was asleep. He wasn't asleep, though; he was on full alert. Kelsey sensed this by the way he cocked his head a little to one side, as he often did when listening for unusual sounds in the night. His head moved ever so slightly as his eyes swept back and forth, scanning the darkened landscape for signs of danger.

Captain Jason Wilder, team leader, and First Lieutenant Kelsey

Barrett, his second-in-command, waited in the tall grasses above their target: a shack in the shallow valley below. They watched for any movement around it, but their interest was centered on one man in particular. They were prepared and ready to carry out the mission their commander had sent them on. Their actions and re-actions tonight could mean the difference between life and death for the team.

He isn't made of stone after all, Kelsey thought as she felt Captain Wilder shift his body. He flexed his forearm and moved his elbows into a different position. His thigh gently bumped against Kelsey's. Tension ran along the muscled length, and an answering tension ran through hers. Kelsey was caught off guard by the contact. She muffled a gasp as unexpected warmth tingled through her body. She didn't move away. Her desire to nestle closer was strong.

The accidental touch and the warmth from Captain Wilder's nearness awakened thoughts Kelsey hadn't allowed herself to have since she deployed to the war zone in Afghanistan—thoughts of male companionship, and thoughts of how much she missed her loved ones back home.

What was this? Was First Lieutenant Kelsey Barrett of the US Army homesick? She was usually successful in fighting off her loneliness or thoughts of home and was always the first to prop up other soldiers when they felt the pressures of deployments. Was she now caving under those same pressures?

Kelsey normally refused to allow her current circumstances to matter, even for a second. She had toughened her mind against loneliness. And yet, while watching her back was a daily require-ment in her job, the conditions and dangers they faced tonight were unsettling. Being plopped down in the middle of enemy territory can give a person a new perspective. Thoughts of happier times were inescapable.

Kelsey exhaled quietly and momentarily gave in as thoughts

of love and home washed over her. She shifted slightly to her side and gazed at Captain Wilder through the darkness. Human contact was what she missed the most. She longed to reach out, to touch him, to guide his arms around her, to lay her head on his shoulder. Tonight, she just wanted to be hugged, and to feel safe and protected by someone who cared just for her.

A simple act of comfort and the connection to another human being would drive away the odd feeling that had fallen over her, the feeling that she was floating alone—an insignificant speck in a vast and dangerous universe—unconnected to anyone. The desire to belong and to be connected to someone was strong in her heart, but her head told her she couldn't act upon the impulse.

Kelsey squashed her sudden urge to reach out to the captain and turned back to face the surveillance target below.

A sigh, barely audible, escaped Captain Wilder's lips. Was he also tired of his solitary existence? Kelsey's father, a retired army colonel, had warned her prior to her first deployment that one of the greatest enemies in a war zone was loneliness. Was Captain Wilder also struggling with this silent enemy tonight?

Maybe the captain was like her, missing his home and the people he loved and those who loved him. Most of the time, Kelsey looked at her situation practically—she had voluntarily joined the army, after all—and she accepted that being unhappy or lonely in her current assignment was a waste of time. As an officer and squad leader, she needed to set an example for the soldiers she led, which included keeping her thoughts and emotions under control and to always stay focused on the job.

But there was something different about tonight. A strange, eerie vibe was in the air, and that strangeness made Kelsey long for the comforts and the normalcy of home. The silence, the darkness, and the dangers they faced from an enemy intent on killing them cast a dark gloom over her. Crazy thoughts were finding space in her head.

Hoping to quell her uneasiness, she let her mind dwell for a moment on her family thousands of miles away. She could almost smell the aromas of her family's holiday dinners drift through the dark Afghan night. When the Barrett family got together, there was always good food and laughter—laughter that filled her grandparents' old, large, wood-framed house in Atlanta. For a brief moment, the scents of home replaced the odor of sweat, sand, and grime that clung to her clothes and body after an overnight march to this spot overlooking the shallow valley below.

Thinking about her loved ones back in the US made her feel better, but memories were a poor substitute for being with them.

Stop! This is a useless exercise, Kelsey silently chastised herself. She quickly blocked all thoughts of home. *You're here because you chose to be. End of story!* She gave herself a mental shake and refocused her wandering thoughts.

This was neither the time nor the place to wish for things that would not be possible any time soon. She couldn't allow herself to be distracted by memories of home... or thoughts of anything else. Plus, the hard metal ring on her left hand reminded her that it would be a mistake to give in to her loneliness. Even if all she wanted was a hug from her handsome fellow soldier, she'd be entering a dangerous minefield, possibly starting something that she might not get out of unscathed.

She didn't know Captain Wilder well in a personal way, which made her urge to snuggle closer to him seem even crazier. He was simply a fellow officer assigned to Major Burton's platoon. They attended meetings together, and she saw him at gathering spots around the post. He was never paired up with another female soldier, so he probably had someone waiting for him back home. He was always friendly when they met, but Kelsey generally kept herself aloof so as to avoid any personal entanglements. She flashed her engagement ring, and he, like all the other men, never moved beyond normal chitchat or army business.

Captain Wilder would be shocked if he knew about her reaction to his touch and the longing it set off. *Accidental touch*, she reminded herself.

Kelsey shrugged. Her earlier runaway thoughts concerning Captain Wilder just proved that underneath the mannish camouflaged uniform and heavy helmet she was a female after all—and one who could appreciate the attributes of an attractive male. And attractive he was. Captain Wilder was tall, trim but muscular, with dark-brown hair and probing dark eyes—the kind of male vision that filled most women's dreams.

Kelsey admitted to herself that in another place and time, she would have been attracted to Captain Wilder. But not here, and not now. A person had to protect their heart as well as their life in a war zone. Kelsey needed to get back to her loved ones in the States with both intact.

Above all else, they were soldiers first, both dedicated to the army and the oath they had taken. Personal relationships were a luxury neither had time to explore, even if they both were willing and ready for a romance. Their normal assignments—leading community-engagement teams—dealt with different segments of the local population. Kelsey's team worked with the women and children, while Captain Wilder worked with the males and tribal leaders. When they were not on patrol, they spent most of their time in debriefings or resting so that they could do it all over again the next day.

The community engagement teams made frequent trips to local villages to meet and talk with locals to gather information, shore up support for the fledgling Afghan government, and blunt any propaganda spread by insurgent organizations such as the Taliban and ISIS. It took patience and long hours of work to earn the trust of the Afghan citizens.

This was the first time Kelsey had served directly under Captain Wilder's command, but she had heard of his reputation. He was bold and smart, but never let heroics get ahead of his brain.

He never asked his team to do anything he wouldn't do himself. When a team member asked a question, Captain Wilder didn't need extra time to think and study, nor did he fumble around for an answer like some team leaders did. He had already done his thinking; had assessed, accepted, or discarded different scenarios and had his answers ready.

"He'll do whatever it takes to protect this team and get the job done in the process," one young soldier told Kelsey when she joined their special mission. She hadn't seen anything that would make her doubt those words.

"I'm going in closer. I can't see anything from here." Captain Wilder's voice pulled Kelsey out of her thoughts. His breath tickled her ear as he leaned close and whispered, "You stay here. Lie low and stay sharp." He rose up on his forearms.

Kelsey shook her head and started to rise. "I'm going, too. Four eyes are better than two," she protested.

"No!" He pushed her back to the ground. "And two bodies are easier to spot than one. Stay here, Lieutenant! Give me the 'owl signal' if you see anything. Can you manage that?" Most of his face was covered by his night-vision googles and camouflage paint, but Kelsey could see his white teeth as he grinned at the inside joke.

The "owl signal" was what the team had decided on when Kelsey admitted that she had never been able to whistle. She could not mimic any of the whistling calls of the birds that were indigenous to the region. The best she could do was the low, moaning, dove-like call of the pallid scops owl. Kelsey's whistling deficiency had made her the butt of many friendly jokes during team meetings, but it was agreed that she and Captain Wilder would make two dove-like calls if the enemy was spotted nearby and three if it was time for the ops squad to move toward the target.

Kelsey acknowledged the captain's command to stay on the plateau, and with that, he was gone, crawling on his stomach as he moved at an angle down the hill. Only a slight swaying of the grass gave any indication that someone was moving closer to the hut in the clearing below. At the moment, he didn't look like Captain Jason "Wildman" Wilder. His team had dubbed him "Wildman" due to his toughness on missions and his willingness to put himself in harm's way for the team. Now, he looked more like "snake man" as he silently slithered down the hill.

Kelsey smiled. She'd have to give him a new nickname when this was over. Back at the post, they would all raise a glass in celebration of a successful operation, and she'd make a toast to his new designation: Captain Jason "Snakeman" Wilder. Perfect! Plus, it would be payback for his teasing reminder about the owl call.

The team had marched through the night to reach the spot on the small plateau where Kelsey now lay. There was a shorter route, one that Major Burton preferred, but Captain Wilder had argued successfully that the shorter route across flat terrain left them exposed and subject to sniper fire. The mountainous route was longer and more difficult, but safer. They had successfully navigated the rough mountain terrain to reach their destination. The rest of the team—the ops squad—was now in position, hidden in the trees and bushes on the western side of the hut, awaiting Captain Wilder's signal to move in.

Kelsey rose higher on her elbows to see if she could spot Captain Wilder. Nothing moved in the direction he had crawled. "Snakeman" had disappeared. She swept her night-vision binoculars across the landscape near the hut. There was nothing but trees, rocks, and bushes. No thermal image came into view through her infrared scope.

Captain Wilder was right: they needed a better angle to identify their quarry than the rise where they had set up surveillance. His point about two people moving down the slope would increase the potential of being spotted was right, too. A lot of work and planning had gone into the operation. They might not get another chance to capture such a high-value target any time soon.

Word from an informant had reached Major Burton that there would be a meeting between one of the tribal leaders, Abdul Khalid, and an ISIS leader, Syed Khan, that night. Khalid was on the verge of cooperating with the US Army and thereby rebuffing the dangerous ideology of the terrorists led by Khan. So why had Khalid agreed to this meeting with Khan? This was a question the army hoped to have an answer to after they captured Khan tonight. They needed to keep the mercurial Khalid moving in the army's directions and prevent him from making a one-eighty turn and pledging his allegiance to Khan. After many years in Afghanistan, the army had learned that allegiances were fluid and could often be bought by the highest bidder. Plus, if they pulled this off, the amount of information they would gain from the ISIS fighter would be enormous.

Major Burton had selected twelve soldiers whom he considered the best for this special mission: two officers, First Lieutenant Barrett and Captain Wilder, and ten sergeants, of which two were also trained as combat medics. Captain Wilder, as the senior ranking member, was the leader of the team. Lieutenant Barrett and Captain Wilder's task was to identify Khan when he arrived at the hut for the meeting and signal for the ops squad to move in.

Kelsey shifted slightly. She was becoming stiff from lying in one position on her stomach. She and Captain Wilder had been on the rise for almost three hours. They were positioned about one hundred yards south of the hut, directly in front of the door, and close enough to hear the voices of the visitors as they approached the hut.

One reason Major Burton had selected Kelsey for this mission was because she understood the language. She had minored in Middle Eastern customs and languages in college and was familiar with Farsi, one of the two official languages of the country. However, there were many local dialects among the Afghan tribes across the country. Kelsey had a working knowledge of the local language through her contact with the tribes and the interpreter assigned to her engagement team. It would be her job to communicate with Khan until he was turned over to the intelligence officer who would do the official interrogation.

Dark clouds covered the moon and blotted out most of the stars. The forecast for the cloudy night was probably why Khalid and Khan had chosen this night for their meeting. The hunter and the hunted needed much the same conditions. But the dark night that permitted the team to move silently into position also limited what they could see, even with night-vision googles.

Several visitors had come and gone from the hut below, but thus far, Kelsey and Captain Wilder had not spotted the insurgent leader among them. Each time the door was opened, all they saw was the small, dim glow of a lantern on a table on one side of the room. The men wore scarves wrapped around the bottom half of their faces, making it virtually impossible to identify them from the plateau.

Captain Wilder's decision to move down the slope would take him closer to the vicinity of the hut and the trail leading to the meeting place. This was a dangerous move, though not outside the "Wildman's" reputation for doing whatever it took to ensure a mission's success. Without the capture of Khan, their mission would be a failure.

A black shadow moved along the path toward the hut. Kelsey sharpened her focus through her binoculars. She strained to hear the voices. A guard greeted the man as he approached. There was a different inflection in the guard's voice as he welcomed this visitor. Respect? Admiration? The guard practically bowed to the visitor.

This had to be Khan. Kelsey felt the certainty in her gut. The new arrival was a tall man, and unlike the earlier arrivals, he moved with purpose and authority. His profile fit the description of Khan. As the door partially closed behind the newcomer, Kelsey raised her head, hoping she could spot Captain Wilder. He would give the signal to the special ops squad. Where was he? Did he also recognize that this was their target?

Kelsey peered through the darkness. Her ears strained to hear the signal. Through the dirt-stained window of the hut, she saw men moving back and forth as they helped themselves to drinks. The sharing of drinks was a welcoming ritual and a good sign that the meeting was now in progress.

A low, moaning, dove-like sound—three calls—came through the darkness from near the front of the hut, where Captain Wilder had gone. This was the signal. Kelsey's heart rate sped up.

It was "go time"! Kelsey rose up onto her knees to get a better view.

At first, there was just a pop and a flash coming from the hill to the northeast of the hut. The sound built quickly, though, and soon roared into a loud boom. A projectile flew through the air and landed on the roof. The roof's dry boards splintered into pieces, adding more kindling to the fire. It spread quickly, and the hut burst into flames.

More explosions followed, much louder than the first. Pieces of debris flew into the air, lost momentum, and then made a fiery descent toward the earth. As the burning fragments of the hut landed on the ground, they set the grass on fire. The flames soon engulfed a wide swath of dried grasses, trees and bushes that surrounded the hut. The dry conditions enabled the fire to race through a large portion of the countryside.

The force of the blasts traveled up the hill and threw Kelsey backward. She landed with a thud several feet away from her lookout post. As her body slammed into the ground, she heard a sharp crack in her right leg, followed by searing pain through her left thigh. Waves of agony burned through her body as the blood poured from the gash on her thigh. A large object came out of nowhere and slammed into her helmet, knocking it to one side of her head. A smaller piece of shrapnel followed and smashed into her temple. The last thing she saw was the silhouette of a body blown high in the air in the midst of the inferno. It was suspended for a moment, outlined by an orange glow from the fire. Then it disintegrated and fell to the ground in pieces.

Kelsey opened her mouth to scream, "Wilder!" but no sound came out. The muffled cries of pain and surprise from the victims filtered through the night, then quickly faded as the sound was overtaken by the roar of the fire. Within minutes, it had destroyed the building, its occupants, and much of the surrounding countryside.

Oh God! No! Not Wilder! Not the team!

As the faces of her mother and father floated before her, blackness descended over Kelsey and blotted out any further sounds of the carnage. Her shocked and injured body slowly slipped into peaceful unconsciousness.

CHAPTER ONE

D ad, you can't keep me locked up here behind a desk forever," Kelsey protested. "It's been three years since my injury. I'm suffocating." She placed her hands on her throat
and coughed to drive home the point.

Her father, Colonel Joseph Barrett, US Army, Retired, rolled
his eyes, unmoved by her playful display. "I'm not giving you anything more dangerous than what you're doing now. You can forget
it."

"What danger am I in now? Falling off my desk chair?" Kelsey
countered.

"I don't want you out in the field," the colonel replied. "End of
discussion."

"But it's just a small contract with a local government." Kelsey
ignored the "end of discussion" comment. "How much danger
could there be?" She rose from her chair and approached her
father's desk.

"There's always danger in surveillance," Colonel Barrett replied. "I wish Richard had never mentioned it to you."

"He didn't tell me much, just that it's in the mountains of

North Carolina—some peaceful, country hummock like Mayberry. By now, I figure Sheriff Taylor has retired and Opie is sheriff." She paced in front of her father's desk. "What could they possibly need? Someone stole a family's pet pig, and the sheriff needs help finding it?"

"Kelsey, this is nothing to joke about. It's far more serious than that. And I repeat, all surveillance can be dangerous. Besides, cybersecurity is a national threat right now, and our contracts in that area increase every day. You're needed here in that job."

"I know it's not funny. I'm only trying to get you to lighten up." She had hoped to make her father laugh by bringing up one of his favorite TV shows, *The Andy Griffith Show*. He still watched the reruns. He claimed it reminded him of his uncomplicated boyhood.

Changing her tone, Kelsey continued, "No one knows more than I how surveillance can go wrong." Her gaze shifted over her father's head and out the window, and she began unconsciously rubbing the scar on her left thigh. She started to count the clouds in the blue Atlanta sky—a helpful distraction she often used to drive the fiery memory from her mind. Images of the explosion and the body blown to pieces, as well as the months she had spent in the hospital after that night were never far from her mind. Kelsey had learned not to dwell upon what happened in Afghanistan, but it didn't take much to bring it all back to her.

She was tired of her father coddling her. She understood that the hours he and her brother, Joe, had spent sitting beside her bed in the army hospital in Landstuhl, Germany, had taken a toll on them. Her condition at first had been tenuous and scary for them. Shortly after her arrival at Landstuhl, the doctors had inserted a monitor into her skull to track the pressure of a hematoma in her brain. The force of the projectile from the blast had knocked off her protective helmet and slammed into the side of her head. Fortunately, the feared brain swelling from the deep bruise never materialized, and the hematoma healed on its own. Her family had been unable to do more than wait and pray for her recovery. The long days of worry had left a mark on them.

Kelsey was eventually well enough to be moved to Walter Reed National Military Medical Center in DC. She faced weeks of physical therapy for her broken leg and injured thigh, but the toughest recovery had been during her many sessions with a staff psychiatrist as she tried to cope with the loss of her team. The doctors were all heroes, but it was the combat medics who had found her unconscious on the plateau and saved her life by stopping the bleeding in her thigh. They had provided first aid for her other injuries until they moved her to the post hospital.

She had survived the ordeal, and now, her father needed to let it go—to not allow his fears to rule his life or hers.

Kelsey's father, Colonel Joseph Barrett, had started Barrett Security Consultants after he retired from the army. He had spent much of his thirty-year career in intelligence, so his experience translated well into the private sector as a security consultant. With the explosion of the information age, ransomware, blackmail threats, and the theft of intellectual property, there were many CEOs who needed his company's expertise.

Colonel Barrett hired experienced people in all areas of security work—both IT and physical security—and worked with foreign and domestic companies. Over the years, Barrett Security Consultants had earned a reputation for getting the job done. Whether it was a simple stakeout, complicated undercover work to root out theft, or uncovering highly organized groups involved in hacking and data security breaches, he had people who knew how to catch the bad guys. There were also some secret operations that even Kelsey was not privy to.

Kelsey had joined her father's company after she left the army. It was a safe place to hide until she could piece her life back together. At first, she had been content to focus on cybersecurity. It offered a diversion from the turbulent thoughts that had taken up residence in her head. Even in her dreams, a video of Captain Wilder being blown high into the air played over and over again.

When the army's medical staff at Walter Reed had cleared Kelsey to return to active duty following her recovery, she was assigned to a desk job in the Special Ops Center at Fort Bragg. This administrative job did not require her skills as an analyst and manager of intelligence data. She had an experienced staff that handled most of the routine duties with ease. Frequently, she felt useless because there was little for her to do except answer questions from the staff, make a few minor decisions, schedule training, and be the liaison between the staff and the commanding officer.

Kelsey felt she was well enough to go back to serving as an engagement team leader in Afghanistan, but with her injuries, it was unlikely that the army would send her back into a combat zone so soon—and perhaps even ever.

She was stuck in a holding pattern, serving in a position created just to keep her out of the way. She sometimes caught herself daydreaming and reliving the camaraderie she had shared with the soldiers she served with in Afghanistan. There had always been a feeling of serving a greater purpose—a one for all, all for one feeling. Now everyone in her office, including herself, were separate units going their separate ways. They were not a cohesive team, where each member was dependent upon the others in a joint endeavor. She missed that part of her former job.

When it came to sharing information about the fatal, failed operation, the army had clammed up "tighter than a tick," to use one of her grandfather's expressions. It was as if it never took place. She was rebuffed each time she tried to find out what had happened to the other team members. All she managed to learn was that at least five members of her team had been killed, though no one would tell her who they were. She also spent considerable time wondering who had survived, where they were, and what they were doing. She thought frequently of Captain Wilder. The image of his body being blown into the air had been burned into her brain forever. It was the worst image left by the carnage that night. She could still see his body suspended in the air, outlined against the bright orange glow of the fire. In the end, the heroic exploits of the "Wildman" hadn't been enough to save him. It was a painful memory, but that didn't keep her from thinking of him. She even imagined she saw him in person a couple of times.

One day, as she was coming back to the office at Fort Bragg after lunch, she saw someone walking toward the Ops Center who looked like Captain Wilder. He was tall and fit, with an athletic build, similar to Captain Wilder. He even sported captain's bars on his shoulders. Her heart quickened, and she walked faster to catch up with him. Her silent plea of, *Please, please, please*, matched the sound of her footsteps as they hit the sidewalk. She needed this man to be Captain Wilder. She needed that confirmation that the images in her mind were wrong and that he hadn't died that night. She was just about to call out to him when the captain stopped and turned to speak with another soldier on the sidewalk. Her heart dropped. It wasn't him. "Wanting him to be alive will not make it happen," she muttered as disappointment flooded through her.

Kelsey still blamed herself for not spotting whomever shot the projectile—it must have been an RPG, a rocket-propelled grenade—at the hut that night. Of course, it was ridiculous to think that she was more skilled than her teammates or the drone operators whose job it was to spot such dangers and call off the operation. And yet, her contrarian self always came back to the knowledge that she had been stationed on the hill as the lookout. So, why hadn't she seen the shooter?

"Failure always breeds what-ifs and questions," Dr. Watson, her therapist at Walter Reed, had explained. "Your subconscious tries to justify what happened or creates some type of action you could have taken to prevent the failure. It's the mind's way of attempting to overlay a failure with a different outcome." Dr. Watson paused, looked at Kelsey, and added, "Sometimes, you have to accept that there's nothing more you could have done."

After many weeks of thinking up different scenarios that could have prevented their failure, Kelsey came to accept that it was also possible, if not probable, that the informant had been working both sides, passing information to both the Americans and the terrorists. It frequently happened. As time passed, the physical injuries she'd sustained in Afghanistan healed. The psychiatry staff at Walter Reed had helped her mentally, teaching her how to deal with the nightmares when they did come. Thankfully, they were infrequent, but she had no control over when they came or what triggered them. But in the light of day, she could handle those, too. Except for her lingering questions about the mission and the horrible scenes from that night that still played through her head at times, Kelsey managed to live a pretty normal life. But she wasn't happy, and she wasn't fulfilled.

Perhaps if she had been given the opportunity to do more as an army officer, that would have replaced the bad taste that lingered in her mouth after the failed Afghan mission. Not long after she was assigned to Fort Bragg, her three-year active duty commitment was over, and she decided to end her time in the army. She couldn't say it was a reluctant decision. She had many reasons for leaving active duty. The memory of that night in Afghanistan was something she never wanted to experience again, yet she longed to use her skills as an intelligence analyst. Everything added up to one conclusion in Kelsey's mind: the failed mission she had been a part of was a black mark on her record. She still had a reserve requirement, but the army's upper echelon seemed happy to see her leave active duty. And so, she chucked her military career and left for civilian life.

Now, her life was normal. Normal, but boring.

And here she was, stuck again. In the three years since her injuries, the memories had faded somewhat, and she was beginning to long for more action—something different that challenged her. She was tired of hiding out within the walls of her office in the middle of Atlanta. She wanted to take on more diverse projects and get out into the field. And she never missed an opportunity to inform her father of this.

Kelsey could now look at what she knew about the Afghan operation more objectively. It was war, and missions in war do not always go as planned. Now, she just had to convince her father that she had moved on from that failure and was ready for this job in North Carolina. It was a small contract, perfect for her to ease back into fieldwork.

It also sounded more interesting and personally rewarding than staring at a computer screen all day. Kelsey longed to interact with people face-to-face in the field again.

Her father, however, treated Kelsey like a delicate flower, always refusing to let her do anything more than monitor computer screens and probe clients' computers for glitches in their software systems. Complaining about the limitations of her job was becoming annoying to both of them. She was tired of nagging him and begging for a different assignment. It was time to change tactics.

"Am I going to have to resign and take a job with a competitor to get to do fieldwork?" Kelsey half-asked, half-threatened. She was not giving up this time. She would keep nagging until she wore him down. "I'm as qualified, if not more qualified than any other person you have in this area. You do know that, right?"

"It's not about you being qualified. You're my daughter. It's my responsibility to protect you."

"That same old tired argument? Can't you at least come up with a new excuse? I'm twenty-nine years old. Who's going to take over the business when you retire? You know Joe plans to make the military his career. He's happy in the army, especially now that he's been promoted to major and transferred to Fort Bragg. You're getting old and can't keep working forever. I'm your best hope, and I need to learn about all aspects of the business." Kelsey grinned, taking the sting out of her words. Her father was the least "old" sixty-two-year-old she knew. Still, it served him right for being so overprotective.

"Joe will still be young enough to come onboard when he retires, just like I was. I plan to leave the company to both of you—with instructions for him to keep you working in-house." He smiled back at her. "I understand your frustrations and your desire for more fieldwork. If I weren't so old, as you put it, I might feel the same way. But, Kelsey, if something happened to you again, I'm not sure I could survive." He got up from his desk and came around to stand in front of her. He sighed. "This old man is just worried about you."

Kelsey reached out and hugged him. "I was only kidding about your age. You're more energetic than someone half your age. Don't worry. I'll be careful."

"Accidents can happen even when you're careful," Colonel Barrett replied. "I wish you would listen to me, but you're just as headstrong as I—and your mother—were at your age. If she were here, I'd have to listen to both of you preach about how women should have the same opportunities as men."

"She would," Kelsey replied softly as her eyes misted. "I miss her, too—even her tirades about women's rights."

Colonel Barrett smiled slightly. "She could get wound up over any injustice." He paused, then asked, "You know my decision isn't about you not being capable of doing the job, don't you?"

Kelsey saw indecision on her father's face. Her arguments must be wearing him down. She went in with her closing argument: "This contract is a one-person job, but if you're nervous about me going alone, send Ron with me. I don't want you to worry, either, so this would give you peace of mind."

"Hmmm." Her father walked to the window and looked out while he sorted through his thoughts. The clogged streets of Atlanta appeared to hold his attention, but Kelsey saw the wheels turning as he mulled over her proposal, weighing the pros and cons. "All right," he finally said, relenting. "But you'd best not do anything risky and nothing without approval from Ron."

"Sheesh!" she snorted, though she did not object to his instructions. "Agreed." A half-loaf was better than no loaf. It was a start. Kelsey hugged her father, then made her way to Ron's office to give him the good news.

Kelsey and Ron had been best friends since fourth grade when he moved in next door. When her father was deployed to other bases, her parents retained ownership of their house just outside Atlanta and rented it to other military families who were passing through for a few years. When Colonel Barrett received orders sending him back to Atlanta, Kelsey and Ron picked up their friendship right where it had left off.

They attended the University of Georgia together, where Ron was a student-athlete on the basketball team. Only when Kelsey joined the army did their paths separate. In the meantime, her father recruited Ron to join his company as soon as he graduated from college with a computer science degree. When she left the army and joined her father's firm, they again picked up their friendship.

Ron had even visited her at Walter Reed. She happened to look up one day, and there he was, standing in the doorway, smiling the crooked smile she had missed while she was deployed. He greeted her with, "What the hell, Barrett?! What happened to you?"

"Nice to see you, too, Blackledge," she retorted. "What took you so long to come and visit me? New girlfriend wouldn't let you leave town?"

They were back to giving each other a hard time, much as they always had. Ron teased her about the tufts of regrowth on the side of her head where her hair had been shaved because of her head injury. She teased him about his recent "life-threatening" injury when he hurt his shoulder playing basketball with a friend at the gym. Kelsey's world partially righted itself as they fell back into these old patterns.

Now, Kelsey stepped into Ron's office, which was located just down the hall from hers. "Guess what," she exclaimed.

"With you, I can't imagine, Kels," he replied as he turned away from his computer screen and smiled. The skin around his blue eyes crinkled in amusement. He still maintained his athlete's physique, and a small scar on his cheek—his "war wound," he claimed, from playing basketball—just added to his handsomeness. It didn't hurt that he had floppy blond hair that was always falling down onto his forehead. Kelsey would never dare tell him this, though. His head would get even bigger than it already was.

In college, her girlfriends had been jealous of her close friendship with Ron. Kelsey always insisted that they were just close friends, but one time, one of her girlfriends responded, "Girl, you're crazy if you don't hook up with that."

"I'm going to North Carolina, and so are you," Kelsey said in answer to Ron's comment.

"The colonel agreed to let you go? And I'm going, too? Are you sure?"

"Yep! He gave me the assignment on the condition that you tag along as my babysitter. We need to see Richard for the details, then plan our strategy."

"Let's go." Ron shut down his computer.

As they exited his office and started down the hallway, Kelsey chatted excitedly about getting out of the office. She was practically walking on air as she matched her steps to Ron's long stride. "I've been wanting to do something different and cut the strings to my computer. It's a small job, but it's a start," she said.

"I know, Kels. You tell me at least once a day," Ron replied with a smile.

They entered Richard's office and sat down across from him. *Richard Frazier*, Kelsey thought, *the most boring man in the world.* She instantly felt ashamed. He was actually a very nice person, but what interested him didn't interest her. She had gone out with him a few times. Her friend Tina was responsible for that.

Lately, Tina had been haranguing Kelsey about going out, having a social life, and forgetting her bad past relationship. She hadn't exactly been a nun and had dated a couple of other men since her return to Atlanta. They were all perfectly nice, accomplished in their chosen fields, and had interesting backgrounds, but the spark she expected from a relationship had been missing.

Kelsey was still wary of becoming permanently involved with anyone. The emotional scars from her breakup with her ex-fiancé, Lucas, had not completely healed. Her disappointment over having placed her absolute trust in someone who then failed her miserably still hurt. It made her wary of trusting anyone again.

Kelsey knew Tina was right, though: she needed to go out more. And so, she gave in and agreed to go to dinner with Richard. After all, it was just dinner. It wasn't as though she were making a long-term commitment. He was a safe choice where her heart was concerned. The problem was that going out to dinner with him meant she had to listen to business talk for two-plus hours straight.

But it wasn't Tina's fault that Kelsey agreed to go on a second date and then a third. Richard seemed so earnest about every-thing—*everything*—especially if it had to do with his job, and she didn't want to hurt his feelings. Unfortunately, not hurting his feelings had given Richard the wrong idea. He now thought and acted as if they were a couple. She had refused his last two re-quests for a date, but he still hadn't gotten the message.

"Here's a copy of the contract," Richard said as he opened a file on his desk. "I made it clear to the colonel that this is a one-person job, so there's no reason for you to go, Kelsey." Richard also sometimes thought he was the company's CEO.

"I asked to go. Just give us the details, so we can finalize our plans." Kelsey didn't mean to be sharp with him, but he struck a nerve. She had exhausted herself arguing with her father, and she didn't need any preaching or harassment from someone who was an employee just like her. She needn't have worried about Richard's reaction to her comment. He usually missed all comments that didn't fit his point of view.

"The sheriff in Haygood County, North Carolina, in the town of Mason Valley, requires an agent for surveillance. He has a situation with two runaways—or maybe not runaways. He doesn't know for sure. The girls in question, two eighteen-year-olds, claim they left home of their own accord."

"Who notified the sheriff?" Kelsey asked.

"Their parents think they've been kidnapped by a local cult. A militia leader—or something along those lines—has set up a camp there in the mountains. A real nut, apparently." Richard paused, then continued. "As I said, the parents think they were kidnapped, but as I told the colonel, we don't need to get involved in a family dispute. He doesn't see it that way, though. He believes we should give law enforcement all the help they ask for." Richard's tightened lips showed that he still disagreed. "The parents have tried to get them to come back home, but they won't."

"Why can't the sheriff handle it?" Ron asked.

"I don't know any more than what I've told you. You'll have to get the details when you arrive." Richard closed the folder and pushed it toward Ron. "I take it you'll be the lead on this little operation? You're the senior member, after all." Did Richard have to make it a point that this was her first field job for the company?

"We'll be co-leads," Ron replied and winked at Kelsey. He stood to leave the office.

"Kelsey, could I speak to you for a few minutes?" Richard asked as she moved to follow Ron.

"Sure. What's up?" Kelsey said, turning toward Richard. Ron closed the door behind him on his way out, but not before Kelsey caught his smirk. She'd kick him later.

"I'd like to take you to dinner tonight. You won't be leaving until tomorrow or the next day so, I've made reservations at—"

Kelsey cut him off. "I'm sorry, Richard, but Ron and I need to go over our plans for the surveillance. There are several things I don't understand about this operation. I need to talk with Ron. You know, get his take on what he thinks we'll find in North Carolina." She couldn't believe Richard's arrogance in making reservations without checking with her first.

"Sure. Sure. I understand. Maybe when you get back."

"Sure," she echoed as she turned toward the door. *You said 'Sure'? Damn!* Kelsey berated herself as she closed Richard's door and started down the hall. Why couldn't she just tell him that their relationship wasn't working and couldn't work. *Coward!* She was disgusted by her own lack of courage in speaking up and saying what she really felt. But she remembered the pain she had experienced when Lucas, whom she thought she'd be spending the rest of her life with, had callously broken her trust and her heart. She didn't want to inflict that kind of pain on anyone—not even annoying Richard.

As Scarlett O'Hara famously said, "Tomorrow is another day." And didn't someone else once say, "Put off until tomorrow what you don't have the guts to do today"? That's how the saying went, wasn't it?

Kelsey made her way to Ron's office. They discussed what the upcoming operation entailed and concocted their cover story. Tina, Kelsey's friend and one of the company's administrative assistants, rented a house for them in Mason Valley under the name of Ron and Kelsey Moore.

They were a married business couple from Atlanta looking for property to lease for the establishment of an executive and corporate retreat. They needed walking trails, terrain suitable for a zip line feature, a lake for fishing, and other appropriate amenities. This would explain their need to explore the woods around town. Hopefully, no one would become suspicious if they spent a lot of time in the woods. They would adjust their plan as they got into the surveillance operation, and as the need arose.

Kelsey set up the image of a happily married couple in her mind and tried to mentally get into the role. Forgetting their undercover names and yelling, "Hey Blackledge," as she was prone to do around the office, would not be a good thing once they reached Mason Valley. They needed to guard their cover from everyone they came into contact with. If the two girls had been abducted, their lives might depend on it.

No slipups, she reminded herself, as her thoughts immediately went to the failed operation in Afghanistan.

CHAPTER TWO

Kelsey and Ron left Atlanta mid-morning the next day. It was approximately a four-hour drive to Mason Valley, located a little north of Asheville. The black BMW SUV they drove was newly leased in the name of Kelsey and Ron Moore—an extra precaution just in case a person with the means and the curiosity decided to run their license plates. "Careful" was the watchword in everything they would do in the coming days.

As they left the state of Georgia and entered North Carolina, there was barely a noticeable change in scenery. But as they drove further north, the terrain became more mountainous, with curving roads and thick stands of trees that hugged the road. As they neared the town of Mason Valley, Kelsey marveled at the beauty of the landscape on either side of the roadway. Late April had brought out spring blossoms and thick vegetation that covered the sides of the mountains. Large stands of wild dogwood and redbud trees painted wide swaths of white and red against the green backdrop of tall pine, elm, and poplar trees. It was beautiful country.

In some places, the road came extremely close to the mountain. Kelsey couldn't stop herself from pressing an imaginary brake pedal when they met oncoming traffic on the narrow two-lane road that wound upward. Each time they encountered a passing car, Kelsey held back a gasp as she peered out the passenger window. Just how close to the gorge on the right was Ron driving? They frequently passed signs that read, "Beware of Rockslides." Ragged cliffs lined the road, a sure sign that rockslides might indeed be a problem.

"I see you have your engagement ring on," Ron said, breaking the companionable silence. "Oh, heh! Looky there! A wedding band, too, this time."

Kelsey stretched out her hand and turned it back and forth. The rings sparkled in the sunshine streaming through the window. She hadn't worn the ring since the medics had removed it to treat her injuries in Afghanistan. "Just playing my part and getting the feel of the ring again," she replied.

"Good idea. Who would have thought I'd be married to the mean girl who threw mud on me the first time we met?" Ron asked with a chuckle. "You ruined my Batman T-shirt."

"You shouldn't have messed with my mud pies. I was building up my inventory for the bakery I planned to open." Kelsey folded her hands in her lap. "Admit it, you started it."

"That mean girl hasn't changed much as she grew up, has she? In fact, she's meaner than ever," Ron teased. "She left poor Richard all alone and went off into the wilds of North Carolina."

"Richard doesn't appreciate my love of adventure," Kelsey replied.

"You mean Richard isn't an adventure himself? Hearing him talk about himself doesn't make your heart jump?"

"Don't pick on Richard. He's a nice guy."

"I hear wedding bells," Ron declared as he laughed loudly.

Kelsey playfully slapped his arm. Ron liked to tease her about Richard, but she teased him back about his vast array of girlfriends. She had stockpiled a lot of ammunition over the years.

They lapsed back into silence, and before long, the road widened into a broad valley. They spotted the town up ahead. As they entered the city limits, a few people turned and watched as the unfamiliar SUV drove by.

A Google search done prior to their departure from Atlanta had told them that Mason Valley was a typical small city with a population of about twenty-five thousand. The town covered several blocks, and its hub was centered around Main Street, with its boutiques, cafés, a theater, a hardware store, a couple of coffee shops, and sundry other small businesses. A travel agency that offered rafting and other tourist excursions stood on the corner of Main and Cherry. Big-box stores were located along the town's periphery, and residents drove to Asheville for items they could not find in Mason Valley.

Saturday shoppers milled around Main Street. They frequently stopped to look at stores' window displays as others exited clutching shopping bags. A woman with two children in tow called down the sidewalk to someone she knew. She retraced her path to chat with her friend.

The town was already like a busy beehive this morning, and Kelsey knew that once the tourist season got into full swing, the crowd would grow to twice its current size. As they passed the courthouse, she noticed small groups of elderly men sitting on benches under the trees and talking. They frequently passed a coffee can down the line, and each man would deposit his tobacco spit into it before it circled back around again.

Kelsey had seen similar activity in the villages of Afghanistan. The marketplaces were the hubs where locals gathered to shop, visit with neighbors, and catch up on gossip. These were two different cultures, but with the same routines.

"Look! There's the sheriff's office," Kelsey said, pointing to a two-story red brick building set at the back of a large parking lot. "I wonder if the sheriff is in today."

"We'll find out later. First, we need to get settled in," Ron replied.

The SUV's navigation system led them down Main Street, then directed them to turn left onto Willow Street. They passed a row of homes that were built in the middle of what Kelsey guessed were large, one-acre lots. Their destination was one of those homes.

"1204 Willow Street. This looks like the one." Ron pulled into the driveway of their rental house, a single-story clapboard home with a front porch. A large, well-maintained lawn that was starting to turn bright green in response to the warm spring days surrounded the house.

"Oh, yay! A porch swing," Kelsey exclaimed. "Just like the one at my grandparents' house."

"This is nice," Ron said as he climbed out of the SUV and looked over the house and property. "One thing about country living: they believe in having lots of space between houses."

"Yes. My grandparents say that Atlanta used to be that way years ago. Not anymore. Or at least not where their house is located."

"Let's take our bags in, get unpacked, and then go see if the sheriff's in," Ron suggested. "I've got questions, and I hope he's got the answers." Ron opened the trunk and retrieved their luggage. "I'll carry everything in. Wouldn't want nosy neighbors seeing the little wifey lug these up the steps."

Kelsey shot him a look. "That's only if we're newlyweds. It might be more credible if you left them all for the wifey to carry in." She knew he was right, though; they needed to always be aware of their cover story. It was showtime, and her feminist independence needed to take a backseat whenever they were in public. It was a habit of hers to play the offended female, especially with Ron because, well, it got under his skin. And she had never been able to pass up an opportunity to needle him.

Ron carried their bags inside while Kelsey held the door. He had to make a second trip for the extra bag that held their weapons and gear for the climb up the mountains. They unpacked and arranged their belongings in the house. Ron insisted Kelsey take the master bedroom with the attached bath. He settled into one of the extra bedrooms. He left a couple of his shirts on a chair and a pair of shoes on the floor of Kelsey's room.

"Just in case a looky-loo happens to wander over," he explained.

"That makes sense." She paused, then added in a teasing voice, "Shoes and shirts scattered around the bedroom? I see you are the typical husband."

"Hey, I don't do this at home! I may have annoying qualities, but messy isn't one of them," Ron shot back. "By the way, your cynicism regarding the male species is unbecoming, Mrs. Moore."

Once they finished unpacking, Kelsey and Ron retraced the route they had taken earlier and parked their SUV in front of the sheriff's office. They made their way to the front door. Ron held the door for Kelsey to proceed him.

A tall, dark-haired man in a tan sheriff's uniform shirt and denim jeans was pulling folders from a filing cabinet against the back wall when they walked in. He turned toward them at the sound of the door opening, a welcoming smile on his face.

Kelsey looked up to greet the sheriff and extended her hand. Her breath caught in her throat, and her outstretched hand froze in midair. The face of a ghost stared back at her. It was the same face she had seen blown to bits time and time again in her dreams: Captain Jason Wilder! There was no mistake. It was him. The piercing eyes—dark orbs in a currently whitened face—stared back at Kelsey. They reflected the shock in her own eyes. A stack of folders tumbled from his hands and landed on the floor with a thud.

"Oh my God! Captain Wilder?" Kelsey's voice was barely above a whisper, but the effort to speak woke her shocked and frozen body. The thaw didn't happen all at once, but slowly traveled up her body in waves. Her knees weakened. Then, her stomach clenched and twisted into knots. Kelsey's hands began to shake, and her lips trembled. Her whole body was shaking as she tried to speak again. She swallowed to dislodge the sobs that burned her throat. "You're dead! I saw you die!" she gasped.

Kelsey's knees buckled, and she stumbled backwards. Only Ron's presence close behind kept her from slumping to the floor. She stared at the captain, unsure of what she was seeing. She shook her head to clear the image of the ghost that stood before her. Was she actually in the middle of another nightmare and she would soon awaken, drenched in perspiration with her heart beating wildly? She leaned weakly against Ron, grateful that he was supporting her.

Sheriff Jason Wilder stared back at Kelsey, with shock written across his face. A woman he hadn't seen for three years was here in his office. He shook his head to dislodge the image as he struggled to breathe. Jason swallowed and forced air to return to his lungs. He closed his eyes for a second, then opened them. She was still there. She was real and not a mirage conjured by wishful thinking. Jason's expression turned to one of wonder, then to curiosity as joy and relief replaced his shock. Color returned to his face.

"Lieutenant Barrett, is it really you?" He moved toward Kelsey, reached out, and gently pulled her away from Ron. He wrapped his arms around her, and his hands roamed over her back as he searched for the feel of human flesh—confirmation that she was real. As he felt the warmth of her body, he clasped her even tighter to his chest. She hadn't disappeared in a puff of smoke when he touched her.

Jason briefly pressed his forehead against Kelsey's, then raised his hands and cupped both sides of her face. He pulled back slightly, and his eyes stared into hers. He gently rubbed his thumbs across her cheeks. "I can't believe it! I thought you were lost," he said, then swallowed and added softly, "in the attack."

Kelsey leaned into the captain and wrapped her arms around his neck. Tears pooled in her eyes as she gazed up at him. "But how?" she asked. "I saw you! In the air." The scenes from that night flared fresh in her mind. She had lived the same moment over and over again in the past three years. The flashbacks were less frequent now, but when they came, they were just as powerful as the night they happened. She again saw his body fly into the air and disintegrate into a hundred pieces. She heard the cries of the wounded and the dying as they seemed to call out to her over and over.

"Shh," Captain Wilder said softly as he gently touched her lips with his fingertips. "Don't think about that now. You're here. I'm here."

The reality of what he said slowly penetrated Kelsey's brain and brought her back to the present. He *was* alive! He *was* here, smiling, and holding her as if the failed operation had never happened. For three years, she had been tortured by the belief that he had died—burned and blown to pieces in a horrible death—and her guilt over not being able to stop it was something she fought constantly to block from her mind.

He's alive! her mind repeated.

A part of her knew it was illogical, but that revelation suddenly made her angry. She had carried the burden that she was in some way to blame for his death, while in reality, he was alive and well and lived less than two hundred miles away.

Kelsey pulled back and looked accusingly at him. "You let me think you were dead!" she accused. She slapped his chest with each word. "Why didn't you find me? Why, Captain? Why didn't you let me know? I saw you die—in my sleep—over and over!"

Kelsey was being unreasonable, her accusations were unfair, and subconsciously, she knew this. But in the moment, she couldn't stop herself. Three years of survivor's guilt overrode reason. She shoved against his chest and jerked free of his arms. "How could you be so cruel?" She took a ragged breath. Prompted by shock, anger, and confusion, her words came tumbling out. "You died! I blamed myself. I should have done something, should have spotted the danger!" She was rambling now. How was he here? "I saw you die," she insisted again.

"Lieutenant, wait!" Captain Wilder reached for her hands, but she pulled away. "There wasn't anything you could've done." His face blanched under his tan. "It was my fault. I was the team leader. I was to blame for the madness that night. If anyone should have anticipated an ambush, it was me." Apparently, the captain's anguish matched her own. "Not you!"

"I can't be here right now," Kelsey muttered. "I need some air." The shock was wearing off, and it was replaced with an anger she didn't quite understand. She felt like she was caught in a time warp. She had finally found peace after a long struggle by accepting that, yes, Captain Wilder had died, along with most of the team. But now, suddenly, here he was in the flesh. He hadn't died. She needed space to sort through what was real and what was embedded in her memory from that night. She shoved her hands through her hair. "I have to think. This... I'm so messed up!"

She turned toward the door, but Ron caught her before she opened it.

"Kelsey! Stop!" He grabbed her by both arms and shook her gently. "Listen to me. He's alive. You're both alive. And that's a good thing, isn't it?" He gently squeezed her arms. "Don't think of what happened that night. That's the past. It's the present that matters."

Kelsey looked up and searched Ron's familiar face. It was filled with concern. She took a deep breath and nodded.

Ron lowered his voice and added softly, "I get that you're in shock, but remember, we have a job to do. Come on, Kels. Focus on why we came here." He smiled and encouraged her. "Right now, you're caught in an emotional whirlpool and aren't thinking straight. Come on! Have I ever steered you wrong?"

As she considered the scene through Ron's eyes, Kelsey's anger dissolved. As a spectator, it must have looked crazy to him. Ron was right, of course. She and Captain Wilder were both alive! That fact deserved celebration, not anger. And Ron was also right in that they had a job they'd been hired to do. She nodded again.

Ron reached out, took her cold clinched fists between his palms, and gently rubbed them to bring back their warmth. "Come on, relax! Do you want to sit down?"

Kelsey shook her head. She pulled one hand free of his grasp and pushed her hair out of her eyes.

Ron's calming words settled some of her jumbled thoughts. Embarrassment over the scene she had caused began to creep in, replacing her shock and anger. Kelsey had traversed a full range of emotions in just minutes.

The captain—*The sheriff*, she corrected herself—stared at her with concern in his eyes. He took a step toward her, but she raised a hand to stop him. She didn't want him to touch her again. She needed to regain her self-control and to do it on her own. Her anger was spent, but she still needed time to process the fact that what she had believed for three years had been completely wrong. If he touched her right now, she wasn't sure how she would react. Her emotions were still raw, and she had embarrassed herself enough for one day.

Losing control like this was unusual for her. She didn't fall apart easily. Most people might excuse her for her reaction over the revelation that Captain Wilder was alive, but she thought herself stronger and steadier than she had just demonstrated. She set a high bar for herself, and she had fallen short. She was her own fiercest critic.

Kelsey's professional demeanor resurfaced, and she silently

advised herself, *Okay, Barrett, you're human. Time to stop beating yourself up.*

Wilder knew her capabilities—knew she was a trained soldier—or at least he knew how steady, calm, and unflappable she had been three years ago. She hadn't been one for histrionics. But he hadn't seen her in three years. He may see this as evidence that she had changed. After her meltdown, she'd have to reassure him that she could handle the job he had hired them to do.

Kelsey felt foolish, even as she forced herself back on track and to concentrate on the job before her and Ron. But she still didn't understand why Captain Wilder, as team leader, hadn't reached out to her to let her know that he was alright. She planned to ask him this at some point, but now was not the time for that.

She was here to represent her father's company. She had boasted to him about her abilities and qualifications, and now, she had screamed at a client simply because he was alive and well. *Put that way*, she thought, *I acted like a crazy lady.*

"Kelsey?" Ron prompted as he reached out and shook her arm.

Kelsey straightened her shoulders and briefly closed her eyes. Color replaced the whiteness of her face. Yes, embarrassment was the emotion she was experiencing now, but she refused to admit—out loud, anyway—that she had overreacted. Not just yet. She could apologize for not controlling her outburst, but not for the shock and the painful memories invoked by seeing him. The image of the captain's body flying into the air, then falling back to earth with his face blown to pieces was not one she could easily replace with that same face alive, well, and now staring at her with concern.

"If you're not up to it, I understand," Ron continued gently. "I can have a replacement sent up by tomorrow."

Kelsey's embarrassment instantly changed to humiliation. She wanted to kick Ron for even mentioning a replacement. Anger at Ron replaced anger at the sheriff and any embarrassment she still felt.

A replacement? Never! If word that she had to be replaced got around among the males at Barrett Security Consultants, it would feed the stereotype of the hysterical female unable to control her emotions and do her job. Her reasons wouldn't matter to the gossip mill. And her father might never trust her again. No, she would not accept humiliation by being replaced on her first field assignment.

As Kelsey considered what a replacement would do to her reputation, she looked at Ron through narrowed eyes. Her friend knew her well and knew exactly how she would react if he mentioned a replacement. After years of close friendship, Ron knew which buttons to push and when to push them.

Kelsey was necessary for the completion of the job that Sheriff Wilder had hired them to do. She had convinced her father that no other agent he employed could do it as well as she. She still believed that. She had her emotions back under control now and was ready to attack the job with all the skills and competence she possessed. She had done difficult jobs in Afghanistan. Wilder would not be disappointed in her job performance in Mason Valley.

On the other hand, Ron needed some payback for even suggesting a replacement. "But Ronnie, dear," she protested. She used the playful, syrupy voice she often employed when correcting him on something foolish he had said or done. "How will you explain when another wife arrives tomorrow? Hmmm?" She playfully reached out and ran her finger down his cheek. "You're stuck with me, sweetie. You've changed and stopped your philandering ways, haven't you? Aren't you a one-woman-man now?" One of Kelsey's favorite things to do was tease Ron about his dating habits. She knew it got under his skin. She smiled sweetly before more seriously adding, "Of course I can do this. You know that."

Ron grimaced but relaxed as his old friend resurfaced.

Kelsey the professional was ready to move past the earlier

emotional scene and get down to discussing why they were here.
That was what mattered at the moment. Kelsey squared her shoulders. She was ready for the meeting with the sheriff to begin.

"Sheriff Wilder, I'm Ron Blackledge, uh, Moore. Nice to meet
you," Ron said. He stepped forward and extended his hand to the
sheriff. He was one-hundred-percent business, as if he hadn't just
witnessed the emotional scene between his partner and his client.

The sheriff shook Ron's hand and glanced at Kelsey. Kelsey felt
her face flush, but she ignored the question in his eyes. She was
ready to hear why she and Ron were here. No more drama. "Let's
get to it, Sheriff Wilder," Kelsey said. "We have a lot of questions."

They gathered around a table in the sheriff's office. "I'm very
glad you're here. Did you have a good trip from Atlanta?" he asked,
speaking to both Ron and Kesey.

"Yes, very uneventful," Ron replied.

Kelsey remained silent. She was unsure how to react to the
sheriff. Her earlier outburst was under control, and she was no
longer angry at him for not letting her know that he had survived
that night. Of course, she was happy about that.

Now that her shock had worn off and Kelsey was thinking
clearly, she realized that anger was not the right word to describe
how she felt upon seeing Wilder again. Disappointment over the
fact that he hadn't found her to put her mind at ease was more accurate. But truthfully, she hadn't been able to find any information
on him, either—and she had tried. She would have thought that,
as team leader, he'd have more sources to contact, but perhaps he
had been stonewalled by the army's secrecy, too.

As Sheriff Wilder turned to pick up the folders he'd dropped
on the floor when they came in, Kelsey took a closer look at him. If
she memorized his face again, perhaps it would replace the horrible images she had carried for so long. He looked much the same
except for a small scar on his chin. Suddenly, he turned back to
the table and caught her eyes on him. Kelsey quickly looked away,

but not before she noticed the warmth in his gaze. She tried not to blush as she felt his eyes linger on her for a long moment.

"So, Sheriff Wilder, I'm curious: why do you need the help of Barrett Consultants?" Kelsey said as he opened his mouth to say something. She needed to keep the conversation businesslike and focused on the job. She wanted—no, needed—to avoid further discussion of the last time they had seen each other. Maybe they could talk about that later, but right now, she needed to prove that she was in control of her emotions and could do the job.

"It's a long story," the sheriff said as he lay down the map he had pulled from the folder and leaned back in his chair. "I've been sheriff here for a little over a year. I was a detective with the Mason Valley police department's criminal division when the former sheriff was removed from office for corruption. I know the mayor. I served in the army with his son at one time. And so, he asked the county commissioner to appoint me sheriff until a new election could be held this fall. I didn't particularly want the job, but they were in a real bind."

Sheriff Wilder got up from the table and removed three bottles of water from a small refrigerator in the corner. He placed one in front of Kelsey and handed another to Ron. He opened the third and took a long drink.

"But that's only part of the story," he continued as he screwed the cap back on the bottle and placed it on the table. "Three of the previous sheriff's deputies were also fired. I'm shorthanded and have been too busy to do background checks and hire replacements. After what happened with the former sheriff, I want to make sure I know who we're hiring this time."

"Wow! That's quite a story," Ron said. "How many deputies do you still have?"

"Three, and they're tied up with serving warrants or helping me with calls that come in. We have three jail staff, but they're not part of the enforcement division. We have over five hundred square miles in our jurisdiction." The sheriff ran his hands through his hair, then rubbed the back of his neck in frustration. "Funds are tight, too. I had to practically promise my firstborn child in exchange for approval to hire you. Thanks to Colonel Barrett's law-enforcement discount, we were able to come up with the money." Jason smiled ruefully. "Taking over after an embezzling sheriff isn't easy."

The sheriff returned to his folder of information and spread out a map of the region. "Here's the problem I hope you can help me with. About four months ago, a militia group, cult, or some other kind of group moved here from Arkansas—at least, that's where they say they came from—and set up camp on Love Vine Mountain, not far from the Big Rock Waterfall, here." He pointed to a spot on the map. "It's about a mile and half up this ridge— two miles' hiking distance by the time you skirt around the rock formations and ravines. There's an old logging road that goes up there, but only part way." Kelsey and Ron leaned over to get a better view. "It's very over-grown, much like a true wilderness."

"Why don't you run them off? Are they squatters?" Kelsey asked.

"No, Herman Coeburn, the leader, owns the property. He bought it from a man who lives out of state. I don't know where he got the money for the purchase. Likely some type of criminal activity, but I'm just guessing about that. I checked the deed records. He paid a pittance for the land, but it all looks legit. He has a legal right to be there, so long as what he does is legal. We may not like it, but that's the law."

"Does he have a criminal background?" Kelsey was now fully engaged in the discussion. She had completely pushed the earlier scene into the back of her mind.

"I haven't found any evidence that he has ever broken the law. Not even a parking ticket."

"Must be pretty cagey to be that squeaky-clean," Ron said.

"You say he bought the property? I thought most of the land around here was part of the national forest."

"A large portion west of the valley belongs to the national forest. Some land around Mason Valley has been sold to environmental or conservation groups. But there are a few tracts that still belong to private citizens." The sheriff paused and twirled his pen around in his fingers. "I just wish the owner of this tract had sold to one of the environmental groups and not to Coeburn."

"Tell us about the two missing girls," Ron suggested. "Has anybody talked to them?"

"Yes. I spoke with both of them shortly after I located them," he replied. "Here's photos. The dark-haired one is Allie, and the blonde one is Maddie. The last time their parents saw them, they had gone to the movies together." He placed pictures of two teenage girls before them.

Kelsey studied their innocent faces. They were so pretty and with the majority of their lives still before them. If they were being held against their will, she and Ron had to free them and return them to their parents. They could not fail them.

"Both said they were there of their own free will," the sheriff continued. "They said they hooked up with two young men from the camp behind their parents' backs. I came away suspicious, because they seemed a little nervous, and their stories felt rehearsed. But a hunch is all I have, not proof. The nervousness could be because they thought they were in trouble. I tried to get them to leave with me, but they wouldn't. They didn't give any indication they were being held captive. It's entirely possible they really did meet up with the two guys at the movie and went off with them willingly."

"How old are they, again?" Kelsey asked, as she picked up the pictures. She wondered what life in this camp might be like for two teenage girls. What were they doing right now?

"They both just turned eighteen. Legal age in North Carolina. They should still be in school and getting ready to graduate in a few weeks. Their parents are sick with worry." Sheriff Wilder turned to face Kelsey directly. "Lieutenant, I mean, Kelsey," he said, "remember when we visited the villages and sat in on the tribal meetings in Afghanistan? And how you could always tell when something in the area was just not right, like the villagers were hiding something...or someone?"

"Yes," Kelsey said, nodding. "There was always that feeling that something was wrong—a darting of the eyes or nervous twitching of the hands—just something off kilter. They were usually lying."

"That's how my meeting with the girls went. Something felt odd, but I can't act because I feel odd vibes."

They moved on to discussing the best way to surveil the camp. Ron and Kelsey shared their undercover plan to pose as a couple from Atlanta looking for property to buy for a business venture.

"Only the county commissioner knows you've been hired, and even Commissioner Bryant doesn't know the details or when the operation will begin," Sheriff Wilder assured them. Then, he sat back, looked at them both, and laid all of his cards on the table: "I've hired you to get proof that the two girls are being held against their will. I don't want you trying to rescue them. That will be the job of myself and the FBI's Crimes against Children and Exploitation division. I've already spoken with the agent in charge in Charlotte. He approves of the surveillance plan and said they could chopper in and be here within minutes once I give them the go-ahead."

One of the sheriff's deputies was on duty the next day, so Sheriff Wilder offered to show them around and familiarize themselves with the town. Then, he'd take them up the mountain to the militia camp.

After the meeting broke up, Kelsey hung back while Ron went ahead to wait for her in the car. She wanted a private word with Sheriff Wilder. He leaned against his desk and waited for her to speak first.

"Sheriff Wilder, I, uh... about my behavior earlier," Kelsey stammered. "That's not my usual way with clients. I can do this job."

"First of all, let's drop the ranks. We're both civilians now, and we're working together. How about just 'Jason'?" he asked. When Kelsey nodded, he continued, "And I know. I'm not your typical client, either. This was a shock to both of us. I—" He paused as his phone rang. He pulled it from his pocket and looked at the caller ID. "This is my deputy, Ferguson. Excuse me. I need to take this... Hey, Ferguson," the sheriff—*Jason*—said as he answered the call. He listened for a moment, then said, "Let me check the schedule." He went over to his desk and opened his computer. "Next Tuesday? Sure, I can work that shift for you. Don't worry about it. Take Melinda out for a nice anniversary dinner." He listened for another minute. "And happy anniversary to you both."

Kelsey took the opportunity to leave while Jason was busy with his call. She quietly closed the door behind her. She wanted to explain and apologize for falling apart earlier but had lost her nerve. She didn't yet trust herself to hold it together if the discussion turned to the night when she thought she had witnessed his death.

Kelsey had assured him that she could do the job, and that was the most pressing issue. They would have their talk, but she wanted to postpone it until he was not on duty and she could bring herself to talk about the nightmare they had both lived through.

CHAPTER THREE

Kelsey and Ron sat on the porch swing the next morning, waiting for Jason to pick them up. He lived at the end of the cul-de-sac on Willow Street, just a few houses down from their rental.

"You want to talk about what happened yesterday?" Ron asked. Kelsey had gone to her room immediately after they had eaten dinner last night. She didn't go to sleep right away and had watched TV late into the evening. She hadn't wanted to talk about the scene in the sheriff's office. Ron had respected her wishes and hadn't asked any of the multitude of questions he almost certainly had.

Kelsey appreciated that Ron was giving her the space and time to sort out her emotions. In the privacy of her bedroom, she had gone over her reaction again and again. Her shock, anger, and embarrassment all stemmed from the same source: the images and sounds that were seared into her brain by the tragic and monumental event she had lived through.

Even this morning, in the bright North Carolina sunshine, Kelsey felt justified in her reaction. She was just embarrassed by the way she had handled the shock.

"No. I'm alright," Kelsey replied. "Really, there's nothing to talk about. The captain—I mean, Jason—is alive, and that's a wonderful thing—better than wonderful, actually." She pushed the swing back and forth as she spoke. "I was never mad at him, just shocked to see him alive. It just threw me. But... I... I thought he was dead." Her voice caught, and she paused momentarily, then went on. "I was confused and couldn't understand why he hadn't contacted us—the team members—I mean, those of us who survived. After all, he was the team leader. It would have changed the pictures in my nightmares."

"You don't have to explain. I understand. It was a normal reaction." Ron stopped the motion of the swing and turned toward her. "He also said that he thought you had died, too, Kels. It seems like a good reason for not contacting you. You need to give him a chance to explain." Ron paused, then added, "As a defender of the male gender, let me just say that when we screw up, it's not intentional. Sometimes we just don't know what we're doing." He paused, as if waiting for her to take the opening he'd left her and make a snarky retort, but she remained silent. "Well, if you want to talk about it, I'm here, just so you know."

"I know," she replied. "It's just... I've lived with the guilt for so long that seeing him alive... I'm just having a hard time wrapping my head around what's real and what I might have imagined."

"It had to be a shock—for both of you." Ron put his arm around her and squeezed her shoulders.

"Here comes the sheriff now," Kelsey said as a pickup pulled into the driveway. She was glad for the interruption. Sympathy from Ron might weaken her resolve to put the difficult topic on hold for the time being.

Ron was a good friend and a good listener, but she had never told him the details of the Afghan operation and how it had gone awry. As far as he knew, it was just a normal patrol that had gone horribly wrong. He had been more concerned with her injuries than how she got them and never pumped her for details.

It'll take time and patience—that's what the therapist always told Kelsey when she asked if she would ever be able to put the attack behind her. It was excellent advice for her current situation.

Ron climbed into the backseat of Jason's pickup, leaving Kelsey to slide into the front seat. Kelsey busied herself with fastening her seat belt.

"Good morning, Kelsey," Jason said, looking over at her.

"Good morning, Jason," Kelsey muttered is response. The drama of yesterday was still between them, but she wanted to forget it and pretend her meltdown had never happened. Kelsey snuck a look at Jason just as he glanced over at her. He smiled warmly as their eyes met, and she blushed. Yes, Jason Wilder was very much alive, and apparently, even after yesterday, he didn't think she was a raving lunatic. This was a good start. She gave him a slight smile before turning to look out the window as they drove through the city. She vowed not to let memories from the past spoil the day.

They drove toward a café, with Jason pointing out local businesses along the way. He gave them a brief history of the town of Mason Valley and how it got its name.

Mason Valley was originally a land grant made to John Mason in 1774 by the royal governor of North Carolina. Despite a treaty with the Indian tribes in the region, the governors sent from England to rule this part of the new world continued to encourage the establishment of white settlements throughout Indian territory. Their hope was that white settlers would eventually outnumber the Indians, limiting conflict between them. In time, available land in the coastal regions of North Carolina became so scarce that John Mason decided to deed parcels of his land to settlers in exchange for a promise that they would clear the land, establish a homestead, and remain on the land for a minimum of five years.

"A community grew as more and more settlers took Mason up

on his offer. The settlement became known as Mason Valley," Jason ended. "And the rest, as they say, is history. We are now a town of approximately twenty-five thousand, with many more during tourist season. There are also approximately 3,500 people living in the county outside of town."

They pulled into an open parking space in front of a red brick building bearing a sign that read "Rita's Café." Jason climbed out of the pickup, and Kelsey and Ron followed him. "This place has the best food in town." He leaned close and added in a whisper, "And if you want your undercover identities to be spread, this is the place to do it. I imagine everyone in town already knows you're from Atlanta."

As he opened the door, the smell of home cooking struck Kelsey's senses and reminded her that she had not eaten much at dinner last night.

"Hey, Sheriff," a middle-aged lady greeted them from behind the counter. "Take a seat. Any one that's empty."

"Thanks, Rita." Jason placed his hand on Kelsey's back and guided her toward a booth by the windows. His touch was warm, and a shiver ran up her back and across her shoulders. She sat down, and Ron slid in beside her. Jason took the empty bench across from them. Once they had placed their orders and downed several gulps of hot coffee, Jason continued his history lesson, describing some of the local businesses and their owners.

"Hi, Jason. Do y'all mind if I join you?"

Kelsey looked up into the face of a strikingly beautiful woman. She was tall, with dark brown hair and sparkly green eyes. Kelsey stared at the stranger. *If reincarnation is real, this is what I want to come back as*, Kelsey thought. She was suddenly conscious of her ponytail, her face free of makeup, and the hiking boots and jeans she wore.

"Sure, Stephanie. Sit down," Jason said as he scooted over to the other end of the bench. He introduced Ron and Kelsey and then indicated the young woman beside him. "This is Stephanie Landry. She's the mayor's daughter. Stephanie is a model and lives in Charlotte most of the time," Jason explained, "but she comes to Mason Valley between modeling shoots to visit her parents."

The waitress soon delivered their food. Kelsey was hungry and didn't let the fact that Stephanie had ordered only coffee keep her from enjoying the full plate the waitress had placed before her. *I have a mountain to climb*, she thought.

Stephanie, who was evidently used to being the center of attention, kept the conversation going as they ate. She entertained them with stories of modeling shoots "gone bad" and described some of the places and countries she had visited. She frequently placed her hand lightly on Jason's arm with a familiarity that piqued Kelsey's curiosity. Were they more than acquaintances?

"Jason, Mamma said to invite you to dinner tonight," Stephanie said at one point. She looked at him expectantly. "And my dad said he has something he wants to discuss with you."

"I'm sorry, Stephanie. I can't make it tonight. We're going to hike up Love Vine Mountain today. Ron and Kelsey are here to pick out a site for a company retreat, and I promised to show them around. Maybe another time. Tomorrow?"

"I have to go back to Charlotte in the morning, and I'm leaving for New York for a shoot the day after tomorrow. But I'll be back in about two weeks." When Jason looked confused, she prompted him. "Remember? Daddy's party is the following weekend."

"You're welcome to go up the mountain with us if you'd like," Kelsey interjected. "That way, you could spend a little time with Jason before you leave." Out of the corner of her eye, Kelsey watched for Jason's reaction. He sat stone-faced. His expression didn't change at all. But was there a slight tightening of his jaw? Well, he should have invited Stephanie himself.

Stephanie gave a delicate shiver. "No thanks! There's snakes and bugs in those woods. And it's humid. Not for me," she replied.

She lifted her long hair off her neck and looked across the table at
Kelsey. Stephanie studied her for a moment. It was the first time
she had looked directly at Kelsey since joining them. Kelsey recognized assessment, then dismissal in the other woman's green eyes.
Stephanie dropped her hair back onto her shoulders and turned
toward Jason. She started another conversation concerning some
of their mutual friends.

Stephanie's chatter became part of the background noise as
Kelsey concentrated on eating her meal and finishing her second
cup of coffee. Kelsey's female antenna picked up that Stephanie's
interest in Jason went beyond being mere acquaintances. It didn't
pick up whether Jason reciprocated that same interest. And it certainly didn't reveal to Kelsey why she was interested in this potential Stephanie-Jason connection.

They soon finished breakfast and said goodbye to Stephanie.
She hugged Jason, rose up on her tiptoes, and lightly kissed him on
the cheek. "I'll see you next weekend?" she asked.

"Probably," Jason answered.

Kelsey, Ron, and Jason drove to the city park located at the
base of Love Vine Mountain and climbed out of Jason's pickup.
Kelsey and Ron hoisted their backpacks on their shoulders and
followed Jason as he led them along a jogging trail that ran westward around the park. Kelsey looked up at the tall, intimidating
mountain before them. Wisps of mist like cotton candy floated up
from the valley floor toward the mountaintop. A buoyant sun had
risen and was trying to break through the low-hanging clouds that
obscured the highest peaks. *The clouds and mist will probably burn
off with the heat of the day*, thought Kelsey, *but Stephanie's right: it'll
be a humid day on the mountain, as well as in the valley.*

"We'll bypass this trail. It's the old logging trail I was telling
you about and the one Coeburn and his people use when they
come down to town." Jason indicated a wide trail that led up
through the trees. There were tire tracks, suggesting that vehicles

could navigate it. "There's a hunting trail a little further up this way that we can use. It's more overgrown than this one, but we'll be less likely to meet anyone."

They entered the woods on an almost invisible trail that led into thick undergrowth. If Jason had not guided them toward it, Kelsey would have walked right by. She pushed tree limbs, vines, and bushes out of her way as she followed Jason and Ron into dark shadows under a tangled canopy of trees. The trail soon widened slightly, but it was obviously used only rarely, if at all. Maybe wild animals came this way, but Kelsey saw no evidence that a human had passed this way recently.

They pushed upward in a steady climb. Jason took the lead, with Ron close behind him. Both men were in good physical condition, so they were not strained by the effort. Kelsey prided herself on staying fit, so the climb was easy for her, too, but it was a fight to move the limbs and undergrowth out of the way. The fallen leaves cushioned their footsteps, so the only sounds were the calls of birds and the wind whistling through the tops of the tall trees.

Just as Kelsey had anticipated, it was humid among the trees. Perspiration dampened Jason's and Ron's hair around the edges of their ball caps and beaded on Kelsey's forehead under the visor she wore. Jason looked back frequently to see if his party was winded or in need of a break. A few times, he held heavy limbs out of the way until Ron and Kelsey had passed, then resumed his position at the head of the line.

Kelsey heard the call of a morning dove from somewhere in the thick growth. The sound brought back memories of the pallid owl and their signal in Afghanistan. *Does Jason remember it, too?* Kelsey wondered. *Probably not*, she decided, since he seemed focused on their destination and nothing else. His muscles worked fluidly beneath his denim shirt, and his jean-clad legs pushed him steadily over the rocky path and up the mountain.

As hard as Kelsey tried, she couldn't seem to get away from memories of her time in Afghanistan. So long as she stayed away from the fiery ending, she could handle it. Seeing Jason in the lead brought back other memories of their climb together up another mountain in Afghanistan. The landscape was different, their mission was different, but Jason's perseverance was the same.

The climb up the Afghan mountain had been slowed not by limbs and bushes, but by the rough and rocky terrain. Jason, as team leader, had relentlessly pushed the team up the mountain, even as their sixty-pound backpacks and body armor weighed heavily on their shoulders. Their load was made even heavier by the communication gear they carried. Sharp, jagged rocks had scraped and cut their fingers as they climbed and skirted the deep crevices along their route. They had maintained a steady pace and only stopped for brief water breaks and to survey the countryside for signs of the enemy.

No one on the team had complained about the speed set by the captain. They reached the top of the mountain and then had to hike back down the other side. The descent was painfully slow and just as difficult as the climb. But the team had moved silently and secretly through the night like ghosts in a graveyard, inching ever closer to their destination.

"Everyone doing okay?" Jason asked as he stopped near an outcropping of rocks and turned back to them. His voice snapped Kelsey back from memories of Afghanistan to Love Vine Mountain. "We'll take a break soon."

"I'm good," Kelsey replied, "though Pretty Boy here might need some help." She grinned at Ron when he looked back at her. He returned her grin, then let go of a long limb that slapped back and caught Kelsey around her waist and thighs. Kelsey made a face at Ron in response, pulled the limb from around her legs, and continued the climb upward.

"If you can joke with each other, obviously, the climb is too easy. Maybe I should pick up the pace," Jason laughed. He turned back to the trail and skirted a large boulder to resume the climb.

Kelsey looked around and took in the beauty of the mountainside as they pushed onward. Her mother had been a plant lover—an amateur botanist, really—and had dragged Kelsey to many garden shows featuring native plants. Kelsey had often helped her mother plant and maintain the potted plants and flower beds around their Atlanta home. She wasn't the plant enthusiast her mother was, but surprisingly, many of her mother's teachings had stuck with her.

Kelsey recognized many of the plants. Rotting leaves and impenetrable shade provided the perfect growing conditions for a variety of wild plants and bushes. Tall maidenhair ferns, wood violets, and wild mushrooms grew in the fertile, damp soil under the trees. Kelsey spotted ginseng and blood root—both herbal plants used in medicines. Large patches of rhododendron opened their blooms to welcome spring.

A peacefulness settled over her. Who would be arrogant enough to think their human problems were important here in the shelter of nature's magnificent creations? Kelsey's frayed emotions and rattled nerves were further calmed and settled by the silence and the spectacular beauty of the scenery around her. Any lingering grievance she had with Jason seeped away. She still had questions as to why he hadn't used his connections as team leader to find her and the other team members, but as Ron had reminded her, the fact that they were both alive was the most important thing.

Kelsey began to pepper Jason with questions about the plants along the trail that she didn't recognize, and he paused to answer each one of them. Eventually, he stopped near a thick growth of the vines that were primarily responsible for their difficult climb and pointed to the dark-green vine with leathery leaves. "I know you recognize this plant: kudzu, also known as 'The Plant That

Ate the South.' Actually, it's not as bad as its reputation, but it can be very invasive." Jason reached up and broke off a long strip of a different, orangey-yellow vine that bore no leaves. It grew in tangled coils throughout the kudzu thicket. "This is love vine. The mountain was named for it. Or that's the story, at any rate. I don't know its botanical name."

"I've never seen a vine like that. It looks like long yellow worms," Kelsey said. "How did a mountain get named for a vine—and an ugly vine, at that?"

"It's folklore, a local legend," Jason replied as he wrapped the vine into a ball. "As far as I know, it originated with the early settlers when they first migrated to this region. There's no shortage of superstition around here, at least among the older generations. Some beliefs were brought by the early settlers from Europe. Voodoo rites came from the Caribbean. And there are Indian beliefs from the original tribes who lived here. They all got mixed together into something unique. Or maybe everyone who lived here didn't have much to occupy their time, so they just made stuff up."

"And the love part?" Ron prompted.

"The story goes that during the valley's early settlement, a flu epidemic wiped out many of the young men in the village. The young women who were left didn't have any men to marry. They appealed to a wise old Indian woman who had lived among them for several years. You might call her the resident shaman, I suppose."

"There's always a wise old Indian in all the legends," Kelsey interrupted.

"And she was the wisest of all, of course," Jason said with a smile as he continued. "She told the young women—and I paraphrase—" Here, his voice changed to mimic his version of the voice of the wise old Indian woman. "Young maidens, you must go quickly while the moon is full. Go up the tallest mountain in the valley. Search until you find the love vine in the shade of very tall trees." Jason switched back to his normal voice and explained, "It grows prolifically up here, so it wouldn't have been difficult to find." He continued the tale, again using the voice of the Indian woman. "Find the vine of love and wind it into a circle as that of the full moon. You must then throw it over your left shoulder. It will bring you great joy. A handsome man will soon arrive for each of you."

Jason switched back to his normal voice. "This exercise, the woman promised, would create great *juju*—sorry, I'm mixing cultures," Jason said with a laugh. "But lo and behold, her prophecy came true. Within days, a group of young men appeared and joined the settlement. Not long after that, there were weddings aplenty. Apparently, it was love at first sight—or just a shortage of both men and women."

"Humph," Kelsey snorted. "A very tall tale, indeed."

"Has it worked since?" Ron asked.

"No one knows for sure," Jason said, "but that doesn't stop people from wishing on the vine, just in case. Personally, I think that if there were even the slightest grain of truth to the legend, it's more likely that the young men were recruited to join the settlement because there was a shortage of workers after the flu wiped out so many. It was a business decision. They didn't arrive because of magic."

"Aww, you don't believe in magic?" Kelsey teased. "Where's your sense of romance, Sheriff Wilder?"

"Oh, I can be romantic," Jason assured her as he tossed the ball of vine toward Kelsey. She reacted just in time to catch it as it hit her chest. "Since you question *my* romantic sensibility, why don't you try it?" he challenged.

Kelsey stared back at him, then closed her eyes for a moment and calmly tossed the balled vine over her left shoulder. She pulled a length of vine from the thicket beside the trail and tossed it back at Jason. "Your turn."

Jason slowly wound the vine into a ball, never taking his eyes off Kelsey. He flashed a mischievous smile, then covered his mouth and mumbled something behind his hand. He tossed the ball of vine over his left shoulder.

"Well, kids, are the objects of your wishes familiar names you can share, or did you wish for a stranger to arrive and sweep you off your feet?" Ron asked. He looked questioningly from Kelsey to Jason. Their interactions had definitely changed since yesterday, and this had not escaped Ron's notice.

"I'll never tell," Jason and Kelsey replied at the same time.

Jason looked down and studied the balled-up vines where they landed. They had come unwound and were caught on some bushes on either side of the trail. "Who knows?" Jason mused. "Just like in the legend, we have a shortage in the sheriff's department. Maybe the vine will bring me some deputies."

"A female deputy?" Kelsey asked.

Jason smiled and quirked an eyebrow at Kelsey before saying, "That would work, but more staff wasn't actually my wish. How about you?"

Kelsey shook her head and remained silent. She was unsure of what they were doing or what Jason meant by involving her in this demonstration. Maybe it didn't mean anything and this was just an attempt to rattle her.

Jason turned back to the trail. "But whatever the truth is concerning the legend, the mayor plans to start holding an annual Love Vine Festival next spring. Our fine mayor never misses an opportunity to advance Mason Valley's visibility—or its money-making opportunities. The legend might be of some use after all, regardless of whether or not love appears."

They resumed their climb. When they reached what was left of an old hunting cabin, Jason dropped his backpack to the ground and sat down on a large lichen-covered rock. He motioned for Kelsey and Ron to sit as well. Kelsey took up position on a fallen log near the edge of the trail. Ron leaned against a large tree trunk nearby.

"You probably shouldn't sit there," Jason said as he moved over and made room on the rock beside him. "Sometimes tree lice live in those rotten logs."

Kelsey quickly jumped up and brushed off the seat of her jeans. She moved toward the rock and sat down beside him. Jason hid a smile, but he couldn't hide the teasing light in his eyes. *Are tree lice actually a thing,* Kelsey wondered, *or is Jason just messing with me and taking advantage of my unfamiliarity with the woods here?* She had to stop letting him fluster her so easily.

"Rest a bit, and then I'll take you to some of the best-tasting fresh water you'll ever drink." Jason pointed over his shoulder as he dug into his backpack and pulled out some drinking cups.

"I'm ready now," Ron said. "My throat is dry as a bone. I have water in my gear bag, but fresh water sounds better."

Jason stood and motioned for them to follow him. He took them several yards east of the cabin and stopped at a tree stump. "Here it is."

Kelsey stepped up beside him. "What? Where?" she asked.

Jason pointed at the stump. Bubbling water came flowing up through the tree stump and over its sides. He filled one of the cups and handed it to Kelsey. "Take a drink."

She quickly drained her cup. "That *is* good water! Who would ever dream that Mother Nature could create her own personal water fountain in the woods?"

"The locals call this a bee gum tree. These trees develop a large hollow inside where bees build their hives. Obviously, this one is over a spring, and the bubbling water ran the bees off. I imagine the water weakened the wood and the top of the tree was broken off by the wind, creating the stump fountain."

Once they had quenched their thirst and replaced the water in their bottles with the fresh water, they returned to the old cabin.

Jason pulled sandwiches and bags of chips from his backpack and handed them to Kelsey and Ron. They ate in silence for a few minutes. The climb had caused them to work up an appetite, so the food tasted especially good.

"Jason," Ron said as he opened his bag of chips. "How come you know so much about these woods? You a native of Mason Valley?"

"Well, I am, sorta," Jason said as he finished the last of his sandwich. He leaned back on his elbows, and his arm brushed against Kelsey's forearm. The same warmth and tingling sensation she had felt earlier at Rita's restaurant traveled up her arm.

As was Kelsey's habit, she chastised herself silently: *Good grief, Barrett! Yesterday, you were mad at him. Today, you're behaving as though you've never touched a man before.* She didn't move away from the pleasant contact with Jason's arm. She didn't want him to know how it affected her. That would only encourage him to do it even more.

"How so?" Ron asked, pulling Kelsey's mind back to the discussion.

"I grew up in Wilmington, but my grandparents owned a farm about ten miles outside of Mason Valley. I used to spend my summers here." He pulled a twig off a nearby bush and began chewing on it. "They've since moved to Florida."

"What happened to the farm?" Kelsey asked. "Did they sell it?"

"In a way. My parents bought it. They live there now. My dad retired from the FBI. He's a gentleman farmer now."

"He farms? That's quite a change: from the FBI to farming." Kelsey finished her chips and tucked the bag into her backpack.

"He grows a few vegetables for personal use and some hay. I think he decided to grow hay just so he could buy a tractor." Jason laughed. "He grows it, cuts it, and what he doesn't use to feed his horses, he donates it to a horse-therapy farm a few miles further out from where they live."

"Horse therapy? Is that like those camps for autistic kids or kids with disabilities?" Ron asked.

"Yes, and elderly people, too. Veterans with PTSD also find it soothing and therapeutic to spend time with horses. Horses can have the same effect as a therapy dog."

"That's great, Jason. I never knew that about you."

"What? You didn't know that I was great or that my dad owned a farm?" Jason chuckled. A blush spread over Kelsey's cheeks. He clearly enjoyed his ability to fluster and rattle her. Kelsey thought about sticking her tongue out at him, but only for a moment. No doubt he'd have a smart comeback that would rattle her further.

"When you're ready, we'll get started again," Jason said as he busied himself with straightening the contents of his backpack. That done, he hoisted it onto his back and motioned for them to follow.

They turned east along a flat ridge. Jason explained that they were about two miles west and a half-mile north of the western edge of the Coeburn property. "I plan to take you there, but first, there's something else I want to show you. It's about a quarter-mile this way." He pointed north.

They traveled in silence. When the path widened, Jason dropped back to fall in beside Kelsey. He looked as if he were going to say something, then changed his mind. Kelsey searched her mind for a topic to bring up that didn't involve their past. "Stephanie seems nice," she said as she ducked to dodge a low-hanging tree limb.

"She's very nice," Jason agreed. Unprompted, he explained, "I've known Stephanie since she was a teenager, and I served with her brother shortly after I joined the army. Chris and I used to ride home together, since we both had family here."

"You probably didn't need to wish for love with the love vine. Stephanie clearly likes you," Kelsey said nonchalantly. She didn't want him to get the wrong idea: that she cared about his relationship with Stephanie.

"Hmmm, you think? But what's not to like about me?" Jason said, grinning at her. "But if that's your way of asking whether we're dating, yes, we've gone out a few times. But she's pretty busy and travels a lot with her modeling career."

A non-denial denial, Kelsey thought. Jason had read her mind before she could even formulate the question and decide how to delicately ask about the nature of his relationship with Stephanie. Apparently, she needed to hide even her thoughts from him.

Jason glanced at her but didn't say anything more. Kelsey remained quiet as they picked their way up the mountain. Soon, the path narrowed again, and with another glance and a slight smile at Kelsey, Jason went around Ron to take the lead again.

As they neared the top of the mountain, they heard a sound before its source came into view. The pounding roar of water grew louder with each step they took. They rounded a bend, and there, spread out before them, was a huge waterfall. Sunshine sparkled off the streaming water as it poured down the rockface into a crystal-clear pool below.

"Big Rock Waterfall," Jason said as he pointed to it. "The Grande Dame of Love Vine Mountain."

"It's breathtaking!" Kelsey gazed at the surrounding landscape. They stood in a flat, meadow-like space filled with large patches of blooming wildflowers. She spotted what she thought were delphiniums and irises mingled with plants and grasses she didn't know.

"Come on," Jason said. "You haven't seen the best part yet." He moved down the rocky bank beside the pool of water and angled toward the side near the waterfall. Ron and Kelsey followed him. Jason stopped near a ledge beside the streaming water.

"Follow me, but watch your step. It can be slippery. Press close to the rock, and you won't get as wet." Jason inched along the ledge toward the waterfall, pressing his back against the rocky face as he stepped sideways. After a few feet, he suddenly disappeared from view. A few seconds later, he reappeared behind the cascading water. Jason stepped back onto the ledge and stretched out his hand toward Kelsey. She clung to it as she inched along the wet ledge for a few feet.

Jason stepped off the ledge and pulled Kelsey to the side. She fell against him and into a dark cavern behind the curtain of water. She quickly righted herself but didn't immediately pull away from Jason's arms. Her heartbeat picked up and her breath caught in her throat as she looked up at Jason. His dark eyes returned her stare.

"I'm alright," Kelsey whispered as she broke eye contact and then slowly backed away. She turned and looked around at the cavern behind them.

"I checked for snakes," Jason said from behind her.

"Snakes?" Kelsey backed up, stopping when she met Jason's chest. His arms came up to wrap around hers. "You're teasing me again, aren't you?" Kelsey turned to face him. His arms threaded around her waist.

"No," Jason replied. "I checked before I helped you in here. Snakes like dark places."

"I'm not afraid of snakes. I just don't want to step on one." She had gone through jungle survival training in the army. She knew how to deal with snakes, but like most people, she didn't want to encounter one accidently.

"I know. I like your reaction, though." Jason didn't drop his arms. In fact, he held her tighter against his chest. The warmth from his hands on her back blocked the chill of the dank cave interior.

"Ahem," Ron said as he stepped through the cave entrance. "What's going on in here?"

Kelsey quickly pulled away from Jason. A guilty blush rose in her cheeks.

"Nothing," Jason replied. "Kelsey stumbled as she stepped off the ledge." He released her and moved a few steps into the cave. "Incredible, isn't it?" He waved his hand to encompass the interior.

Incredible, indeed! They were in a cave behind the waterfall! Their eyes soon adjusted to the darkness, and they could now clearly see the room they were standing in: a very large room with a smooth rock floor. Patches of algae grew near the entrance.

Ron turned and looked at the screen of water pouring down in front of the cave. "It's like looking out a window during a very bad rainstorm." He stepped closer to the edge and looked down at the pool below. "I would never have guessed this was here," he said in amazement as he turned back to Jason and Kelsey. "How did you find it?"

"Only a few people know it's here—mostly old-timers. I arrested an elderly homeless man early last winter just to get him in out of the cold. He wouldn't take shelter otherwise. I guess he was lonely, because he started taking about the 'good ole days' and told me stories about hunting up this way. Then he mentioned the cave behind Big Rock Waterfall. I thought he was delusional at the time, but then decided to come and see for myself. He was right. It's something, isn't it?"

"How far back does it go?" Ron asked as he started moving toward the cave's dark interior. He pulled out a flashlight as he walked. Kelsey and Jason followed. The walls were damp from tiny rivulets of water that trickled down the sides. A small stream flowed along one side of the floor toward the falling water.

"It makes a turn but ends about twenty-five feet back there," Jason said. "There's a rockslide back there that may have blocked other spaces beyond it."

Kelsey looked around the elongated room and recalled what little she knew about caves. Normally, water was the force behind their creation. The water would find a crack and begin to trickle through, carving a path by dissolving the limestone rock in the mountain. This would eventually sculpt a cave. Standing right in

WHEN THE MOURNING DOVE CALLS

the middle of one was amazing. How many years had it taken to carve out a room this large? Kelsey walked around, looking for writing on the cave walls or other evidence that former explorers and visitors had been here—perhaps native American Indians— but she didn't find any.

After briefly exploring the cave, they exited and slowly worked their way back along the ledge hidden behind the waterfall until they reached the embankment. They climbed back up to the meadow to resume their hike toward the Coeburn property. Jason now turned them in a southeastern direction.

"Today," Jason said, "I just want you to get a general layout of the compound and to familiarize yourselves with the property lines. That way, you won't accidently stray into the compound."

When they came to the northwestern edge of the property, Jason pointed out landmarks that would help them keep their bearings when they made the trip alone. "There's no fence or barrier around the compound. Apparently, Coeburn is counting on the thick undergrowth and rock formations to keep intruders out. And since he owns the property, I guess that gives him some additional sense of security."

They found a break in the trees where they could observe the center of the compound. There was a fair amount of activity. It looked as though the compound was expanding. There were several buildings—some finished and some still in progress—on the plateau below. From their vantage point, they could see a clearing where trees had been cut down and several men were busy constructing crude cabins. The sound of saws and hammers, mixed with occasional voices, carried through the morning air.

"Judging by what I've seen, the residents of the compound follow the old ways of life," Jason whispered. "They dress and live in ways most people would call outdated and left behind decades ago. Self-sustaining communities are rare these days, except for some religious cults."

"Do you think that's all Coeburn's compound is about—religion?" Ron asked. "Or is it something different?"

"I don't know," Jason said. "It makes my job more difficult if religion is involved. So long as they don't break any laws, I can't shut them down just because I don't like the way they practice their faith."

"Looks like the Coeburnites are building permanent structures," Kelsey observed.

"Yes, and that worries me," Jason said. "They're settling in for the long haul." He stood with his hands on his hips and stared intently at the camp below. "I know they're up to no good. I've got a call in to a sheriff's office in Mountain Home, Arkansas. The clerk at the courthouse said Coeburn told her that's where they came from. I hope the sheriff can give me some information on them and why they left there. Bottom line: I've got to get those girls out of there. My gut tells me that Coeburn is nothing but trouble."

They spent a few more minutes discussing the size of the property and how far east and south it ran. Kelsey took a picture of the camp before they left to begin their descent down Love Vine Mountain. They traveled along the western edge of the Coeburn land and angled toward a spot west of the old logging road. They exited the woods onto the jogging path that circled the park.

When they reached Jason's pickup truck, Kelsey slumped in the front seat, pulled the band off her ponytail, and shook her hair free. "That was some hike, but worth every aching muscle I'll have later. I've never seen a place more beautiful than that meadow and the waterfall."

"Yes. Thanks, Jason, for showing it to us," Ron agreed.

"Love Vine Mountain is rugged, but she's a beauty. You can almost understand why she's the center of a legend, whether it's true or not," Jason said.

He dropped them off at their rental property with a reminder to call if they needed anything or had additional questions. Kelsey waved goodbye as Jason drove toward his house down the street.

It was nearing dinner time, but Kelsey and Ron collapsed on the sofa in the living room to rest before deciding what they wanted to eat. They quickly agreed that a sandwich and a cold beer was more than adequate for dinner. Neither felt like cooking or moving from the sofa to go out for dinner.

"That was quite a day and quite a hike," Ron said as he pulled off his shoes and dropped them on the floor. He took a long drink of his beer. "Next time, we do it alone."

***

Jason rose from his bed and walked to the bedroom window. It was early morning, just past two a.m. according to the clock on the TV stand. He looked out at the peaceful starry night. The late April moon was bright. It lit the tops of the mountains, creating shadowy creases in the surrounding valleys. Nothing moved in his view from the window.

The landscape was serene, unlike the dream that had awoken him moments before. Remnants of it still floated before his vision. The dream seemed so real. Jason placed his hands on the windowsill and dropped his head to his chest. His heart still raced as he closed his eyes and tried to dislodge the images from his mind.

Jason's dream had taken him up to the top of Love Vine Mountain. He was dressed in his camouflaged army fatigues. The weight of his heavy backpack and body armor bore down on him and sapped his strength. Jason ignored his tired muscles and fought on. He clawed a path toward the inferno that raged through the trees in front of him.

The wildfire blazed high and expanded its reach every second as the dry underbrush exploded. Flames spread across the mountainside. Sweat pooled under his body armor as the heat and smoke threatened to suffocate him. He tore at the branches and limbs of the undergrowth in a panic. He could not—would not—

fail!

He had to reach the woman in the line of the fire.

Orangey-yellow vines suddenly came alive, an extension of the fiery blaze. Their flaming tentacles reached out and wrapped around his arms and legs, binding him in place. It was impossible to move, no matter how hard he struggled. He could see Kelsey ahead in a clearing, dressed in army fatigues and lying on the ground, injured. She was surrounded by the raging fire, and it moved ever closer to her. He tried to scream at her, "Run!" but no sound came from his mouth.

As Jason desperately tried to reach Kelsey, his struggles and pounding heart woke him. His bedsheets were twisted and soaked with perspiration. He sat up and clutched his head as he looked around his bedroom, trying to get his bearings. He slipped from the bed and made his way to the window. He leaned his head against the cool glass, a relief from the heat of the fiery dream.

Jason had been here before, and he had learned what to do when the bad dreams came. He breathed in deeply, filling his lungs with air, and then slowly let it out. He repeated this several times until his breathing slowed and returned to normal. Next, he needed to focus on something external that would replace the nightmare's images in his mind. Jason forced his attention on the stars that filled the night sky. He began naming the constellations he could see from where he stood. These calming exercises soon had the desired effects. His heart rate was brought under control. His pulse slowed.

Jason ran his hands through his hair and over his face. He hadn't had a nightmare for almost two years now. He was shaken by its vividness and how real it had seemed. *But,* he reminded himself, *that's was all it was: a dream.*

Jason drew upon another technique he had learned to deal with his nightmares. He began to analyze what the dream meant. *Why now? Why this particular dream?*

Seeing Kelsey again had revived old memories and brought back the past they shared. The trip up Love Vine Mountain had transferred the events in Afghanistan to a more immediate time and place. His mind had needed an outlet, a way to deal with the shock of seeing her again after he had spent years thinking she had died.

Jason relaxed. This analysis made sense—or at least as much sense as anything else he could come up with. This episode didn't mean his nightmares had returned. It didn't mean he'd be back to where he was before: afraid to close his eyes at night in order to keep the nightmares at bay. He was physically stronger now and had coping skills that would prevent such an outcome. This was just a one-off brought on by suddenly seeing Kelsey again.

Having analyzed and pushed his nightmare to the back of his mind, Jason's thoughts turned to the real-life Kelsey. What had she been doing in the three years since he left her on that Afghan hill? How badly had she been injured? Was she completely healed? Had she built a happy life since then? Did she marry the man she was engaged to? Was Blackledge that man?

Jason saw a deep fondness between Kelsey and Ron, but he didn't see the spark *he* wanted in *his* relationship. But some people might be satisfied with a marriage based on fondness. He was certainly no expert on romance, and after only two days of observation, he could be very wrong about Kelsey and Ron.

Kelsey appeared to be the same on the outside. She seemed to be the attractive and intelligent woman he had known in Afghanistan, always confident in her abilities, and someone you could count on at all times. But how much had she changed on the inside? The experience had changed him in some ways; it must have affected her, too. How could such an experience not change someone?

The fact that Kelsey was here on a job meant she was getting on with her life. He was, too. He was taking things day-by-day and trying not to get mired down in the past, but there were unresolved issues that still nagged at him. What had caused their special mission to turn into such a disaster was still a mystery. And the army's refusal to share any details aroused his suspicions. What were they hiding? Jason vowed to renew his efforts to find out.

Jason had known Kelsey for a long time, but in reality, he didn't know her at all. She had always been skittish around him back in Afghanistan. Whenever he came near her in a setting other than an official one, she was standoffish and very private. Of course, she wasn't just like that with him. She always seemed guarded and never furthered a friendship with any of the men in the platoon. He had assumed it was because of her fiancé who waited back home.

Kelsey had been angry with him when they met at his office. Had it really been only two days ago? He didn't blame her. He had been shocked, too, and her anger was a natural reaction to the shock of unexpantly seeing him again, here in remote North Carolina. The fact that she was one of the survivors from the team had dramatically brightened his day, and even her outburst couldn't change that.

But had he noticed a thaw or softening toward him today? He hoped so. Perhaps, in time, there would be a complete thaw. The experience they had shared—and survived—was surely something they could build a friendship on.

Friendship? Was it truly a desire for just friendship that gave him such pleasure when he was with her—when he teased her? Was friendship the reason he was analyzing her and Ron's relationship? What was it that made crazy thoughts pop unbidden into his mind whenever she was around?

If she was married or engaged now, Jason promised himself that he would firmly lock down thoughts of anything other than friendship, despite his thoughts of or wishes for more than friendship. He wouldn't allow himself to indulge in anything that stupid. And even if it turned out that Kelsey was free, the situation with Coeburn and her undercover work was calling the shots at the present time.

"You're such a jerk, Wilder," Jason muttered, then sighed. "Your assumption that Kelsey might be interested in you as more than a friend could be another area where you're dead wrong."

The sky was already lightening around the top of Love Vine Mountain when Jason turned away from the window. He pulled his uniform from the closet, laid it on the bed, and then made his way to the bathroom to shower. It would be a waste of time to go back to bed. He wouldn't be able to sleep. The extra time spent at the sheriff's office would be more useful than tossing and turning. There was always paperwork or something at the office that needed to be done.

As a small-town sheriff, many things demanded his attention. Many were small issues, but some were large—and very complicated. And sadly, they combined to mean that there was no time for a personal life.

CHAPTER FOUR

Over the next two weeks, Kelsey and Ron settled into their rental home and began the search for amenities in the area that would fit their business venture. The people of Mason Valley soon became used to seeing Kelsey and Ron head into the mountains in the morning with backpacks slung over their shoulders and return in the afternoon. No one questioned the Moores' reason for coming to Mason Valley.

In fact, Mason Valley, a picturesque place for summer vacations, saw a lot of out-of-town visitors, so two more didn't raise any red flags. In their minds, it truly was the perfect place for corporate employees to destress, renew their bodies and souls, and strengthen their relationships with their coworkers.

In reality, Ron and Kelsey hikes took them up to the Coeburn compound each morning. They chose a different entry point into the forest each time, but always angled toward the property once they were safely away from the road and civilization. They began their surveillance as close to the camp as they safely could and moved their observation spot frequently. Over time, they became familiar with the camp's layout and routine.

They were usually back home by mid-afternoon and used the rest of the day to visit businesses around town, asking questions about the area and the people. They hoped someone would share information, whether accidently or as gossip, about the Coeburn clan.

Through their observations, Kelsey and Ron determined that the group lived mostly off the land. They hunted, fished, and had started a garden on a patch of cleared ground at the compound. Some of the men occasionally went into town for additional supplies, but they were never accompanied by any of the women. The men were easy to spot in town because they all dressed similarly. It was as if the long-sleeved button-up shirts and denim work pants they wore were a uniform. They were unshaven and wore dirty baseball caps over their longish hair.

"These guys could have starred in the movie *Deliverance*," Ron observed one day from their spot on the north side of the compound.

One morning, as Kelsey and Ron came out of Rita's Café, they spotted three members of the cult in town on a resupply trip. Ron and Kelsey trailed them through the business district. The men acted just like any of the other shoppers in town that day. The only places they visited were the hardware store and the supermarket. They nodded to people they passed on the sidewalk but didn't stop to talk with anyone.

Kelsey and Ron, in keeping with their cover story, visited the travel agent's office one day to get information about local fishing spots, rock-climbing excursions, and any horse farms that offered trail rides to tourists. Doug Peterson, the travel agent, was effusive in his praise of what his town could offer a fledging business like theirs. He even gave them tips on other activities that seasonal visitors to the area found interesting.

Kelsey and Ron visited a few places Doug recommended. Kelsey felt guilty each time she met with someone and had to

pretend that she was someone else and that they were indeed a
business couple looking for a retreat location in Mason Valley. She
forcibly reminded herself of the real reason they were here in the
valley. That was more important than any lies she told.

During their trips to the compound on the mountain, Kelsey
and Ron witnessed lots of daily activity as Coeburn built up his
camp. Their high-powered binoculars gave them a sharp view of
everything. The men spent a lot of time cutting down trees. Some
of the logs were chopped into firewood, while others were hewed
and used to construct crude cabins on leveled sites carved out on
the hillside. They cleared away stumps and enlarged the gardening
plot. The women spent their days cooking and gardening. They
planted, hoed, and weeded the rows of vegetables that had begun
to grow in neat rows across the clearing.

It wasn't until their third trip up the mountain that Kelsey and
Ron spotted Allie and Maddie, the two girls they had been hired
to surveil. They didn't see anything that suggested the girls were
hostages. That day, as on subsequent sightings, Allie and Maddie
were surrounded by other women and young girls who worked
around the camp. Allie and Maddie never gave any indication that
they were looking for a chance to escape. Like all the women in
the camp, they wore long, nineteenth-century, prairie-style dresses. Obviously, Coeburn took his belief in "the old ways" seriously,
even down to the way the women dressed.

Herman Coeburn was always easy to spot among the other
men in the compound. He issued commands and ordered the
other members around. They responded to his orders quickly and
without objection. No one ever disobeyed him.

As Kelsey and Ron continued their daily surveillance of the
camp, it soon became clear that one middle-aged woman was
in charge of the young women. She yelled out assignments like
a boot-camp sergeant and screamed at those who didn't move
fast enough to suit her. She was never without a long stick in her

hands. Sometimes, she raised it threateningly, but mostly, she just leaned upon it for support. The women and girls were busily engaged in camp chores by the time Kelsey and Ron arrived at the edge of the compound each day. Kelsey suspected that if they kept up such a pace all day, it was likely the woman needed something to lean on.

"I wonder if she ever actually uses that stick against the girls," Kelsey said one morning as they watched the woman travel back and forth between groups of young women. She kept them at their tasks, never letting up. They never took a break until she gave them permission.

"My thoughts, exactly," Ron murmured. This morning, they were near the southern end of the property. He focused his binoculars on the woman's cane. "Whether she actually hits them with it or not, I think she mostly uses it to intimidate and threaten them."

"She must be Mrs. Coeburn—his second-in-command or maybe just another workhorse, but with more authority," Kelsey whispered. They watched as the woman yelled out more instructions to the younger women. They stood in the center of the clearing, washing clothes by hand and then hanging them on bushes to dry. "Or *one* of his wives, if they're polygamists. That's just another form of slave labor under the guise of religion," Kelsey spit out.

After several days of observing the camp, it became evident that it had a daily routine that rarely changed. A large group of young women would cook breakfast over an open fire and then serve it to several men who gathered around a large makeshift table set up under the trees. Some of the young men frequently made what looked like passes at or even grabbed the young women, pulling them onto their laps as they served the men breakfast.

Coeburn never let the men go beyond grabbing and tormenting the girls, though. One word from him prompted the men to let the girls go, but he never prevented it from starting. Kelsey and

Ron could hear the masculine laughter from their spot on the hill. The men clearly enjoyed their antics.

"I'd like to stuff their breakfasts down their throats and shut them up," Kelsey muttered. "Make the women do all the work! Grab and paw! We should storm the compound and liberate them all right now."

"Whoa, slow down, Warrior Princess," Ron said as he turned and looked at her. "I agree, and it's hard to watch." He turned back toward the camp and continued taking pictures. "It's difficult to understand why some women are okay with abuse like that. I know it happens and happens frequently."

"It's simple, really: Stockholm syndrome, where a captive develops an attachment to their captor," Kelsey said. "The men in charge become like father figures through the power they hold over the women. The women are brainwashed into thinking they don't deserve better. Sometimes, they're intimidated and abused until they're broken, have lost all contact with loved ones, and have no other place to go." Kelsey's knuckles turned white as she clenched her binoculars. "The evil that men do, and I repeat— *men*."

"Yes. It's a power game. I find it hard to understand how men could possibly find pleasure in abusing anyone, much less women."

"It's because you're a decent man, Ron. Not all men think like you."

He placed a hand over Kelsey's. "Kels, we will get what we're here for, I'm sure of it. Just be patient." He adjusted his binoculars and swung them around to get a view from another direction.

Kelsey and Ron's surveillance of the Coeburn compound moved into the first week of May. They had now been in Mason Valley for two weeks and were getting impatient in their efforts to find evidence that Allie and Maddie were being held against their will.

Kelsey was increasingly certain that the girls were not there willingly. Why would two teenage girls give up their summer routine of movies, swimming parties, and visiting with friends? It didn't seem probable that two happy teens would suddenly give up a stable life to follow a ragtag group into the mountains.

But Kelsey also knew it wouldn't be the first time. There was no explaining the power of a charismatic and persuasive cult leader over some people. A few years back, one cult leader had such a strong hold on his people that he led them to mass suicide in the jungles of South America.

Thus far, all they saw were Allie and Maddie going about their daily chores of taking care of the camp, just like the other young women there. At times, they even seemed happy and joined in singing and laughing with the group.

Kelsey and Ron gave Jason frequent updates on what they saw—and didn't see—in the compound. Jason was disappointed, too. Like Kelsey, he thought it unlikely that the girls had chosen the hard life of the camp willingly. They both had to remind themselves not to let their desire to remove Allie and Maddie and shut Coeburn down override the evidence.

Jason encouraged them to continue with their plan. "A break could come at any time," he said, "often when you least expect it."

Kelsey and Ron estimated that the group was composed of about twenty-five-to-thirty people. It was difficult to get a hard number because there were almost always a few away acting as guards, hunting in the woods, or going down the mountain to town.

One thing not in doubt was that Sergeant Coeburnite—as Kelsey had dubbed the older woman—worked the girls hard. It was constant work. Providing for that many people required a lot of cooking, gardening, and laundry.

Despite their disappointment over not being able to quickly accomplish their mission, Kelsey and Ron persisted in their efforts.

One morning at the beginning of their third week, they entered the woods near the park as usual but decided to circle around the north side of the camp and set up their surveillance post for the day further east on a different side of the compound. Once they found a good location, they settled down in a thicket and focused their binoculars on the camp.

Coeburn sat at a table with several other men. "The town council," Ron whispered sarcastically. "I wonder what's on the agenda today."

They watched as Coeburn yelled for his wife—or the woman they had dubbed his wife—to join them. She and several young women were cooking breakfast not far from where Coeburn sat. Sergeant Coeburnite left her place at the campfire and came to stand in front of him. Coeburn grabbed her and pulled her onto his lap. He began kissing and groping her, hiking her skirt above her knees, and running his hands along her thighs. When she pushed against his hand to force her dress back down over her knees, he slapped her.

His groping and pawing continued. It was not a display of affection. As with most abusers, Coeburn's purpose was to show who held the power. His main objective was to humiliate the woman on his lap. His secondary purpose was to entertain the other men.

From their position on the hill, Kelsey and Ron heard hoots of laughter from the men seated around the table. Coeburn soon tired of his game and shoved the woman off his lap and onto the ground. She slowly pulled herself up.

"Go, slut. Bring our breakfast!" Coeburn shouted in a voice that Kelsey thought must be his "king of the castle" tone. His voice rang out clearly in the morning air and carried up the hill to where Kelsey and Ron were hidden. Laughter from his men followed.

Sergeant Coeburnite—who may well have been Mrs. Coeburn—slowly walked away from Coeburn, her head bowed in shame from his treatment. She didn't move fast enough for him, though. Coeburn rose, picked up his rifle, and began poking her in the back with the butt of the gun. She stumbled from the force of his blows but he kept prodding and pushing her along like an animal. More laughter came from the men.

Finding Coeburn's cruelty hard to watch, Kelsey slammed her fist into the ground. Ron reached out and put his hand on Kelsey's. She desperately wanted to rush the compound and take out Coeburn and the group of men seated around the table. Ron held her hand. "Not now," was all he said. Kelsey released her breath in a furious huff.

"It's not enough that he embarrassed her with his pawing," she whispered. "He had to throw in pain and more humiliation, too. What a despicable human being—if he even is human." She breathed deeply, in and out, several times, until she brought her anger under control.

Soon, Sergeant Coeburnite was back, followed by the young women who carried dishes of food, which they set before the men. The women then took up positions behind the men at the table to await further instructions on what the men might want next. They remained at their posts until the men finished eating. When the men left the table, the women began to clear the dishes. Then, they moved to spot away from the table, sat down on the ground, and began eating their own breakfasts.

"Classic reinforcement of the subjugation of females," Kelsey observed. "The men eat while the women wait nearby to serve them. They are only permitted to eat after the men are done." Not only was she angry, but she was also disgusted that anyone could treat another person the way Coeburn was treating his wife and the other women. "Who does he think he is?" Kelsey demanded. "Lord of the manor? He's nothing but a very sick man!"

"I agree," Ron said in disgust. "The women may have come to the camp voluntarily, but surely, they didn't come for or expect this."

As Kelsey and Ron continued spying on the camp, four men they had not seen before were escorted into the clearing by one of Coeburn's men. Coeburn welcomed them and called for his wife to bring them all drinks. They settled into a quiet discussion around the cleared breakfast table.

Kelsey and Ron were too far away to hear their conversation, but they immediately recognized that, from Coeburn's perspective, it was important. Ron pointed his camera toward the group and snapped a picture of the men.

Coeburn ran the meeting. Kelsey and Ron could see him gesturing a great deal. Sometimes, they all laughed. "I wish we could hear what they're saying," Kelsey whispered. "This has all the looks of a business meeting." Ron nodded his agreement.

After several minutes spent talking to his visitors, Coeburn waved to his wife, signaling for her to come forward. She approached the group, herding four of the young women before her. Allie and Maddie were not among them. Sergeant Coeburnite pushed the girls forward until they stood before the men. Coeburn directed them to sway their hips, turn around and present their backs, before facing the men again and striking model poses. They talked briefly and appeared to answer questions posed by the men. The girls smiled and laughed as they spoke with the visitors. When Coeburn motioned them away, they all waved goodbye to the men and then disappeared behind one of the buildings.

"What's that about?" Kelsey asked. "At first, I thought this would be more public humiliation and abuse."

"Yes," Ron agreed, "but they didn't appear to be coerced. They seemed genuinely happy to be there and enjoying their talk with the men. But the physical exhibition Coeburn put them through is odd. It worries me."

"And you can't always tell by obedient and happy appearances," Kelsey said. "I'm not saying this is the same or even similar, but in Afghanistan, I ran across situations where families arranged marriages for or even sold their young daughters to men older than their own fathers. The girls rarely, if ever, objected because they had been taught that this was normal. I tried to convince the families I had built relationships with that there were other ways to make money, but it's hard to change traditions that have lasted for centuries. In this case, in this country, tradition has nothing to do with it."

Kelsey and Ron continued to watch the camp, but the activity soon subsided. The young women who had been in charge of breakfast were shooed away by Sergeant Coeburnite. *Off to other chores*, Kelsey speculated. According to the usual pattern, they would keep busy all day and probably would not stop until they went to their quarters that night. Kelsey was about to suggest that they may as well leave and begin their trip back to town when she heard a noise.

"Do you hear that?" she whispered. She grabbed Ron's arm and motioned for him to be quiet. "Listen." They heard footsteps and the rustling of leaves not far away. Two men who appeared to be in their mid-twenties and were dressed in what Kelsey had begun to think of as the cult uniform came up through the bushes. They both had rifles slung over their shoulders. They were not trying to be quiet.

Kelsey and Ron flattened themselves against the soil and let the limbs of the bushes spring back into place. The bushes closed around them and hid their position. They held their breath as the young men passed within six feet of where they lay.

"Pops said we have to relieve the guards on the north side," one of the men complained as he plodded up the hill. He was obviously unhappy with this assignment. "Why do we need guards? Who does he think will bother us here? We own the land. They can't run us off this time."

"I know what you'd rather do than be on guard duty," the

other man retorted. "I saw you trying to kiss Maddie yesterday. It didn't look like she was interested in someone as ugly as you." He laughed at his insult.

"She's just a tease. She'll warm up when she gets to know me better. Speaking of ugly, you didn't seem to be doing any better with Allie. Maybe we should swap." They slapped each other on the back as they roared with laughter. Their conversation trailed off as they continued their climb up the mountain.

"Great guards!" Kelsey whispered. The men could be heard crashing through the bushes on their way up the hill. Obviously, they were confident that no one would bother them—or the compound. "Creepy!" she added.

"Yep," Ron agreed. "I don't think that's just empty boasting from those two. We need to talk with Jason and possibly adjust our plans. I don't completely understand everything we just saw and heard, but Allie and Maddie may be in danger. I don't want to lie here in the woods while they're assaulted... or worse."

His comments raised goosebumps on Kelsey's arms. They echoed her own thoughts. "We still don't have any proof that they're there against their will. They may not even realize they're in danger. I agree. We definitely need a new strategy. Our current plan is not working."

That evening, after they had showered away the day's grime and as they ate dinner, Kelsey and Ron discussed their options and different tactics they might use against the compound. They decided to check in with Jason, update him on the day's events, and present their new plan. Jason was working late, and when Ron called, he informed them that he would be in the office if they wanted to come by.

Kelsey was putting on her sneakers when the doorbell rang. She answered the door and was surprised to see that a woman she had never seen before was standing on the porch. "Can I help you?"

"I hope so. I'm Mrs. Bridges. I know you're looking to buy land. I have a piece of bottom land I'd like to show you. I think it would be perfect for your business headquarters."

"Uh, I..." Kelsey stammered. "My husband and I were just about to go out. Can it wait? Maybe sometime next week?"

"Please, Mrs. Moore," the woman said, wringing her hands. "The bank is going to foreclose. We'll lose everything unless we catch up on our payments. My husband has been sick and can't work. I don't know what else to do. Selling some of our land would save our home." She paused, sucked in a shaky breath, and pulled nervously at the bottom of her shirt.

Kelsey saw the fear and desperation in the woman's face. She felt like a fraud. She didn't actually have the money to purchase or lease any land, but she couldn't tell the woman that. "Let me speak with my husband," she said. The woman nodded and remained where she was. Kelsey returned to the living room where Ron was waiting.

"I heard," Ron said when he saw Kelsey's face. "Look, the only thing we can do is have you go with her and take a look at the land. I'll meet with Jason and discuss our next move." He lowered his voice. "I hate this farce as much as you do."

"Okay. I suppose that is best," Kelsey agreed. She added softly, "But I don't have to like it." She picked up her purse, waved good-bye to Ron, and joined Mrs. Bridges on the porch.

"I'll drive," the other woman offered, "since I know the way."

CHAPTER FIVE

While Jason waited for Ron to arrive, he worked through some administrative duties. He had not seen Kelsey or Ron since their hike up Love Vine mountain together. They stayed busy with their surveillance of the Coeburn camp, and it took up most of their days. Jason was busy, too. He often felt like he needed to be cloned in order to keep up with his duties. He had not had a full day off in the last two weeks.

Mason Valley was a peaceful community, but that didn't mean it didn't have its share of incidents that required the sheriff's attention. Mixed in with teenage mischief, false reports, and a couple of domestic disturbances, there had been a break-in and robbery at Harper's Feed Store outside of town on the Charlotte highway.

It had taken Jason over a week to solve the case. This was mostly due to Mr. Harper not sharing crucial details of the crime and instead trying to protect the identity of the robber. Mr. Harper had filed a police report so he could make an insurance claim for the broken door and busted safe, but that was before he found out that his nephew, Lenny, was the robber. It wasn't until a friend of Lenny's came forward that the robber was identified. That meant that Jason now had two cases to put together before he could turn them over to the district attorney: the robbery by the nephew and obstruction of justice by the uncle.

At long last, Jason signed off on the report and closed his laptop. He put his hands behind his head and leaned back in his chair. He wanted to close his eyes, put his feet up on the desk, and take a nap. He let the urge pass. The citizens of Mason Valley would not approve of their sheriff sleeping on the job, no matter how sleep-deprived he was.

Jason opened his eyes and sat up as Ron walked into the sheriff's office. "What's up?" he asked. "Where's Kelsey?" He hid his disappointment that she wasn't with Ron. He spoke with her frequently on the phone when she reported in and updated him on what was happening at the Coeburn compound, but that wasn't the same as seeing her.

"Kelsey went to look over a piece of property," Ron said, explaining about Mrs. Bridges's sudden appearance at their house. He slumped into a chair across from Jason and picked up a map of Love Vine Mountain that lay open on his desk. He began to study it, particularly the area around the Coeburn compound. He launched right into business. "Kelsey and I both think our surveillance is moving too slowly. What we need is a closer look at what's going on inside the compound. We could split up and take different shifts, but we don't think that will provide much more insight than what we've got now."

"What do you have in mind?" Jason asked.

"What I'd like to do is make a quick trip to Atlanta tomorrow and pick up some listening and video equipment. If we can plant a camera inside the compound, we'll have a better chance of getting some real information about what goes on there. We'd hear actual conversations and be able to record sound and video, which will be the best evidence."

Jason leaned back in his chair and ran a hand through his hair. "But you'd have to make a trip into the compound to hide the equipment. That's much riskier than originally planned and illegal unless we have a warrant."

"Look," Ron said, "I spoke with Richard at the office, and he said he has some new stuff that just came in. It's very high tech and more powerful than anything we've used in the past. We can activate the devices with our cell phones."

"You think you can get close enough to plant them? Without getting caught?" Jason seemed skeptical. "I'm sure they have guards posted around the property."

"They have guards," Ron said, "but I'm not sure how capable they are." He went on to give Jason an account of what they had witnessed that morning. "We need a different, bolder strategy than what we're doing now."

"I agree." Jason pursed his lips. This was a dangerous idea, but there didn't seem to be another way. "It's time we found out what Coeburn's operation is about. I'm listening. What's your plan?"

"We've noticed there's a building where the single women sleep. It's probably the best place to plant a bug. It's located a little closer to the property line than the other buildings, so it's slightly more accessible. We could pick up the women's private conversations."

"And you think their conversations would tell us what we want to know?"

"Maybe," Ron said. "They might share stories at night that would give us some insight into their pasts, how they got there, and what goes on in the camp."

"Would bugging the women's quarters be better than bugging the single male's?"

"I think so. Most of what young men brag about among themselves will be exaggerated and nowhere near the truth."

"True," Jason agreed. "I'd have to get a court order to make this legal, but I think Judge Kline would give us one after what you witnessed this morning. Coeburn's abuse of his wife, or maybe wife, and your suspicion that the young women were being shopped to the men should be enough for surveillance warrant." Still, Jason was uneasy about this plan. A memory of Afghanistan popped into his mind.

"Of course," Ron agreed.

"Okay. If you think this is the best option, let's proceed." Jason leaned forward. "You're right: we have to do something. But I need to stress that both you and Kelsey need to be extremely cautious."

Ron and Jason discussed the plan further and the logistics of getting into the compound.

"By the way," Jason said during a lull in the conversation. He paused, considered the question he was about to ask, nodded, and decided to proceed. With his heavy workload, he might not get another chance for a private conversation with Ron anytime soon. "I've been wanting to ask," Jason said, "are you and Kelsey, uh, are you dating? I'm just curious..." His voice trailed off. Questions about Kelsey's life over the last three years had been chasing their tails around and around in his mind ever since she first appeared in his office.

"Just curious, eh?" Ron asked. "Me and Kelsey, dating? How do you know we're not married, like in our cover story?"

"Because the day you arrived, I pulled her away from you." Jason paused and shrugged his shoulders. "If you had been her husband, you would have decked me for overstepping and practically mauling your wife."

"It was pretty intense," Ron agreed, "but I figured unexpectedly reconnecting with an old friend like that justified your actions."

"Regardless of the circumstances, I would have reacted differently if she were my wife," Jason continued. "I have wondered, though, if you are a couple or were a couple." He looked down and fingered the papers on his desk. "I mean... you seem close."

Jason lifted his eyes and looked squarely at Ron. He might be disappointed by the answer, but he needed to spit out the question. Answers rarely changed, even if you put them off. At the moment, all he had invested in the answer was an interest in how Kelsey's life had unfolded over the last three years.

"Yes, we are close. Very close, in fact." Ron drew out his comment, teasing with his answer. Jason sat stone-faced, momentarily regretting his question. Ron continued slowly, "I've known Kelsey for most of my life, and we do love each other."

Jason's stony expression changed only slightly.

"Okay, I'll stop toying with you—poor guy! Kels and I a couple? Ha! Kelsey would explode with laughter at that idea. No way! Just ask my wife, Victoria."

"Wife? But I thought..." Jason began. "Kelsey is always ragging on you about other women, as if she's jealous."

"Yep, Vick and I will celebrate our one-year anniversary next month. You added two and two and got five, buddy. Kelsey never misses a chance to tease me about my past dating habits. I dated a lot—I mean, *a lot*—while in college, but I got tired of that life." Ron leaned back in his chair, steepled his hands under his chin, and smiled. "When I met Victoria, I knew that she was the one I'd been searching for. I was ready to marry her six weeks after we met, but we dated for another year before I managed to convince her that my reputation as a serial dater was only because I hadn't met her yet and that I was ready to settle down—but only with her." Ron clearly enjoyed talking about Victoria. His face lit up as he reminisced. He likely missed her, and talking about her was the next best thing to being with her.

Ron shifted in his chair, then leaned forward. "Look, man, I'd do anything for Kelsey. I think she'd do the same for me, but we never dated or even thought about dating. She's like a sister. I was her substitute brother when Joe went off to college."

Jason relaxed, but then Ron gave him an additional jolt. "Now,

Richard is the one you should be worried about. The guy's probably planning the wedding as we speak."

Before Jason could respond, Ron continued, "So, you're interested in Kelsey? Did you... uh... did you date... in Afghanistan? I
mean, you say Kelsey and I seem close, but you two appear to have
some sort of connection, too."

Jason waved off Ron's suggestion with a shake of the head.

"And your flirting with her on the mountain didn't go unnoticed," Ron added.

Jason tried to keep a guilty look from flitting across his face.
"Me and Kelsey in Afghanistan? Are you kidding?" he asked, direct-
ing the conversation away from their hike up Love Vine Mountain.
"Every time I came near her, she looked ready to bolt. Even if I just
said hello, she'd stick that diamond engagement ring in my face. It
meant 'Back off,' so I did. We were all army business, all the time.
Our 'special connection,' as you call it, is common between fellow
soldiers. It's called depending on each other for your life."

"I can understand that, but you're not fishing for information
now just to make idle conversation, are you?" Ron pressed.

"I won't deny that I thought she was beautiful and intelligent—I still do—but a war zone is no place for romance. In a war
zone, you can't separate fact from fiction, loneliness from love,
love from lust. I didn't want to leave there with a broken heart or
inflict one upon someone else."

"We ask a lot of our troops," Ron said softly.

"When I deployed, I decided to stick to business and get home
in one piece, both physically and emotionally. I got one out of
two." Jason fidgeted with the papers on his desk, then decided to
finish his questions. "But... Kelsey didn't marry the guy who gave
her the ring?"

"Oh, Kelsey and her ring!" Ron shook his head. "If you'd looked
closely, you'd have seen it wasn't real. Well, maybe you'd need to
be a jeweler to see that it's zirconium. It's the same one she has on

now."

"I don't understand," Jason said.

"She had a bad breakup in college," Ron explained. "A serious two-year relationship hit the rocks. Lucas, her fiancé, broke her heart. He was a real douchebag. She was hurt very badly."

"Oh..." Jason said. "She never let me get close enough to check out the ring. So, she was engaged at one time?"

"Yes. Lucas was her first serious relationship. I tried to warn her about him, but she wouldn't listen. All I could do was be there for her after the engagement crashed and burned. She bought that phony ring to wear, as her shield—a way of protecting herself from being approached by other men and having a repeat. I think she took it to the extreme, but I'm not her. I don't know how I'd react in a similar situation."

Ron leaned back in his chair. A frown wrinkled his brow. "But, look, man, you really should be talking to Kelsey if you have questions about her love life. I know her well, but she doesn't share all the intimate details. My advice? Speak up if you're interested."

Jason didn't respond to that. He could say that his interest went no deeper than friendship, but was that actually true? Ron's advice was sound. Jason was not completely clueless about the dating game—the game in which men and women danced around each other, working up or losing the courage to approach someone. Jason wasn't a coward, but the right time had to present itself. Kelsey wasn't married or engaged to Richard—yet—so she was basically single. But now wasn't the right time—in so many ways—to make any kind of move. To the public, Kelsey was Ron's wife.

"There's Richard, now, huh?" Jason asked ruefully. "Well, for all your advice and analysis of our 'connection,' I have no idea what Kelsey thinks of me. For all I know, I'm nothing but an army buddy. I hope we can become friends, at least."

"Friends," Ron snorted. "Sure, buddy! You never know until you try." Ron leaned forward and looked intently at Jason. "One last piece of advice. My momma has a saying: 'Life-changing opportunities come around rarely. Never waste them or fail to take advantage when they do come.' To put it another way, as I learned while playing basketball, you can't make the basket if you don't take the shot."

"With all due respect to your momma, I can't take any shots until the Coeburn situation is resolved. I can't blow your cover, and after what Mason Valley went through with the last sheriff, they don't need to think their replacement sheriff is a philanderer and a home-wrecker." Jason paused for a moment, then added. "Looks like I'll have to stick with the status quo for now."

"Yeah, I see your predicament. I don't want to fight you to defend my wife's honor," Ron laughed. "I don't want to hurt you. I've done some boxing in my past."

"But I carry a gun, remember?" Jason challenged with a grin before waving off the comment. "Rest easy. I can control myself. I won't let it come to that. Friendship will be enough."

With that, Jason changed the conversation back to the surveillance operation. "We'll get the warrant tomorrow while you're away. Then we'll decide how and when to get into the compound."

Ron nodded. "Since we're in agreement then, if it's alright with you, I think I'll leave for home tonight. I'm anxious to see Vick. I'll be back sometime in the afternoon. I'll call Kelsey and let her know."

"Sure. No problem. Have a good trip."

Ron stood and moved toward the door. He opened it, but then turned back toward Jason. "One more thing. Kelsey is staying here in case something comes up. She'll be without a car tomorrow, so can you see that she has a way to get around while I'm gone?" At Jason's nod, he added, "And remember what I said: never waste those rare opportunities. All great loves started with friendship."

"Goodbye Ron," Jason pointedly dismissed the other man. As Ron closed the door, the twinkle in his eye and his smug expression did not escape Jason's notice.

Jason wasn't sure whether he had convinced Ron that his only interest in Kelsey lay in the possibility of friendship. If he were being honest, Jason wasn't convinced, himself. Yes, he was attracted to Kelsey, but his personal life had to take a backseat to the thorn in his side: Coeburn.

Jason heard Ron whistling happily as he walked toward his car in the parking lot. Did his happiness come from riling up Jason or was it due to being on his way to Atlanta—or both? The more Jason got to know Ron, the more he liked him. He was glad Ron was Kelsey's partner. He would watch her back, and after working alongside her in the army, Jason knew she would reciprocate. They made a good team.

Jason still had work to do before ending his day. He forced thoughts of his personal life from his mind and picked up the camera SD card that Ron had left with him. It contained pictures Ron had taken on his and Kelsey's trip to the Coeburn compound that morning. Jason was particularly interested in the four visitors the pair had observed meeting with Coeburn.

Jason thoughtfully turned the card over in his palm, then got up from his desk, walked to the evidence room, and unlocked the door. The front office was sometimes like Grand Central Station, with passersby coming in to chat if they saw Jason in the office. He used the secure evidence room whenever he had a job to do that required privacy.

Jason entered the room and approached a desktop computer that was connected to two large monitors sitting on a desk at the rear of the room. He started up the computer, inserted the SD card, and scrolled through the pictures. He stopped when he came to images of the four men seated at the table with Coeburn. Jason enlarged the photos, copied them to a separate drive, and displayed their faces on one of the monitors.

The pictures were not the best quality, as parts of their faces were blocked by Coeburn and one of his henchmen. But Jason had enough detail that he might be able to find them on traffic camera footage. It was worth a shot.

Jason logged into the city server and began searching through the traffic camera footage—the only local database he had access to that contained photos. Looking through all the footage would be a slow process, like searching for the proverbial needle in a haystack. He'd start with today's footage and work backward a few days. Hopefully, the cameras had captured images of the four men driving around the city. If he could get a license plate number, he could identify them—or at least get a clue as to where to look next.

Jason searched through the past few days without success. It was possible that the men came in on roads that didn't have cameras. If they were involved in some kind of criminal activity, they would know to avoid the busiest streets. Jason did spot the truck that belonged to the Coeburn compound, but there was only the driver inside. He wasn't one of the men in the pictures.

Jason looked at the clock. It was almost eleven p.m. His eyes were starting to blur, and he hadn't spotted anyone that even resembled the four men.

Ron had said that the men came from the south side of the compound, so they must have used the old logging trail. He made a mental note to have Ferguson check the logging road tomorrow to see if the men might have tossed out a water bottle or candy wrapper—anything that might contain DNA. Of course, even if they found something, getting DNA results back would take longer than Jason wanted to wait.

Jason—or one of his deputies—would also check local lodging places on the off chance that someone had seen any of the four men. That was a long shot. In Jason's experience, if the men had come to Mason Valley for nefarious reasons, they wouldn't linger in town long enough to spend the night.

It was time for Plan B.

Jason downloaded the photos and sent them to Agent Baker, his contact at the FBI field office in Charlotte, as an email attachment. Agent Baker was the lead agent for the Violent Crimes Against Children and Child Exploitation Division in Charlotte, and he had access to the FBI's facial-recognition databases, which might contain information on the men. All Jason needed was a name. Then, he could search the National Crime Information Center, or NCIC, database for more detailed information on the men. If they had ever been in trouble with a law-enforcement agency, their information would be in the NCIC database.

As Jason hit 'Send' on his email, he resigned himself to the fact that all he could do with the photos for now was wait for the FBI to respond. He asked Agent Baker to make his request a priority. It was an entirely proper request, but there was probably a long list of similar requests in front of his.

The slow pace of the investigation was beginning to wear on Jason's nerves. It was becoming harder to keep his frustrations in check. They needed a break and needed it soon.

Kelsey and Ron's plan to plant surveillance cameras in the compound meant things were moving into territory more dangerous than what Jason had wanted, but Ron's graphic description of what he and Kelsey had witnessed that morning had Jason's mind and gut working overtime.

This operation had reached a critical phase, and his instincts warned him that nothing good was going on at the Coeburn compound on Love Vine Mountain.

CHAPTER SIX

Kelsey yawned, stretched, and turned over in bed. The house was quiet. Ron usually got up first and had the coffee made by the time she made her way to the kitchen. She normally woke to the sound of him dropping things, rattling around in the kitchen cupboards, and muttering to himself.

Ron got up early so he could do his workout routine of push-ups, sit-ups, and other calisthenics. Kelsey preferred to exercise outdoors and usually went for an early run along the path by the park.

She looked at the clock. Eight-thirty. She had slept later than usual. She stretched again. She felt lazy. She decided to skip the run today. The temperature outside would be warming up by now, and with the warmth came humidity.

Instead, she could get dressed, go into town, and do some shopping. *Oh crap! No car,* she reminded herself. She could walk into town. It wasn't far. After all the mountain-climbing she'd been doing recently, a walk into town would be a breeze. Of course, Ron had said before he left town that Jason would give her a ride wherever she wanted to go, but she didn't feel right imposing on him. He had more important things to do than driving her around town like the titular Miss Daisy.

She would get dressed first and then decide what to do. The whole day stretched out before her.

Kelsey showered and pulled a white sleeveless beachy dress out of her closet. She was well-rested and felt happy this morning. The swath of red poppies across the front of the dress's skirt fit her cheerful mood. She slid her feet into strappy sandals and left her hair hanging loose in soft curls around her shoulders. Just for fun, she added some makeup and a squirt of perfume. After the constant ponytail, bug spray, and hiking clothes, it felt good to wear something cool—to do something extra to feel feminine.

Kelsey thought of Stephanie as she looked herself over in the full-length bedroom mirror. She doubted Stephanie would be impressed by the image reflected in the mirror. Her dress wasn't from a designer label, but Kelsey felt good in it.

Kelsey made coffee, and once she had a steaming mug, creamed just the way she liked it—a rich caramel color—she grabbed a croissant, from the counter, slathered it with raspberry jam and went out to the porch swing to enjoy her breakfast. The morning was quiet and peaceful. Kelsey pushed herself back and forth, lifting her feet each time the swing moved forward. The soft breeze felt heavenly as it blew through her loosened hair.

What did she want to do today? Nothing came to mind. Kelsey scolded herself for being so lazy. She was completely unmotivated to get up from the swing and do anything. Instead, she closed her eyes and nestled deeper into the cushions on the swing.

At the sound of a vehicle, she opened her eyes and sat up. Jason's pickup was turning into the driveway, and he was wearing his sheriff's uniform.

"Is this an official call, Sheriff?" she called out playfully as he approached the steps to the porch. "I swear, I didn't rob that bank." After their hike up the mountain together, she and Jason had settled into an easy friendship. She hadn't seen him and only spoke with him on the phone, but she no longer worried that she would panic and dissolve into a puddle of hysteria when she looked at him. His very-much-alive face no longer conjured the sound of explosions or the image of his body flying through the air.

They had shared an experience that others couldn't understand and that most wouldn't believe was true, but all that mattered was that they had both survived. As Ron had suggested on their first day in Mason Valley, she could wait for Jason's explanation as to why he hadn't used his connections as team leader to search for her and the other team members. The Jason she knew and trusted would have a logical explanation.

"It looks like I could arrest you for loitering in the sunshine on this beautiful spring morning." Jason smiled as he climbed the steps and sat down in a nearby rocking chair. He relaxed into it and began moving the chair, making the boards on the porch squeak with each rock.

Jason closed his eyes and rested his head on the back of the chair as he continued to rock. Kelsey studied him for a moment. He looked tired. His job couldn't be easy with such a small staff. And now, he had new worries ever since Coeburn set up his compound in his backyard.

During the time Kelsey had served with Jason in Afghanistan, he had always been the consummate professional soldier. His first priority was caring for those under his command. He tirelessly trained his team as he readied them for dangerous patrols, as well as for the special mission he and Kelsey had led together.

It was tragic that their special operation had ended under such dreadful circumstances. All of Jason's previous successes were tainted by that failure. Kelsey's military career hadn't been as long as Jason's, but hers had ended under a cloud, too. As his second-in-command, she felt responsible for the mission's failure. As the team leader, he must have felt even more responsible.

Except for a few more fine lines around his eyes and the scar on his chin, Jason looked much the same as he had when they served together. His hair was a little longer, and there was a touch of gray in his temples that hadn't been there before. Whether the longer hair was from personal preference or because he didn't have time to get it trimmed, Kelsey could only guess. But he still had the piercing dark-brown eyes, strong jaw, and tall, lithe, athletic build he'd had when she first met him. In Kelsey's assessment, Jason Wilder was the complete package: smart, funny, caring, and kind, all rolled into a handsome body.

He suddenly opened his eyes and caught her looking at him. He smiled when he saw her blush. "I won't arrest you today, Mrs. Moore, but I've come with orders from higher up. I would have called first, but I was afraid you were a flight risk. You need to come with me," he said as he raised his head from the chair back. "Preferably without a struggle, but I have handcuffs, if necessary."

Kelsey blushed again. "Why, whatever do you mean, Sheriff?" she asked in a feigned Southern accent. "No crime, no time—isn't that the sheriff's code?"

"I'm sure I can come up with a crime." Jason's dark eyes sparkled as he teased her. "My parents have requested that you come out to the farm for an early dinner. I'll have you back home by the time Ron returns. I'm on-duty today, but Ferguson is in the office. He'll call me if something comes up that he can't handle."

"But your parents don't even know me," Kelsey pointed out.

"They know of you, but that doesn't matter. There aren't any strangers where my parents and grandparents are concerned. Come on. You have the day off with Ron in Atlanta. Besides, you need a break." He stood and held out his hand.

"Okay, you convinced me," Kelsey agreed. She reached out, took the hand Jason offered, and let him pull her up from the swing. His hand on hers was firm and warm. He dropped her hand when they stepped out of the shadows of the porch. They walked side-by-side to the truck, and Jason helped her into it.

"I have to warn you: my sister, Cate, and her husband, Ken, are there with their two munchkins. Also, my Wilder grandparents are there."

"What's the occasion? Someone's birthday or an anniversary?"

"My family doesn't need an occasion to get together, but the out-of-towners came to attend the mayor's annual Spring Fling tomorrow." Jason put the truck in reverse, backed out onto the street, and started driving east. "My grandfather served on the city council with the mayor up until about five years ago. The mayor always invites him. Grandpa was sick last year and couldn't make it."

"I'm glad he's better and could come this year. Mayor Landry invited me and Ron, too. I guess it would look strange if we didn't go," Kelsey said.

"Yes, you need to go. It's a chance to network. It's the event of the season, but that's a pretty low bar, since Mason Valley doesn't have that many events to compare it to." Jason chuckled.

As they drove east through town and out into the countryside, the valley widened into a flat plain. Kelsey could see mountains with purple-shadowed valleys in the distance, but this plain was where all the farming took place. They drove past the Bridges farm, which Kelsey had visited the night before.

"Jason, what happened to Mr. Bridges? He was sick?" Mrs. Bridges had not shared what was wrong with her husband, and Kelsey hadn't wanted to pry.

"No, he was injured. He fell off a ladder while cleaning the gutters and broke his hip. They do truck farming and own a produce stand. With him laid up, they couldn't plant their fields this spring. Mrs. Bridges is trying to keep it going, but without anything to harvest, I don't see how she can do it much longer."

"I feel sorry for them. I wish I could help. She showed me a nice piece of property, but unfortunately, I don't need any land—

anywhere."

"I know. It's a real tragedy. There's not much work around here unless you're connected to the tourism industry, and when you lose the job you do have, it's devastating."

They drove in silence for a while after that, each busy with their private thoughts.

"Kelsey," Jason said at last. He seemed to search for words. "This Richard you work with... I, uh... when I first called about contracting with you for the job at the compound, I asked to speak with your father. He flatly refused. He said that I didn't need to do business with anyone but him and that all new surveillance contracts fell under his department."

"Richard can be a little rude. Actually, a lot rude." *And self-important*, Kelsey thought. "But why did you want to speak with my father?"

"I wanted to ask him about you." Jason glanced at her and then looked away. "I remembered you mentioning that your father had a security consulting firm in Atlanta. That's why I chose his firm for this job. I thought, 'How many Barrett security firms can there be?'"

"Did you insist that Richard connect you?" Kelsey saw a dressing-down from her father in Richard's future.

"I didn't push the issue." Jason paused. "I don't know. I wanted to find out what happened to you, but I think I was afraid of the answer. I didn't want to upset your father with my questions, either."

They both lapsed back into silence, each caught up in memories of that night when everything went wrong. Kelsey refused to let the familiar visions of fire and explosions take up space in her mind. The day was too beautiful to ruin. She gazed out the window at the countryside. At one time, it hadn't taken much to drag her back into that night. It was easier to block the images now because she knew that the body blown into the air wasn't Jason's.

"I'm sorry." Jason reached over and squeezed her hand. "Sorry for what you went through."

She squeezed back. "It was war, and as they say, war is hell." No truer statement could describe that night. For several minutes, Kelsey wrestled with whether to ask a question that had been on her mind for years. Now, she hesitated, afraid of the answer. She gave herself a mental shove and blurted out, "What happened that night, Jason? What went wrong?"

"I honestly don't know," Jason said sadly. "I've gone over everything a million times. I just don't know."

"I thought you had died when I saw that body fly into the air," Kelsey said slowly, her voice barely above a whisper. "The body... it was in pieces. It was so... horrible," she ended weakly.

Jason pulled the truck off the road and brought it to a stop on a bypass lane. He leaned over the console and pulled her into his arms. "Shh. I'm here. It must have been the guard you saw. He was right in front of the hut." He ran his left hand up and down Kelsey's right arm.

"I saw a flash. I knew instantly that it was a shoulder-fired missile," Jason said, sharing what he experienced that night. "I ran toward an outcropping of rocks, but unfortunately, the blast caught up with me. It sent me head-first into the jagged pile. The rocks saved my life and also injured me. If I had stayed where I was, I really would have been blown to bits."

Kelsey felt Jason's arms tense, but he continued. "I was badly injured, but not dead." He paused and swallowed. "I replay that scene over and over again in my mind. I was probably unconscious and missed a lot of it. I'm sorry you had to witness what you did. It's inadequate, but I'm sorry."

Kelsey nodded her head, unable to speak.

"I completely understand why you went to pieces that day in my office." Jason hugged her tighter, then gently kissed her forehead.

"Thank God you moved out of the blast zone," Kelsey said. "I struggled to understand what happened after I recovered from my injuries. Even with the passage of time, I can't let it go. I'd like to know what went wrong. That's what still bothers me the most. I thought we had planned for all contingencies." Kelsey dropped her head to Jason's shoulder.

The pulse in his throat beat against her forehead. The scent of his cologne—light sandalwood with a hint of citrus—filled her nostrils. The warmth from his body spread through her, and the odd tingling sensation she experienced whenever he touched her ran along her spine. She had the urge to nestle closer. She felt safe in his arms, and the tension caused by reliving that explosive night drained from her body.

They sat silently like this for another moment, both comforted by the contact and occupied with thoughts of their personal nightmares.

Jason finally broke the silence. "It took me quite a while to recover from my injuries. I was in the hospital for what felt like years, but I guess it was only a few months. It took me even longer to work up the courage to ask what went wrong. I knew the answers would be bad," Jason admitted.

"And were they?" Kelsey looked up at Jason. His face was strained.

"I couldn't get *any* answers," he said. "After I was well enough to remember portions of that night, I started asking questions. No one would tell me anything. I couldn't even find information on Major Burton—on where he was or what he was doing."

"What would be the purpose of that?" Kelsey asked.

"I honestly don't know." Jason's hand stopped moving up and down Kelsey's arm, and rested on her forearm as he remembered. "The army acted as though I was out of my mind. There were times when I thought I was crazy, and in truth, maybe sometimes I was. It took me a long time to get my physical health back, but that was a piece of cake compared to getting my mind straight."

Kelsey placed her hand on Jason's and rubbed his knuckles gently. He took a deep breath and continued, "The thought that it was my fault and that I had led the team to their deaths was almost more than I could bear at times."

"Jason," Kelsey said gently, "I'm ashamed that I accused you of not looking for me."

"It's okay. You didn't say anything I haven't said to myself. Questions plagued me for months. How could I have done things differently? What went wrong? Why hadn't I anticipated what happened?" He fell silent, and the shallowness of his breath proved that he hadn't completely come to terms with it yet

Kelsey broke the silence. "It wasn't your fault any more than mine. I'm finally able to accept that there wasn't anything either of us could have done. I got the same reaction from the army when I asked what happened. Nothing! Zilch! I thought you might have had better luck with finding out what happened than I could," she said. "I'm sorry." Her eyes glistened with unshed tears as she thought of Jason and the other men on the team. Five had not survived that night.

Kelsey swiped at her eyes with her fingers and took a shaky breath. She hadn't had a meltdown, which was a definite improvement.

Jason tightened his arms around Kelsey's shoulders. "I've exhausted all my resources and ideas in searching for the truth. My father said he'd try to find out something through his old contacts. Maybe he'll finally get to the truth. We'll all feel better if we know."

"Really? Has your dad found anything?"

"Not yet. I just recently asked him if he would try. After I discovered that you were alive, I decided it was time to find out who else survived. I'll let you know when I hear something."

Jason placed a finger beneath her chin, raised her head, and looked into her eyes. "Better?" he asked. At her nod, Jason's eyes moved across her face before coming to rest on her lips. Kelsey held her breath.

Honking from a passing car made them both jump apart. Jason quickly removed his arms from around her shoulders.

"Damn!" Jason slapped the steering wheel, quickly put the truck in drive, and pulled back onto the highway. "I hope that wasn't a citizen of Mason Valley thinking he just passed the sheriff making out along the side of the highway. And with a married woman, no less."

"Not very smart," a flustered Kelsey agreed. "I mean... I need to protect my cover story. Let's hope they didn't recognize us or your truck." She breathed in deeply as she tried to slow her racing heart. Was it the honking car horn or the fact that Jason looked like he was about to kiss her that had her heart racing? Could she honestly deny she had wanted him to kiss her?

What are you doing, Barrett? she asked herself. *Remember the reason you're here in Mason Valley!* It certainly wasn't the kiss she had been ready to accept and return just a few moments ago. She was here on business, and Jason was her client. They had just gotten caught up in comforting each other, that's all. But the people in the passing car wouldn't know that.

As they drove toward Jason's parents' house, he returned to the topic of what had happened to him after he recovered from his injuries and was released back to active duty. The only job the army offered him was a desk job in the Pentagon.

"My superiors sent me a not-so-subtle message," he said with a grimace. "As the leader of the team that night—and with such a massive failure on my record—I was stuck in a desk job and at the rank of captain for the foreseeable future—maybe forever. I decided not to wait around for the army to kick me out. My commitment was up, so after eight years of service, I resigned my commission and came home to Mason Valley."

Kelsey reached over and placed her hand on his arm. "You

know it wasn't your fault, right? I keep repeating that I'm sorry, but I don't know what else to say. You lost your military career."

"Nah. It was time I came home anyway. Living with the knowledge that someone was trying to kill me twenty-four-seven was getting old," Jason replied with a rueful smile.

They turned to lighter subjects and chatted happily as they drove the rest of the way to Jason's parents' house. Kelsey was relieved and even happy to catch up on everything that had happened in the years since they had last seen each other. Ron had been right: Jason had tried to find her, but as with her, the army had blocked all information.

Jason pointed out landmarks as they drove toward his parents' house. He identified who owned which farm, who had young kids, and who were empty nesters. Their mood was light by the time Jason turned onto a long driveway that wound toward a two-story red brick house. Large trees shaded an expansive lawn where two small children wrestled and played. Several outbuildings strategically placed around the property housed farm equipment. Kelsey noted that one was a greenhouse.

"I texted them that we were coming, so be prepared to be fell upon by many Wilders."

Just as Jason spoke, a stream of adults came out the front door and onto the porch. They lined up and watched as Jason parked the truck. The two children came running toward them, yelling, "Uncle Jason! Uncle Jason!" A petite woman broke from the group of adults and also approached them.

Kelsey immediately guessed that the woman was Jason's mother. Her dark hair and dark eyes, so much like Jason's, were obvious clues. Jason gathered the children in his arms, swung them around, and gave them each a hug. Then, he put them down and turned to hug his mother. She next turned to Kelsey and, as if she had known her for years, wrapped Kelsey in a warm embrace before Jason even introduced them.

"Kelsey, this is my mom, Carolyn." The others approached, and Jason introduced them as well. "And my dad, Ben. My grandparents Barbara and John Wilder. My sister, Cate. Her husband, Ken. And these two miscreants are Missy and KJ—or Kenneth Jason when he gets into trouble."

Kelsey was engulfed in hugs as Jason's family greeted her. If she didn't know better, she'd think she was at a Barrett reunion. The Wilder family's gathering reminded her very much of her visits to her grandparents.

After refreshments were served in the shade of the front porch and they had all chatted for a while, Jason invited Kelsey to take a tour of the farm with him. They walked toward the vegetable garden and passed a chicken coop on the way. They stopped in front of the greenhouse.

"My mother grows vegetable seedlings in here and then plants them in the spring when the weather is right. The flowers you see blooming around the property were also started in the greenhouse," he explained.

They walked on and paused by the neat rows of vegetables in the garden. Some of the vegetables were just beginning to peek above the ground, but the early crops like radishes, lettuce, and carrots were ready to be picked. Jason bent down and pulled up a handful of carrots, knocked off the dirt, and handed some to Kelsey.

"Let's go to the barn. There's someone there I want you to meet," he said. He led her toward the large structure not far from the garden. As they stepped into the dark shadows of the barn, Kelsey heard the sound of horses neighing as they welcomed the visitors. Two horses stuck their heads out of the stalls and neighed again as Kelsey and Jason approached.

"Easy girl," Jason said as he reached up and rubbed the white blaze running down the nose of a beautiful reddish-brown mare. "This is Ginger," he said as Kelsey reached out to rub the horse's neck.

"That's an appropriate name. She's a beautiful color."

"She has a beautiful disposition, too." Jason held out the carrots, and Ginger gobbled them up within seconds. Then, she turned and nosed Kelsey's hand.

"Don't be greedy," Kelsey laughed even as she gave one of the carrots to the horse. She turned to the other stall. "And who's this?" She held out the remaining carrot to the light-brown horse with a thick black mane in the adjoining stall. He tossed his mane in greeting.

"This is Sam," Jason said as he fed the horse the remainder of his carrots. "They're both quarter horses—great riding companions. Do you ride?"

"Not since I was very young," Kelsey replied. She added with a laugh, "I'd probably need to be tied to the saddle now to keep from falling off."

"We'll have to give it a try sometime and see. That just might be worth the price of admission to watch." Jason grinned.

They left the barn and were strolling back to the house when Kelsey asked, "Is one of the horses yours?"

"Technically, no. They belong to my parents, but I rode often when I first got out of the army. Remember how I told you that my dad donates his hay to the therapy horse farm? Well, the director told my folks that riding was good for wounded veterans, too—those that are physically able to ride, anyway. They pestered me until I decided to give it a try."

"Did it help?"

"Surprisingly, yeah. It did," he said. "I could get on Sam, give him the reins, and just let him go wherever he chose. No thinking on my part, no decisions to be made. I was free—just along for the ride. I'd let him choose the trail and set the pace. Sometimes, he'd gallop, and other times, he'd plod along. After a while, when we both got tired, he'd bring me back to the barn."

"That does sounds very therapeutic." Kelsey matched her steps with Jason's as they crossed the lawn toward the house.

"It was. And I think it did more to help me heal mentally than anything else I tried."

Kelsey looked over at Jason. He appeared relaxed. The tension she had noticed in his shoulders when they talked on the roadside was gone. His stride was easy as they climbed the sloped embankment up to the house.

Kelsey suddenly realized that she, too, was relaxed, and happy. Her conversation with Jason had cleared the air as they shared what they had each gone through in the aftermath of the Afghan mission's failure. Her heart was soothed by knowing that Jason had not forgotten the team members. He was still trying to find information about them.

"I'm happy to hear that you found something that helped," Kelsey whispered as she lightly touched his arm. He placed his hand over hers and let it linger for a few seconds.

"Me too. Riding Sam helped me regain the sparkling personality you see today," he quipped. He squeezed her hand then dropped his back to his side as they neared the porch where the family sat watching them.

"Sparkling? I wouldn't get ahead of myself if I were you, Wildman," Kelsey said. They were both laughing as they neared the steps to the porch.

"Jason," Ben said, "we were just waiting for you. Want to join us in a game of horseshoes in the backyard?"

"Sure, but only if you're prepared to lose," Jason challenged. With that, Ben, John, and Ken got up, left the porch, and walked toward the backyard horseshoe pit.

Kelsey followed them and watched for a few minutes as they good-naturedly bickered and challenged each other. Then, she turned and entered the kitchen through the back door. She asked if she could help Carolyn, Barbara, and Cate with the dinner preparations. She expected to be shooed away, but instead quickly found herself helping Cate peel potatoes and doing other jobs as meted out by Carolyn. The women's warmth brought back memories of similar activities she had enjoyed when her mom was alive.

Dinner was ready and on the table by mid-afternoon. It was a traditional Southern dinner—usually reserved for Sundays and holidays—a meal too large to be lunch but too early to be called supper or dinner.

Today was not a holiday, and it was a Friday, but with Kelsey as their guest, Carolyn had prepared a special meal. A huge beef tenderloin roast took center stage on the long dining table. The main course was surrounded by dishes filled with mashed potatoes, gravy, sautéed yellow squash, green beans, homemade bread, and a variety of homemade pickles.

Everyone selected their seats, apparently according to a long Wilder tradition at family dinners. John and Barbara sat at each end of the table, with Carolyn and Ben on either side of John. Kelsey was seated beside Jason. Cate and Ken were seated on either side of the children, ready to restore order if either got out of control. Kelsey noted that the parents did not shush the kids but let them join into any conversation so long as they modulated their voices.

There was lots of laughter as they began passing the dishes around the table. There was one uncomfortable moment for Kelsey and Jason, though, when Missy asked, "Are you Uncle Jason's girlfriend?"

Before anyone could shush her, KJ added, "Are you going to be my Aunt Kelsey?"

"Missy, KJ," Cate said, "Miss Kelsey already has a husband." She turned to Kelsey. "I apologize. The kids want their Uncle Jason to find them an aunt." She narrowed her eyes accusingly at Jason and added loudly, "But he won't cooperate."

Jason scowled back at her.

"Leave Jason alone, Cate," Ken said. "He'll fall into the love trap one day and find himself ensnared like the rest of us." Cate glared at her husband. He smiled, then added, "That's not a complaint, sweetheart. I like being snared... though only by you."

"Nice save," Cate said with a laugh as she shook her head. She leaned over Missy and KJ and gave Ken a quick kiss.

John spoke up. "It's not as if Jason doesn't have any options. Stephanie is a beautiful girl, and you can tell she's in love with Jason—or wants to be."

"Grandpa," Jason cautioned as he quickly glanced at Kelsey.

Color rose in her cheeks as she thought about the moment on the side of the road earlier when Jason may or may not have been about to kiss her—which she may or may not have wanted.

"My sister needs to stop bringing up my bachelor status." Jason narrowed his eyes at Cate. "I don't need her help."

Cate made a face at her brother, picked up her wine glass, and stood. Her movement broke the uncomfortable silence that had settled over the table. "I want to propose a toast." Cate paused until everyone had raised their glasses. "I want to welcome our guest, Kelsey, into this Wilder chaos. Believe it or not, Kelsey, it can get even crazier than this. Also, I want to say to my brother, we love you. You work too much, but we're glad you found your way home today."

There were cheers all around the table. Kelsey and Jason both nodded in recognition of the toast.

"Kelsey," Barbara said after they had sipped their beverages, "it's too bad your husband had to go to Atlanta on business and couldn't join us. We'd like to meet him."

Again, Kelsey felt the weight of her and Ron's pretense, and heat rose in her cheeks. Apparently, today was her day to experience awkward moments. Of course, Barbara didn't know it was awkward. Kelsey opened her mouth to reply but stopped when she realized that she didn't know what to say.

"Would anyone like more sweet tea?" Carolyn suddenly asked. She rose from her chair and turned toward the sideboard where a pitcher of tea rested.

"Grandma," Jason said, "Ron will be at the Landrys' tomorrow. You can meet him then."

Kelsey relaxed and tried not to sigh in relief. She hated not being completely honest with this wonderful family, but she couldn't tell them the truth. Lies, even those with a useful purpose, had a way of tagging along wherever you went. She hoped they would forgive her when they learned the truth.

Later, Kelsey helped clear the table and then began helping Carolyn clean the kitchen. As they stacked plates on the kitchen counter, Carolyn leaned close and whispered, "Relax. I know you must feel bad about the deception."

"What?" Kelsey asked. "You know?" There was no use pretending that she didn't know what Carolyn meant.

"Jason told me. He knew I'd have questions about you. Don't worry. Your secret is safe with me and Ben. You can't have been married to an FBI agent for thirty-five years and not know how to keep secrets."

As Kelsey digested this information, Carolyn put the leftovers in the refrigerator. That done, she turned back to the younger woman. "I don't know if you know how badly Jason was injured in Afghanistan," she said. "At first, we were afraid we would lose him." She twisted her apron around her hands, an indication of the depth of her worry just after Jason had been injured. "He doesn't like to talk about it, but he was in a medically induced coma for about four weeks due to brain swelling. He injured his neck, and there was concern that he might not walk again."

Kelsey gasped and put her hand over her mouth. "I didn't know that."

"Thankfully, that resolved itself once the swelling went down in his cervical vertebrae. But it seemed to take forever before we knew whether his mobility would return. I think I aged twenty years during that time." She reached out and placed a hand on Kelsey's arm. "He'd be angry if he knew I was telling you this." It was a silent request to keep it between the two of them.

"I'm so sorry for what you went though. Thank you for telling me," Kelsey said. "I won't bring it up."

Carolyn nodded, then continued, "He spent another three months immobilized due to bruised lungs and a variety of broken bones in his back, hips, and ribs."

Kelsey reached out and put her arms around Carolyn's shoulders. Jason's injuries put her own into perspective. Hers had been bad, but mild compared to his.

"The doctors did a good job of piecing his broken bones back together, but it took him almost a year to completely heal—longer, if you count the physical therapy. And then the nightmares began." Carolyn shivered, looked away for few moments, then added, "He told me that he thought you had died. Did you know that? I know it haunted him."

"I know. He told me. I thought he had died, too." Kelsey paused to steady her voice.

Carolyn turned toward her and studied her face. "He seems better—more cheerful—since he learned you're alive. It's a victory: one less person for him to think he let down." Kelsey nodded. "And I repeat: you can relax about the pretense. I understand that you have a job to do."

Kelsey did relax—some—as Carolyn suggested. Part of the tension that had wound her up like a spring at the dinner table faded away. Jason's mother knew about the deception and why she was here. Carolyn knew she wasn't "cavorting with another man while her husband was out of town," as Kelsey's Grandmother Gilbert, the English teacher and queen of formal words, would say. It was only dinner with a friend's family, but some in the community might get the wrong idea. The people in the honking car, for instance. Sometimes, the largest commodity produced in a small town was gossip. That Carolyn knew the truth was a relief.

But perhaps the lie about her and Ron's marriage wasn't the only thing stressing her out. Maybe part of the problem was constantly having to be on guard against a slipup in her interactions with Jason.

It wasn't long before Jason joined them in the kitchen. He persuaded his mother to leave the clean-up to him and Kelsey. Carolyn left the kitchen for the porch while Kelsey and Jason fought over who did what.

Kelsey and Jason laughed and reminisced about funny things that had happened at the army base in Afghanistan. They avoided any discussion of the night it had all ended. Working together, they soon had the dishwasher loaded and running and the pots and pans scrubbed clean. They stacked the pots and pans on the counter so that Carolyn could put them away where she wanted.

"Your mom will thank us for not attempting to guess where they belong," Kelsey said.

Once the kitchen was in order, Kelsey and Jason joined the rest of the family on the front porch. Kelsey sat down beside Carolyn and Barbara. Barbara had a large framed hoop with a quilting a block fastened in the frame.

"Is that a wedding-ring pattern?" Kelsey asked.

"Yes, it is," Barbara replied, clearly surprised. "Do you quilt?"

"No, but my grandmothers do."

"It's very relaxing. I started a quilting circle in Palm Beach. Those ladies actually do know how to do more than golf," Barbara said with a laugh. "I belonged to one when I lived here, and now, I've talked Carolyn into joining it."

"I'm trying, but I'm not the expert you are," Carolyn said. "I'm starting out slow on something simpler than that wedding-ring pattern."

"You should have been doing it all along. If there's one person who needs a hobby to relax them, it's a nurse."

"You were a nurse?" Kelsey asked Carolyn.

"I was a surgical nurse up until Ben decided to retire," Carolyn explained.

"Then you definitely needed something to relax you," Kelsey agreed. She nodded as it sank in that Carolyn would have known the depth and severity of Jason's injuries without having the doctors tell her. Kelsey turned back to Barbara and asked, "Can I cut some of those pieces for you?"

Barbara handed some fabric, scissors, and a pattern to Kelsey. She instructed the younger woman on how to cut the pieces for the quilt blocks. Kelsey settled back in the wicker chair and began snipping the fabric around the pattern.

***

"Jason," his grandfather said when Jason had barely taken a seat on the porch, "take a walk with me."

"Sure," Jason replied. He looked around for Kelsey to let her know that he was leaving the porch, but she was occupied with his grandmother, who was giving her directions on quilting. No doubt his grandmother would keep Kelsey busy until he got back. He stood up and followed John out into the yard.

They walked across the lawn and down toward the pasture, stopping near the fence that circled the paddock. The spot John chose was a signal to Jason that this was more than just a leisurely stroll. His grandfather had something on his mind. *It's serious—to him, at least,* Jason thought. His grandfather had that frown between his eyes that always indicated there were important things to be discussed.

Jason's grandfather had brought him to this very location in the past for many important discussions and lectures. When he was a teenager, his mother never threatened him with "Wait until your father gets home," like many mothers did. Instead, it was,

"Do you want me to have Grandpa take you to the pasture?" She knew the power of that threat, even when they lived in Wilmington and his grandparents lived in Mason Valley.

Their conversations by the pasture had covered a wide range of topics over the years. Some had been about the stupid things Jason had done as a teenager, some were about girl troubles, and others were about topics such as his future and his career choices. Sometimes, their talks even centered around financial advice.

Just before Jason deployed to Afghanistan, his grandfather had brought him to this spot and shared his experiences fighting in the Vietnamese jungle as a young man. His parting advice had been, "Always keep your mind sharp and alert. Protect your squad, and they will protect you."

Jason's grandfather became an attorney after he was discharged from the army. He was never short on advice or shy about sharing his thoughts. Jason respected his grandfather's opinions and knew he always had Jason's best interests at heart.

Now, Jason braced himself for the lecture he knew was coming. *What'll it be about today?* he wondered.

"Jason, you're a good boy," John began.

Jason tried not to smile. Even at thirty-three years old and six-foot-three, his grandfather still thought of him as a boy. He didn't respond and waited for the older man to go on.

"Kelsey is a lovely young woman, but she's married to another man. You know this is not going to work out well for you." John paused. "I don't want to see you get hurt. It was bad enough seeing you injured in the war, but the heart can get injured, too, just like the body. Sometimes, it's even harder to recover from a broken heart than a broken body."

John exhaled, evidently relieved to have said what he felt needed to be said. "I know I probably sound like an outdated curmudgeon, but my love for you will never be outdated. I will always warn you if I see danger in your path. And the path you're on right now is dangerous."

"Grandpa," Jason said, interrupting him, "it's not what you think."

"Jason, I may be an old man, but I remember looking at your grandma the same way you look at Kelsey."

Jason scrubbed his boot across the grass, making a brown gash across the green surface. He suddenly felt like a teenager again, like he'd been caught sneaking in after a clandestine meeting with a girl his father had forbidden him to see.

Jason was taken aback by his grandfather's comment. His thoughts spun like a top. In two days, two different people had shared an observation that even Jason wasn't fully aware of: that his interest in Kelsey was clearly more than a desire for friendship. *Sure*, Jason admitted, *I've had a couple of thoughts about exploring the connection between us and seeing where it leads.*

But even though Kelsey wasn't married to Ron, that didn't mean she was available. There was still the question about her and her coworker, Richard. Where did that leave Jason? Headed for disappointment in a one-sided romance? But it hadn't gone that far yet. Had it?

Ron and Grandpa could be right, Jason concluded. He was trying to deny what others saw: that he was already in deep and that his feelings for Kelsey went beyond just friendship.

Jason concluded his introspection and found himself right back where he and Ron had ended their discussion the night before. Until the Coeburn situation was finished, he had to forego taking his "shot," as Ron had advised. Also, he had to be more careful about hiding any developing feelings for Kelsey. If he muddled Kelsey and Ron's cover story, he'd blow their chance of ever solving the Coeburn case.

"Don't worry," Jason finally said. "It'll be alright. I'll be careful. I know what I'm doing."

They turned and started to walk back toward the house.

"Humph!" John said. "Young people always think they know what they're doing. They have it all figured out and under control. I just want you to be careful, Jason." John stopped and looked at his grandson earnestly. "Take it from an old man: the heart is rarely careful where love is concerned."

CHAPTER SEVEN

Ron had returned to Mason Valley by the time Jason dropped Kelsey off at the rental house. Jason walked Kelsey toward the front porch and paused at the top of the steps.

"Thanks for inviting me to dinner and to meet your family," she said. "I had a wonderful day. Your family is so warm and welcoming. They made me feel right at home."

"Everyone liked you, too," Jason said, "though Grandpa warned me about falling for a married woman." He laughed. "He still thinks I'm sixteen and susceptible to pretty women—even pretty married women. I told him it wasn't how it looked, but that never keeps Grandpa from giving his opinion or advice. I felt like a heel for not being able to completely level with him."

"I'm glad you at least told your mother and father the truth," Kelsey said. "Otherwise, your mom would have questioned why I didn't go to Atlanta with my husband."

"If my mother thought I had designs on another man's wife, she would do more than give me a sermon, like Grandpa did. I told her the truth, but I told the others that you had an early-morning appointment today and that Ron went to a meeting in Atlanta alone."

"I feel like a fraud pretending I'm someone I'm not," Kelsey said. "I'll be glad when this is over."

"I couldn't agree more," Jason agreed. "I need to resolve this case and either exonerate Coeburn or put him in jail." He smiled and added, "Plus, I need to get Grandpa off my tail."

"It's sweet that he cares enough to look out for you," Kelsey said. "He and Barbara are both lovely people."

"They are. So, I guess I'll see you and Ron at the mayor's party tomorrow?" Jason asked. They walked across the porch and stopped in front of the door.

"Yes, we'll be there," Kelsey said with a nod.

Jason made a motion toward her. Kelsey readied herself for a friendly hug or even a quick kiss on the cheek. But then, Jason stopped and stepped away from her. "Neighbors," he said quietly before he turned and walked down the steps and back to his pick-up. Kelsey waited by the door until Jason had backed out of the driveway. She waved to him as he pulled away.

"It wasn't a date, Barrett," she muttered as she tamped down her disappointment that Jason had not kissed her goodbye. Of course, he was right that someone might see them. The houses on this street were separated by large lawns, so no one could hear their conversation, but they might drive by or see them if they were out in their yards.

Kelsey opened the door and went inside to see what Ron had brought back from Atlanta.

Ron loved gadgets of all kinds, and he now had an array of devices spread across the kitchen table. They sorted through the equipment together as Ron explained each device and how it would be used in their surveillance.

"According to Richard, this is the latest in security equipment. The manufacturer gave it to us at no cost, provided we field-test it." Ron picked up a small device and held it out to Kelsey. "The cameras are waterproof and practically indestructible. The batteries have extended life. We have two cameras, plus a backup. They work with mobile or Wi-Fi and have audio and video capabilities that can be streamed to our cell phones."

"I'm not the gadget guru you are, but that sounds exactly like what we need," Kelsey said.

"Two special phones are also included, and they're already activated, so we won't have to involve our personal phones. I agree; they're perfect for our plan." Ron paused, then opened another package. "I also got us new binoculars that are more high-powered than our other ones and more powerful cameras."

They checked and double-checked everything to make sure they had all the pieces they'd need. Extra batteries and chargers and the additional camera were further insurance against mischance. They hoped to have all the recordings and videos they'd need before the attached battery needed to be charged or replaced.

They tested the equipment until they were satisfied that it was working correctly. A camera failure would mean a second risky trip into the compound. One trip would be dangerous enough; a second trip would be pushing their luck

Next came the hard part: the decision on when and how to plant the devices within the compound.

After discussing and discarding several options, Kelsey and Ron decided that the next night would probably work. It was time they concluded this operation and extracted the girls from what they worried was a dangerous situation—or at least show some progress toward that goal. The lack of progress was frustrating everyone involved. If the girls were captives and something bad happened to them, that frustration would turn into devastation.

"We can leave the Landrys' party in the early evening while most everyone's there and occupied," Kelsey suggested.

"That's a good idea: a married couple sneaks away from the party for some private time. I'll be extremely affectionate so no one gets suspicious," he teased, then added, "Speaking of affection, Richard asked about you. He said he misses you."

Kelsey shot him a dirty look.

"What?" he asked innocently. "I'm just paying you back for all your tormenting over the years."

"Let me make this clear," Kelsey said. "I miss Richard like I miss that deer tick I pulled out of your arm the other day."

They packed up their gear and readied their backpacks for the next night's climb up the mountain. According to the weather service, it was expected to be cloudy. Kelsey tried not to think about—and did not mention to Ron—the fact that they had also chosen a cloudy night for the operation in Afghanistan three years ago. Things could go wrong in the dark, too. She had learned that lesson the hard way.

They went over their checklist twice more to make sure they hadn't missed anything. Then, once they were satisfied that they had packed everything they would need, Ron called Jason to advise him of the plan. It wasn't foolproof—no plan was ever completely foolproof—but it would safely get them into and out of the compound to plant the security cameras. Kelsey let Ron make the call to Jason. She always enjoyed talking to him, but tonight, she wanted to avoid any reminders of old failures.

When Ron finished his call, he gave Kelsey a thumbs-up; Jason was on board. They poured themselves glasses of wine and headed out to the porch swing. After he had filled Kelsey in on his trip to Atlanta and how everyone was—Vickie, her father, Tina, Richard, and their other coworkers—Ron suddenly turned serious. "Vickie wants to have a baby," he blurted out. "I admit it, Kelsey, I'm scared. What if I'm not a good father?"

"You big oaf!" Kelsey chided and slapped him on the shoulder. "You'll make a great father, and Vickie would make a great mother. When is this earth-shattering event going to happen?"

"I promised Vickie that we'd discuss it once this operation is complete. Maybe I'll be used to the idea by then."

"Well, it doesn't happen overnight, you know? You'll get used to the idea," Kelsey said. She laughed gently. "Daddy Ron! You're just a big kid yourself, you know, so you'll be a great dad."

Kelsey and Ron settled into peaceful silence. In Kelsey's view, Vickie was the perfect mate for Ron. She took his teasing in stride and gave it back to him ten-fold. Kelsey had been Ron's 'best woman' at their wedding. A baby would complete their world, and she had no doubt that they would be perfect parents.

Kelsey briefly wondered whether she would ever find what Ron and Vicki had.

Ron, she mused, was good at everything he attempted, but his voice had held real concern when he mentioned being a father. He was intimidated by a tiny bundle that would be no bigger than his two palms put together.

Kelsey knew he would come around to the idea, and whether it was a boy or a girl, he'd be building sandboxes and swing sets in the backyard even before it was even born. And, of course, there'd be a basketball hoop and the baby decked out in University of Georgia T-shirts and ball caps by the time it was six months old—maybe even sooner. Of this, she was certain. Ron never did anything halfway.

Kelsey and Ron were the best of friends and could tell each other anything, but Kelsey had withheld the gruesome details of the operation in Afghanistan. She hadn't wanted his sympathy or for him to know how vulnerable she felt when she first got home. With that one exception, they had shared most of their sad times and their happy times. They had been there for each other at every important stage of their lives. Tomorrow night, they would depend on each other as never before.

The next day, Ron and Kelsey arrived at the mayor's house around mid-morning. The Spring Fling was a picnic and pool party, and everyone, whether or not they were a resident, was invited.

Mayor Landry was running for reelection in the fall, so all voters—particularly the movers and shakers of Mason Valley—were welcome.

The mayor's home was located on a large flat knoll overlooking a small lake. A boat was tied up at the private dock, and it was gassed up and ready to take anyone for a ride across the water. The property consisted of several acres of trees, with at least two acres of landscaped lawn, which surrounded a large heated swimming pool.

A maid escorted Kelsey and Ron through the house and out onto the patio. Kelsey spotted Jason immediately. He was involved in a heated volleyball game with some people she didn't know. Several guests sat in the shade, while others played horseshoes, beanbag toss, and croquet. A few guests were in the swimming pool or sunbathing on the chairs lined up on the pool deck. Kelsey decided to join the Wilders, who were watching the activities from under the shade of a large oak tree.

"Here, let me help the little wifey down these tall steps," Ron whispered as he took Kelsey by the elbow. "Wouldn't want you to fall."

Kelsey looked at him and struggled not to stick her tongue out. "Most old married men would make their wives walk six paces behind, don't you think?" she retorted.

Ron stopped her and turned her to face him. Anyone watching would think they were having a sweet moment before joining the crowd. Ron kept smiling, but his eyes were serious as he said, "Kelsey, Lucas was a dirtbag. You can't judge all men by him. I'm not like that, and since I've gotten to know Jason, I can tell that he isn't, either. It's time to let your cynicism go."

Kelsey nodded. "I know. I was only kidding. I didn't mean to sound like a shrew," she apologized. Too frequently, she let her retorts get away from her, especially with Ron. It got under his Southern skin when she implied that he wasn't a gentleman. Her comments were losing their humor, even to her.

Her tongue had been sharpened by all the emotions that churned inside her after she and Lucas broke off their engagement. He had professed to love her, and yet, he had broken her trust. It had devasted her at the time. That was now old news, but she had developed a habit of making snide retorts where men were concerned.

"I didn't actually mean what I just said," Kelsey continued. "I was joking. Not funny, huh? I promise, I'll stop—break my bad habit."

"You sure? Maybe you're just that mean girl I've known all my life," Ron retorted. "Leopards can't change their spots, you know?"

"Funny!" Kelsey reached up and patted his cheek. "You know I love you, don't you? I'll do better. Come on, let me introduce you around, sweetie."

"Richard will straighten you out once you're married," Ron said as he took her hand to help her down the steps. Kelsey tried to pull away so that she could punch him on the shoulder, but Ron refused to release her hand.

"Easy! Otherwise, you'll fall." Ron squeezed her hand harder. It didn't hurt, but it was his way of getting in the last word.

Kelsey and Ron were laughing as they walked up to the Wilder clan under the tree. After introductions, Ron excused himself to join the group on the volleyball court. They welcomed him, and before long, there were loud taunts and cheers coming from the court.

Kelsey's attention was pulled away from the volleyball court when she turned to reply to a question from Carolyn. Grandpa Wilder sat at the other end of the table. His face was shadowed by the leaves of the oak tree, but Kelsey caught him watching her. She smiled at him. He gave her a polite smile in return, but even after she turned back to Carolyn, Kelsey felt his eyes on her. No cheating wives would be permitted to roam freely today. Grandpa was on guard duty.

Kelsey talked with Carolyn and Barbara for a while, then turned her chair around so she could watch the volleyball match. Ron and Jason were on opposite teams. *Oh, this should be worth the price of admission*, she thought. *Two men with equal athletic prowess trying to outdo the other.* However, good-natured banter was all that came from the two men as each tried to spike the ball on the other.

Drinks were soon passed around by the catering staff, and Kelsey chose a glass of white wine. She would nurse it for the rest of the day, keeping her faculties sharp for the trip up the mountain that night while still appearing to be engaged with the party. She shivered, even though the day was warm. This night would be their best shot, and if they were caught, it would all be over. *I won't let that happen*, she silently vowed.

The smells of barbecued pork, beef, and chicken wafted over to Kelsey. She was already getting hungry by the time the cooks rang the dinner bell. She followed the crowd across the lawn to the tables of food. She looked around for Ron as she filled her plate from the large buffet.

Ron and Ben were making their way across the lawn together, angling toward the buffet line. As she was about to call out, Kelsey felt a warm hand at her waist. A familiar tingle quickened her breath. She didn't have to look around to know that Jason was standing beside her.

"Grandpa's watching," she mumbled from the side of her mouth.

"I know," Jason returned. "And here he comes."

From the corner of her eye, Kelsey spotted John, with Stephanie in tow, making his way toward them.

"Jason," John called out, "Stephanie has been looking for you."

Jason smirked at Kelsey and mumbled, "Not very subtle, Grandpa." Then, louder, he said, "Hey, Stephanie. How was New

York?" He turned to join his grandfather and Stephanie.

After successfully completing his maneuver, John filled his plate and returned to sit with Barbara under the tree. Jason and Stephanie found a table by the pool and sat down together.

Kelsey returned to her place in the shade with the Wilders, and Ron joined her. Her eyes wandered over to where Jason and Stephanie were laughing and enjoying their meals together. *What is the nature of their relationship?* Kelsey wondered. Jason said he had dated Stephanie, but was that still going on? *You couldn't be feeling a twinge of jealousy, could you, Barrett?* she asked herself before looking away from the pair.

Ron was the consummate conversationalist and had never met anyone he couldn't find something in common to talk about. Today was no exception, and he entertained their tablemates with his stories. His knowledge ranged from politics and current events, to NASCAR racing and, of course, basketball. Ron even engaged John in a discussion about the practice of law. Ron had always been this way: a font of knowledge whenever she needed it. She had no idea how he did it. Barbara and John were enthralled by such a charismatic young man. Yet even as John talked with Ron, he still managed to keep his eyes on Kelsey—the sentinel standing guard for his grandson.

Kelsey let Ron carry the conversational ball. Occasionally, he would reach out and touch Kelsey's arm or shoulder in a husband-ly manner. He even occasionally picked up her hand and kissed the back of it. *Gag,* she thought—and as they used to say as kids whenever they saw a couple kissing. She knew he did it just to get under her skin, but he also did it every time she let her eyes wan-der toward Jason.

She recognized many of the townsfolk who were present. She was relieved that she didn't see the Bridgeses, because she knew they would want an answer from her about the land sale. God, she couldn't wait until this ruse was over. Well—over, so long as they were able to safely free the two girls and shut down the compound.

At one point, Kelsey spotted the mayor and Jason sitting on the patio, huddled in a discussion. Mayor Landry's hands were flying around as he made his points. Jason sat listening quietly, but he was too far away for Kelsey to see his expression or to hear what was said. Hopefully, they were talking about getting Jason some help at the sheriff's office.

When Kelsey had finished her dinner, she left the shelter of the trees and the Wilders to deposit her plate in the trash. That task accomplished, she walked toward the swimming pool, where Jason and Stephanie were tossing a ball around in the water with another couple.

Jason spotted her. "Come in and join us," he called out.

"Not now. Maybe later," she replied, then mouthed, "Grandpa." Jason nodded and grinned. Kelsey was wearing her bathing suit beneath a sarong that was slung low around her hips, but she wasn't in the mood for swimming. *And,* she chided herself, *it has nothing to do with the fact that Stephanie is a stunner in her two-piece bikini.* Unsurprisingly, she struck a pose—likely from her repertoire of modeling poses—each time she climbed onto the diving board.

No, Stephanie wasn't the reason why Kelsey didn't want to join in the fun in the pool. Instead, she was thinking about what she and Ron had planned for later tonight. They had sketched out a plan, but as with all operations, they would likely need to adjust it once they reached the compound. She was thinking over different options—discarding some and looking more deeply at others—and planning contingencies should any of them fail. She was psyching herself up for what lay ahead. She didn't want any distractions to take her out of that mindset.

Kelsey started to leave the pool area to find a cold drink when the ball the swimmers were tossing around came flying toward

Jason. Kelsey watched as he turned and jumped high to smack the ball back to the other couple. In the process, he turned his back to her, and Kelsey saw that a long, thin white scar ran down his back from his right shoulder blade, across his ribs, and down into his swim trunks.

Her eyes remained on him as she recalled what his mother had told her of his injuries. Her own struggle to heal had been difficult, but Jason's would have been much harder. *Lest we forget the scars of war are real*, she thought as she turned away and went back to her spot beside Ron.

Kelsey and Ron stayed at the Landrys' place until the sun started to descend behind the mountains. By then, a band had set up behind the dance floor and were tuning up their instruments and getting ready to play. Kelsey would have enjoyed staying for a few dances, but she and Ron needed to get home, rest a little, and go over their plans again. They would also review their checklist one last time before starting the climb up the mountain.

As they left through the front door and headed toward their car, Jason caught up with them on the front porch. He stopped near Kelsey. "The warrant was issued this morning. You're good to go, but be careful out there," he said quietly. He looked at Kelsey and started to reach out to her but stopped himself. "You have my phone number. Call if you get into a situation. And call immediately when you get back."

"Of course," Kelsey and Ron replied in unison. They left Jason standing on the front porch and walked to their car.

"Oh, by the way," Jason called after them as he came down the steps toward the car. Kelsey and Ron paused to wait for him. "I finally heard back from the sheriff's office in Arkansas," he said quietly. "The sheriff is out of town due to a family emergency but should be back this coming week. His staff promised he would call."

"Good. I hope he can fill us in on whatever evilness Coeburn is up to," Ron said.

"Be careful," Jason cautioned one last time. "I know you know what you're doing but stay on the alert."

"We will, Sheriff. Don't worry," Kelsey assured him.

Jason stood there and watched as Kelsey and Ron drove away. He was still there when their car turned along a curve, disappearing from sight.

It was getting dark by the time Ron and Kelsey arrived at the park and entered the woods off the jogging trail. Once they were out of view of any potential passersby, they pulled on black sweatshirts and black caps and painted their faces with camouflaged paint. That done, they began to pick their way up the rocky, overgrown mountainside. They were moving along a trail they had not traveled before. It was blocked by tangled roots, vines, and young sapling trees.

They angled toward the lower edge of Coeburn's property. It was not their final destination, but they would work their way up from there as they checked the positions of the guards along the way. Their trajectory would eventually take them to a spot near the girls' quarters.

They took turns being on point so that they could conserve as much energy as possible. Clearing any new trail was always difficult, but this area was extremely challenging with its thickets of vines and tangled underbrush.

Kelsey was in the lead and they were halfway to their destination when she heard an expletive from behind her. "What's going on?" she whispered as she crawled back toward Ron. Their black clothing, their painted faces, and the darkness under the trees made it hard to see him from more than two feet away.

"These damn mosquitoes are eating me alive." Ron quietly clapped his hand against his neck.

"I told you not to put on that cologne this morning."

"I didn't put on cologne," Ron whispered back in irritation.

"But these little buggers are still biting me."

"They aren't bothering me. They must like male sweat. Here, use this," Kelsey said, handing him a disposable wipe soaked in bug repellant. "Do you think you're strong enough to make it the rest of the way?" she teased.

Ron shoved her back up the trail. "Get! We have work to do."

They climbed the rest of the way in silence, and before long, they were close enough to spot the shack that served as the girls' sleeping quarters. Using the night-vision scope on their new binoculars, they studied the area's layout. A guard was posted, but there was only one tonight. He stood with a rifle over his shoulder not far from the building. They usually saw two guards together, so one was a good sign. It would make getting into the compound unseen easier.

Their plan was for Ron to distract the guard while Kelsey planted the cameras and listening devices. Ron could handle the guard, should he be spotted, and Kelsey's small frame would be less obvious as she snuck toward the building. She could maneuver around far easier than someone Ron's size.

On previous surveillance trips, they had noticed large gaps in the boards used to build the shack. At the time, Kelsey had wondered how Coeburn planned to heat the building during the winter months. It could be extremely cold at this elevation. Surely, he didn't expect the girls to sleep in there without heat. Maybe the scumbag didn't care. Whatever Coeburn's reasons for the poorly constructed shack, the gaps in the boards might give Kelsey a view into the cabin.

Ron pulled the devices from his backpack and handed them to Kelsey. "Be careful."

"You, too. I'll see you back here in a few minutes."

Kelsey surveyed the area around the shack, along with the position of the guard. His back was turned to her. She began to slowly crawl toward a stand of shrubbery not far from the rear of the shack. She froze and pressed her body to the ground when she heard movement from the guard. She held her breath and waited. She would be exposed if he turned in her direction. The guard shuffled his feet, then leaned against a tree. It wasn't long before he slid down the trunk, sat on the ground, and settled his back against the trunk, facing away from Kelsey.

Attaboy. Take a nap, Kelsey silently encouraged the guard. She pushed up on all fours and scampered behind the row of bushes. From there, she paused, waited, and listened. The guard was still sitting by the tree, seemingly unaware of her presence not far away.

Kelsey's next move was to quickly get closer to the building. Any minute now, Ron would create a diversion that would pull the guard away from his post.

Sure enough, a loud noise came from the right of the sitting guard. A loud *thunk* sounded as something bounced off a tree not far from where he sat. He rose, grabbed his rifle, cocked it, and turned in the direction of the noise. The guard gazed upward, searching for the source of the noise in the trees. He waited. Then, the noise came again, a double *thunk* in quick succession, slightly farther away from the first noise. He started moving toward the sounds.

It's now or never, Barrett, she told herself. She started crawling across the open ground between the bushes and the shack. *Quickly*, she reminded herself, *plant the cameras and get back to the rendezvous point before the guard catches on.* As she felt around the wall of the shack in the darkness, her hand found one of the large slits between the boards. She peered through the crack. It was large enough that she had an unobstructed view of the room.

The room was dimly lit, but she could make out the ends of bunk beds lined up against the wall. No feminine touches were anywhere in view. The room was very sparse and utilitarian. She couldn't tell whether there were any sleeping bodies beneath the dark covers on the beds.

The end of the room near the front door was in shadow. Under the bed that sat nearest the door would be a good place to hide the camera. Kelsey would need to only partially open the front door, lean through on her knees, and plant the device under the foot of the bed. From that location, the camera would capture much of the room.

But first, Kelsey decided to see whether the crack she was looking through ran all the way to the floor or was wider further down. She stuck her fingers through it and moved them downward. She came to a rounded hole where a knot in the wood had fallen out. The enlarged opening was big enough for her to push her hand through.

Kelsey twisted her hand to the left and down toward the floor. It came into hard contact with a small chest. She bit her lip to stifle a cry, but then she smiled. She couldn't believe her good luck. This was the perfect hiding place: inside and in a spot where they could get useful video and audio. She didn't even need to go into the cabin.

Kelsey pulled her hand back out and reached into her pocket for the camera. She slid it and the attached battery through the knothole and down toward the floor. She pushed the unit under the side of the chest and toward the front. The device wouldn't be easily spotted under the low chest. Someone would have to move the chest to uncover it.

With the camera in place, Kelsey started backtracking the way she had come. There was a rustling in the leaves further down the hill, followed by more loud noises. Ron was making a racket, and as they had hoped, it was drawing the guard further away from his post. Kelsey silently prayed that the guard wouldn't suddenly wonder why so many pine cones were falling tonight—and all at the same time.

Kelsey still had to find a place for the second camera. She

looked around, her heart racing. She spotted a rock near the bushes she had hidden behind earlier. If she set up a camera there, it would point toward the clearing and the western end of the girls' quarters. She needed to be quick. Sooner or later, the guard would grow tired of chasing Ron's pinecones and return to his post. If he did, she would be directly in his line of sight.

Kelsey dropped to her knees, pulled hard, and pried the rock loose. Her fingers shook as she slipped the camera and its battery into the ground under one side of the rock. She partially covered it with leaves, leaving only the camera's eye uncovered. Finished, she ducked behind the row of bushes and hugged the ground just as the guard turned and walked back toward his original post. She froze and barely breathed.

There was more noise from a different spot not far away. The guard sighed and turned toward the new disturbance. Kelsey used that moment to begin crawling back toward the trees near the edge of the property. As she crept toward safety, she strained to listen for the sound of the guard's footsteps. She heard more loud rustling in the leaves and a thrashing of bushes.

Was that a growl she heard? A wild animal? The guard stopped walking, raised his gun, and pointed it toward the noise, his back to Kelsey. She chose that moment to cross the open space. She stayed low and moved quickly until she cleared the open space. Then, she stood and ran toward the rendezvous spot.

It felt like hours, but it was only seconds before she was back in the thick underbrush where they had entered the property. *Success!* Kelsey held her breath and waited for Ron as the minutes ticked by. She jumped when a hand touched her back. She turned to see Ron right beside her. *How did a man that large move so quietly?* she wondered. He would have made an excellent special forces soldier. "Done!" she mouthed.

They looked toward the shack. Now that the noises had ceased, the guard had returned to his original post. He was once again slumped at the base of the tree. Kelsey guessed that he would soon be asleep, completely oblivious that someone had invaded the compound.

Ron signaled for Kelsey to follow him, and they started their journey back down the trail. They moved slowly and in silence while on the lookout for debris—breaking sticks or rolling rocks— that might disturb and alert the sleeping compound. They didn't stop or speak until they were about a half-mile away from the Coeburn property.

"No one will even know we were there," Ron asserted. "If it were me, I'd fire that guard. I could almost see him shaking in his boots when he heard that growl. He probably thought it was a panther or a mountain lion, but he wasn't brave enough to find out."

"Throwing the pinecones was a good idea. I didn't know they made such a loud noise on impact," Kelsey said.

"It's the strong arm behind the throw, Barrett," Ron said. Kelsey snorted. "I'm disappointed. It takes the fun out of sneaking around like this when your enemy is so inept," he complained. "I was expecting more excitement or a chase. I was really looking forward to slugging someone."

"I wasn't," Kelsey replied. "But you're right. It was easier than I expected."

"Yep!" Ron agreed. "They're either inept or just confident in their isolation up here."

Before exiting the woods near the park, Kelsey and Ron removed their dark clothing and wiped off as much of the camouflaged paint as they could. They didn't want to be spotted looking suspicious with their painted faces. It was the middle of the night and camouflage paint worn by two business people from Atlanta might be hard to explain.

They drove home satisfied. They had successfully completed what they set out to do tonight. The next stage would be to get the pictures and videos that would reveal what Coeburn was up to at his compound on Love Vine Mountain.

CHAPTER EIGHT

Jason left the mayor's party shortly after he said goodbye to Kelsey and Ron. Stephanie asked him to stay longer and watch a movie, but he declined. His mind was fixated on Kelsey and Ron and the danger they were putting themselves into up on the mountain. Jason felt antsy, and he didn't have the patience to listen to Stephanie's chatter tonight—or for watching a movie. He had a lot on his mind and needed a quiet place to think.

As much as he dreaded it, he needed to have a private talk with Stephanie. Soon. Maybe he was reading the signs wrong, but he didn't think so. Stephanie was hinting at wanting more from him than he was prepared to give. They had gone out a few times—to movies and football games—but he never really viewed her as a romantic partner. In his mind, they were friends and nothing more. That wasn't likely to change. He'd like to remain friends and didn't want to hurt her, but accepting his offer of friendship would be a decision left to her after they talked.

When he first left the army and came home, he had badly needed a friend like Stephanie's brother, Chris. Jason and Chris hung out together. They fished and played pool and video games.

Jason regularly visited the Landry household, which was a friendly place, until Chris moved to South Carolina. He never meant to give Stephanie the wrong idea.

It was getting dark by the time Jason reached his house. He looked up at Love Vine Mountain, where darkness had already descended over the ridge. Clouds were moving in and had already blurred the mountaintops, blocking most of the moon's light. Kelsey and Ron had probably started or were about to start their climb up to the compound. God, he hoped they were careful tonight.

On the spur of the moment, Jason went out to the garage and picked up his fishing pole and tackle box. Fishing was a hobby that relaxed him and helped him clear his head. His head definitely needed both relaxing and clearing tonight. Did fish bite on cloudy nights? He'd find out, but even if they didn't, hooking a big one wasn't his objective, anyway. He just needed something to do and a place that would distract his thoughts from the constant replay of all the things that could go wrong on a dangerous mission.

He wished he had gone with Ron and Kelsey, but admittedly, he didn't have a role in what they were doing.

Jason drove almost all the way to his parents' house before pulling his truck off the road. It was very dark when he exited the truck. Jason pulled out a penlight to light his path as he pushed his way through the weeds and vines that grew along the fence. He angled his way toward the fishing hole. The long grasses and weeds wrapped around his legs, slowing him, but he pushed them aside and kept walking until he came to a worn path that led to the pond.

He was on his parents' property, at the spot where he had spent many happy days during the summers of his youth. He hadn't stopped to let them know he was here. His need for solitude tonight included being away from his parents and grandparents. He just didn't want to talk with anyone right now.

Jason lay the penlight on the ground at his feet and baited the fishing hook by its light. He cast the line into the water and watched the breeze blow the bobber about on the water's surface, going this way, then back that way. *Like me,* he thought, *just bobbing along without a purpose or clear direction.*

Jason considered the job of sheriff an important one, but was it really what he wanted to do for the rest of his life? He liked law enforcement, but he wasn't a fan of the politics that sometimes seemed more important than maintaining order and enforcing the law. He had never learned to play the political game, but he liked the camaraderie of working with a group of professionals who stopped bad actors from hurting or taking advantage of people—be it as a leader or member of the team. "Whatever it takes" was still his motto.

Jason was just generally disgruntled with his life tonight. He blamed himself for the rut he currently felt stuck in. He hadn't been proactive in making decisions about his life ever since he left the army, whether it be about his career, his love life, or anything else. He had simply been reacting.

He hadn't actively sought out his current position as sheriff, but he had accepted it when it was pushed on him. Most of the time, the job was more time-consuming than challenging. It had fit his purpose when he was still trying to piece his life back together after what had happened to his military career, but maybe it was now time to look for more.

Jason smiled ruefully. He was being hard on himself tonight, but self-flagellation matched his mood. He wanted to kick something, and since he was the only thing around that wouldn't complain, he was a prime target.

Jason pulled the fishing line out of the water and recast it, sending it farther out into the pond. He wasn't sure where his current mood had come from or when it had descended upon him. Maybe it came from seeing Kelsey today and having to stand

back and pretend she was Ron's wife. Maybe it was due to his
wondering about her and this Richard guy in Atlanta. Or wondering whether she was still hung up on the guy who broke her heart.
Or wondering what she thought of Jason Wilder, the man. Was he
still just Captain Wilder, her army buddy, to her? His head was full
of questions tonight, and he didn't have answers to any of them.
They all annoyed and bothered him for some reason.

Or, said a voice inside his head, *maybe you're brooding because
Kelsey and Ron are now up on the mountain—with your approval—
and exposed to danger.* Jason knew that a million things could go
wrong up there. One slipup, and they could be caught, injured,
or even killed. Even if nothing like that happened to them, if they
were discovered inside the compound, it might make Coeburn flee
once again. Jason had agreed to their plan, but he hadn't liked it,
and now, any failures that might result from tonight's operation
would be because of him.

Maybe his brooding tonight was brought on by memories of a
failure in the past.

When he had contracted with Barrett Security, Jason had no
idea that Kelsey was even alive, let alone that she'd be one of the
agents he hired. Had he known, he probably would have gone to
another firm or done it himself in the evenings after work. *You
forget, your evenings are usually spent working, too. Remember?*

They'll be okay, he assured himself for the hundredth time.
They're trained for this job and know what they're doing. He didn't
know Ron's qualifications beyond the fact that Barrett Security
said he was one of their best, most-experienced agents, but he did
know that Kelsey was well-trained for dangerous assignments.
After all, he had seen her in action in Afghanistan. With that
thought, Jason relaxed a little. They would be alright; he had to
believe that.

He heard a twig snap behind him, and he became perfectly
still. For a moment, he actually hoped it was an assailant. He had

run out of things to pummel himself with, so a new target would be welcome.

"Why'd you sneak down here alone?" his father said from behind him.

"How did you find me?"

"Neighborhood watch, remember? If you see something, say something." Mr. Wilder laughed. "Mr. Carson drove by and saw your truck. He called and described it, and I knew the identity of my trespasser. Otherwise, I'd have called the sheriff."

"You're a comedian tonight, aren't you?" Jason moved over on his perch, giving his father room to sit down. "I came here to think. I just didn't want to be around anyone."

"Want me to leave?"

"No, I've pretty much beaten myself to a pulp," Jason said with a smile. "I'm tired. Maybe you can take over."

"Girl trouble?" Ben asked. "We haven't had one of these talks in years."

"Girl trouble, work trouble, friend trouble, you name it," Jason said. "But I think I'm over it now. I talked it through with myself. I didn't come to any conclusions except that problems are easy to identify and solutions are even easier to put off. I'll get back to them later."

"Procrastinate—always a good strategy," Ben agreed.

"I'm just wound up tonight, and it's not clear why." The wind blew Jason's fishing line toward the edge of the pond, where it tangled in the weeds. He yanked on it until he had it straightened, but he didn't recast the line.

"Maybe I can help clear that up," Ben replied.

Jason waved away the offer. He didn't want further discussion of what had brought him out to the pond on a dark night.

His father ignored him, however. "By 'girl trouble,' I don't think you're talking about Stephanie, are you?" Ben stated it as a fact, not a question. "I've seen you two together enough to know there's no spark there. Now, I'm just guessing here, but maybe it's Kelsey trouble?"

"In a way, it is Stephanie," Jason said, sighing. He might as well accept that his father—the former FBI investigator—wasn't going to let him dodge his questions. "You're right. There's no spark. I need to make it clear that we're not a couple and never will be. I shouldn't have waited this long."

"The heart knows what the heart knows," his father chuckled.

"Feeling wise tonight, huh, Dad? A comedian *and* a philosopher," Jason laughed. He reeled in his fishing line. His bait was still on the hook. Nothing was biting tonight—just his father nibbling around and fishing for answers. "As for Kelsey, I don't know what her heart knows. That's part of my problem."

"I don't know, either," Ben said, "but if I were a betting man, I'd say your odds are better than fifty-fifty."

"What makes you say that?"

"I was an FBI investigator, remember? I notice things. Your grandfather wouldn't be twisting himself into a pretzel trying to keep you two apart if he hadn't seen something between you. The fact that he thinks she's married and that you have feelings for her has him in a tizzy." Ben picked up a small rock and skipped it across the dark water.

"You don't just ask questions, you surmise things, too," Jason observed. "I hate that I can't tell Grandpa the truth. I know he has my best interests at heart."

"Your grandfather has excellent intuition in the love department. He knew your mom was my soul mate even before I did. He maneuvered us together every chance he got," Ben said with a laugh. "It worked out pretty well, don't you think?"

"It worked for you," Jason said, still not convinced about himself. "I'm going to make some decisions about a lot of things as soon as this Coeburn case is closed." Jason shifted his position on the rock and uttered a long sigh. He didn't even try to hide the worry that his voice contained.

Ben looked at his son's face. He hesitated, then asked, "You're not having flashbacks again, are you? You know... from seeing Kelsey?"

Jason thought for a moment as he considered how to answer his father's question. He didn't want to worry him and decided not to tell him about the nightmare he'd had after the hike up Love Vine Mountain with Kelsey and Ron. He hadn't had another dream like it since and assumed it had been a one-time thing.

"No. I'm alright. It was a huge shock seeing her again, and it brought up a lot of memories, many of them bad. But, actually, seeing her has helped. Knowing she survived has definitely been a positive thing for me. As team leader, I still feel responsible, but I've accepted that sometimes things go off the rails, regardless of how much you prepare."

Jason reeled his line all the way in, removed the bait from the hook, and started putting his gear back into his tackle box. "I'll just be glad when the Coeburn compound is shut down and the situation is over. I don't like Kelsey and Ron up there exposed to danger." He looked up toward Love Vine Mountain. The clouds had now completely obscured the mountaintop and the moon.

Wanting an experienced opinion on what they were planning with the cameras, Jason had run the details of the operation by his father in advance. Ben Wilder had a vast knowledge of clandestine operations, and the majority had been successful. Ben had agreed with Jason, Ron, and Kelsey's assessment: it was time to try something new to bring the case to an end.

"Waiting for someone with a dangerous job to come home is a heavy burden. Just ask your mother. I guess you and I have put most of the gray in her hair. But she was the strong one when you were in the hospital."

"Mom is a trooper," Jason agreed. Ben's mention of jobs reminded Jason of the other topic on his mind tonight. "I've been thinking about my future and my job, about what I want to do. I have to make some decisions on that, too."

"Someone with your experience has a lot of options. You could follow your old man and join the FBI or follow your grandfather and go to law school. Plus, any police department in the country would be happy to hire you."

"I know I have options," Jason said. "I just have to work out what I want to do. But I'm hamstrung on that decision, too. I can't do anything until Coeburn is either cleared or taken down."

"I'm sure you'll make the right choice," Ben said. He stood up. "Well, I'm going back to the house. Come by if you get tired of your own company."

"I'm going home, too. Thanks, Dad." Jason picked up his fishing gear and began walking back to his truck.

As he drove past Kelsey and Ron's house, he saw that their SUV was not in the driveway. There were no lights on in the house. He reminded himself that it would take hours for them to get up the mountain, plant the cameras, and then hike back down.

Jason arrived home, took a shower, and stretched out on the sofa with his cell phone nearby, waiting for their phone call.

It was almost two in the morning when his phone finally rang. His body went limp with relief when he saw Kelsey's name on the caller ID. A giddy Kelsey bypassed the normal greetings when Jason answered the phone and immediately launched into a play-by-play description of how she and Ron had completed their mission. The cameras had been planted, and Ron was now busy setting up the two cell phones he'd brought from Atlanta.

"Thank God," Jason said when Kelsey stopped talking long enough for him to respond. "I was starting to worry. No, that's not true. I've been worrying since you drove off from Landry's."

Jason shared Kelsey's happiness. That the dangerous operation had gone smoothly was terrific news, but it was the sound of Kelsey's voice that thrummed through Jason's blood and made his heart beat fast.

As he had laid on the sofa awaiting Kelsey's call, Jason had replayed his conversation with his father in his mind. If Grandpa was right, there was hope that Kelsey might feel something more than friendship for him and more than a connection from the past. The possibility was worth exploring, regardless of how it turned out. Ron's axiom, "You can't make the basket, if you don't take the shot," was true.

Kelsey was describing how the guard at the compound had reacted to Ron's diversion tactics when Jason heard an expletive from Ron in the background. Kelsey paused, then said, "Something's wrong. Ron needs to talk with you." She handed her phone to Ron.

"The cameras are working, but I'm getting a message that the signal is weak," Ron said. "Richard said this can sometimes happen with mobile cameras in a place like Mason Valley. Cell phone reception can be interrupted and spotty. But these phones are specially designed for our purpose. They're upgraded beyond standard cell phones."

"What can we do?" Jason asked. His disappointment matched Ron and Kelsey's.

"My guess is that it's a weak signal and not the fault of the phones." Ron paused, then added, "But don't worry. There's got to be something we can do. We'll make this work." He handed the phone back to Kelsey, but not before Jason heard Ron say with disgust, "I should've known better than to trust Richard."

"He's good at his job," Kelsey replied. "My father wouldn't have hired him if he wasn't. This isn't his fault."

"Yeah, he's good at his job. He'll tell you just how good he is anytime you're around him," Ron replied. Frustration and disappointment dripped from his voice.

Kelsey picked up the conversation with Jason again. "Ron is checking the cell phone again," she said, "but judging by his face,

I don't think there'll be any change. I'm sure these would work in better conditions, but you can't always pick the perfect conditions. We'll give it some thought and come up with a work-around. Don't worry."

"We'll come up with something, Jason!" Ron yelled from the background.

"I know you will," Jason agreed. "If all else fails, you can keep doing visual surveillance until you work something out."

"We aren't going to let this stop us. It's just a minor hitch," Kelsey assured him. She paused for a moment, then added, "Maybe we can find a spot up on the mountain where we can pick up a stronger signal. The point is to get pictures and videos, regardless of how we do it."

"That might work," Jason agreed. He added with a chuckle, "You were feeling bad about missing that daily climb, weren't you?"

"Whatever it takes, Wildman," Kelsey replied with an answering laugh. "Whatever it takes."

CHAPTER NINE

Kelsey finished her morning run, showered, and pulled on her jeans in preparation for a trip up Love Vine Mountain. She and Ron planned to check out the cell-phone reception from the spy cameras in a spot closer to the compound. Two days of stormy weather had kept them off the mountain and added more frustration to the problem of what to do about the faulty reception.

Today was their first chance to see whether the reception was better on the mountain. Down in the valley, the reception on the cell phones paired with the spy cameras had not improved. It was a blow to what had seemed like a good plan. The only work-around they had been able to come up with was Kelsey's suggestion of getting closer to the compound and hoping for better reception. If this didn't work, and they had to take another trip into the compound to replace the cameras, well, that's just what they would do.

Kelsey's phone rang as she was taking inventory of her equipment in her gear bag. It was Jason.

"Guess what?" he greeted her. "Your father is here in my office with Richard and my dad."

"What? Why?" Kelsey asked. "Dad didn't say anything about coming to Mason Valley."

"I think it was a last-minute decision he coordinated with my father. They have some information on the Afghan operation. Are you free right now to discuss it?"

"Sure," Kelsey said. "Give me about fifteen minutes to finish getting dressed, and I'll be ready."

Ben Wilder, Colonel Barrett, Richard, and Jason arrived at the rental house about twenty minutes later. Kelsey hugged her father, Ben Wilder, and then Richard. She pulled away sharply when Richard tried to prolong his hug. Kelsey smiled at Jason but didn't include him in her welcoming hugs.

"I accompanied Colonel Barrett to check on the surveillance equipment," Richard said as Kelsey pulled away from his embrace. She wouldn't have missed him if he had stayed home, but she conceded that he might be of use in getting the equipment to work properly. "Any progress?"

"Not yet," Kelsey admitted as she motioned them all toward a pot of coffee she had just made and cinnamon rolls that Ron had picked up earlier that morning from Rita's Café. "It's disappointing, but we aren't giving up. We're still trying to find a way to make the cameras work."

They filled their coffee mugs and took a seat as Jason explained why the rest of them were there. "My father and your father have been working together these past few weeks, and they've found some information they want to share with us."

"Yes, you'll find this very illuminating," Ben Wilder said. "I decided to go to someone who might have more insight into how the army works. I contacted Colonel Barrett, and he reached out to an old army buddy still at the Pentagon."

"It took some prodding," Colonel Barrett confessed, "but he eventually gave us the name of a major—someone in your platoon in Afghanistan. This major was the chief-of-staff to the commanding officer at the base you two were stationed at. The major is retiring at the end of the month. He was reluctant to disregard the official army position, but after I told him how unfair this was to you and the other survivors, he agreed to meet with Ben."

Ben picked up the story. "I think his conscience was uncomfortable with what the army had done. He agreed to tell me what he knew so long as I promised to keep it off-the-record and not share it with the media. I agreed and met with him yesterday in DC."

"Ben contacted me last night. I wanted to be here when he told you what he learned," Colonel Barrett added, "so Richard and I drove up this morning."

"Kels," Ron said from the kitchen. He had just finished loading their breakfast dishes into the dishwasher and came into the living room carrying his backpack. "I can go up the mountain by myself today."

"Are you sure?" she asked.

"I just plan to check the cell phone reception and take a quick look around," Ron replied. "Judging by the sky, it's going to rain again today. Looks like it's already started up on the mountain. It'll be a chore plowing through wet underbrush."

"Okay." Kelsey looked up at Ron from her seat on the sofa. She and Jason sat side-by-side facing their visitors, who were seated in chairs across from them. "I do want to hear what Mr. Wilder found out."

"Sounds good. See you later, babe." Ron bent to kiss her on the forehead.

"Mr. Wilder knows," she said as she ducked and shoved Ron away.

"Oh! Good! In that case…" Ron said. He reached out, grabbed Jason's hand, and placed it over Kelsey's. "Opportunities, man! Action gets reaction. Take those shots!" He chanted as he marched toward the door.

"What was that about?" Kelsey asked, looking at Jason. *What is Ron up to now?* she wondered. *Is he coaching Jason on basketball or on opportunities?* The touch of Jason's hand on hers sent warmth tingling up her arm. Her reaction to Jason's touch indicated that *she* didn't need any coaching on how to react to *him.*

Jason shrugged. "I've found that, with Ron, you never know." He smiled warmly at Kelsey, squeezed her hand, and then pulled his hand away.

"Very true," Kelsey agreed with a smile. "Go on, Mr. Wilder. What did you find?" Kelsey avoided looking at Richard, but she could feel his stare focused on her and Jason.

Ben launched into details about the operation in Afghanistan. His report shocked both Kelsey and Jason, but it did not come as a complete surprise. They had both been stonewalled at every turn, so they already suspected there was a cover-up of some type.

According to the major who had spoken with Ben, Major Burton had sent the team out on an unauthorized mission. He hadn't shared the informant's tip about the meeting between Khalid and Khan with his commander. Instead, he kept it to himself so that he could take full credit when the operation was over.

Major Burton's secrecy had kept him from drawing up a back-up plan just in case something went wrong. He was certain that a crack team—such as the one he had assembled—could get in and get out without mishap. But nothing was ever easy or went exactly as planned in Afghanistan. A mission commander had to plan for all contingencies. Burton had failed miserably in that regard.

"I told Major Burton that he needed to split up the ops team or send another team to the north side," Jason said bitterly. "Any military tactician knows you don't stage everyone in one spot. A second team could have scouted the area and perhaps spotted the man with the RPG. But Major Burton thought that having the ops team together and positioned in the trees closest to the hut would make it easier to overwhelm all the meeting's participants and capture Khan." Jason slapped his knee with his fist. "We even had an argument over that point. He wouldn't listen and ordered me to shut up and go with his plan or he'd remove me from the team. I couldn't do that to them."

Kelsey remembered the planning meeting when Jason had asked to speak with Major Burton in the hallway. She had heard raised voices through the closed door. When both men returned to the room, they appeared calm and ready to get on with the meeting. Kelsey had looked questioningly at Jason as he sat down beside her. Through a clenched jaw, all he had said was, "Operational matters." That must have been the argument he was referring to now.

Colonel Barrett interjected, "My guess is that Major Burton feared that if he expanded the operation and added another scout team, more people would be involved, thus increasing the chances of a leak. Since he was already planning it without authorization, he couldn't let that happen."

Unfortunately, the single ops team on the west side of the hut had been in the missile's—and the explosion's—direct line of fire. Five members of the ops team were killed, as were all occupants of the hut, including their target.

Mr. Wilder went on with the story the major had relayed to him. "If the team had been successful in capturing Khan, Major Burton would have been called a hero. But since the mission turned into a disaster, he was disciplined... though not in the way he should have been."

"What happened to him?" Jason asked. "I tried to find him, but no one knew where he was."

"He was relieved of his command and reassigned to a remote outpost on a tiny island in the Indian Ocean," Mr. Wilder answered. "In the army's view, it was the best punishment they could give him without going public. It's a miserable assignment."

"It was a hiding place—hiding him from us and from anyone who had questions," Kelsey stated bluntly.

"Major Burton believed he was a shrewd tactician. We butted heads often. He probably expected to be rewarded with a promotion once we captured Khan." Jason shook his head in disgust. "All he wanted was glory. He put his career over the lives of his men. I should have fought harder when I felt he was wrong... But he would've just replaced me with someone that might not have fought for the team at all."

"Jason, you did all you could. I was there. I saw how you always had the team's safety in mind." Kelsey reached out and clasped Jason's hand in hers. He didn't pull away.

"Major Burton should have faced trial and been convicted of dereliction of duty, but the army's main goal was to avoid publicity. They didn't want to be forced to explain the useless loss of life," Mr. Wilder said. "Instead, he was exiled to one of the most isolated outposts the army could find. Like most cowards, he cut and run. At his first opportunity, he resigned his commission and left the military." Mr. Wilder's mouth tightened. "I can think of several things I'd do to him, if I had the chance."

"Since the Vietnam War, the military has been wary of public opinion turning against them," Colonel Barrett explained. "It's egregious, but some commanders—unfit ones, in my book—try to minimize the amount of information that gets out to the public. They'd rather handle it in-house. My guess is that with people already questioning why we're still in Afghanistan so many years after 9/11, the army felt that trying Burton would only increase the pressure to bring all the troops home." Colonel Barrett paused, took a breath, and then added sadly, "These days, the military quietly brings the bodies of soldiers killed on foreign soil back to the US through Dover Air Force Base without a hero's welcome or special recognition. I'm sure they think it's for the best, but to me, it's worse than some of the failures of the Vietnam conflict."

Kelsey and Jason nodded in agreement. "Do we know who fired the RPG? How did Jason and I miss it with the thermal imaging?" Kelsey asked. She glanced over at Jason. His jaws were tight, and angry white lines showed around his mouth. Kelsey squeezed his hand tighter, and Jason worked his fingers between hers. Kelsey felt the tension leave his arm. He gradually relaxed and rubbed his thumb back-and- forth across her knuckles.

"The major I spoke with says the army is certain it was an RPG, and was fired by a member of the Taliban," replied Mr. Wilder. "You missed it because he may have only arrived minutes before he fired it. It was a hit and run, so to speak. That's what makes the RPG so dangerous—it can be moved into position quickly, do its damage, and the enemy escapes before you realize what has happened. Another possibility is he might have used a shield that thermal imaging can't penetrate. It's something the insurgents in Afghanistan have been using lately."

"That's why protection on your northern flank would have been so important," Colonel Barrett said, "and why Major Burton's plan was doomed to failure from the start. He should have had drone coverage, too."

"He promised me that he had all that lined up," Jason protested.

"Well, he lied to you," Mr. Wilder said. "He didn't line up anything of the sort. To get that, he would have needed the approval of his commander." Mr. Wilder paused to let that sink in. Then, he wrapped up his story. "The army's investigation found evidence that there were several members of the Taliban in the area that night. At one point, they had used the shack to build IEDs. It was filled with enough explosives to blow up a good portion of a town the size of Mason Valley."

"That must have been the secondary explosion I heard," Kelsey said. "But I don't understand. Why would one insurgent group attack another?"

"The major isn't privy to the US's official intelligence, but his personal guess is that the Taliban was—and is—warring with ISIS over who will control the region when the United States military pulls out. Their conflict may be secret right now, but it'll become nation-wide chaos if the Afghan military can't gain control of the situation."

"And," Colonel Barrett added, "knowing what I do about that region, I can say that it would be even worse for the civilians if these two groups were to make a pact dividing up the territory." Colonel Barrett's experience did not paint a pretty picture.

"Jason, Kelsey," Mr. Wilder said as he leaned back in his chair. He looked tired and drained after recounting the story of how his son and Kelsey had been injured and of the useless deaths of their teammates. "Neither of you is to blame for what happened that night. It was war under a feckless commander. Major Burton carries full responsibility. Now that you know what happened, I hope you'll be able to let it go. Just accept that you did your best under untenable conditions."

Kelsey and Jason nodded.

"Do you know which of our team members were killed that night and which escaped? Do you have any information on their families?" Jason asked his father.

"Yes, actually. In fact, one of the casualties had family near Raleigh, and another two were from Charlotte. The other two were from California. I have all of their names and addresses—or, at least the addresses from their official records," Ben said. "I'll text them to you."

Ron returned just as Mr. Wilder and Colonel Barrett finished their story. Water dripped from his hair, and his clothes were soaked from the storm in the mountains. The rain had not yet reached the valley, but they could hear the rumble of thunder in the distance as it moved toward them.

"The signal is strong up on the mountain," Ron reported.

"There's a cell tower on the ridge a few miles from the compound. But the picture and sound are still jumbled and distorted on the video. I got flashes of images, but nothing of any consequences—just a guard relieving himself in the bushes. Then, the picture went all crazy. In the girls' quarters, all I got was shadows. They're quiet in there, too. I got nothing but static on audio."

"Maybe your camera isn't the only one in the building," Jason said. "That would explain why they're not talking."

Ron nodded. "I decided to leave one of the phones hidden up there just to make sure we could pick up the signal. Maybe we'll record something, at least. After the storms pass, the video and audio might improve."

"Richard," Colonel Barrett said, "contact the manufacturer and see if they know what might be wrong. Get replacements if necessary."

Richard nodded, pulled his phone from his pocket, and went out onto the porch. It wasn't long before he was back. "I called the sales rep and explained our problems. He said he hadn't heard of this sort of thing happening before, but it's new technology. He promised to have his tech guys look into it and get back to us ASAP."

"Stay on top of it, Richard," the colonel said.

"Yes, sir. I will."

With that, Mr. Wilder, Colonel Barrett, Richard, and Jason prepared to leave.

"I'll be back later, Kelsey," her father said, "to see you before I leave town. Ben has invited me and Richard to his house for lunch today. Your brother may meet us later if he can get away from Fort Bragg."

"Great," Kelsey said. "I should be home by late afternoon. I'd love to see Joe."

"You're welcome to join us for lunch," Mr. Wilder offered.

"I'd love to, but we can't. Ron and I have an appointment with a tour director—for our 'business,'" Kelsey explained. "With Ron's flare for manipulating conversations, we hope the director might divulge something, like any odd or suspicious visitors to the area recently."

"I heard that!" Ron yelled from the utility room. The sound of the washer lid closing indicated that he was washing his wet, muddy clothes from his hike up the mountain.

"But thank you, and give my love to Carolyn and your parents," Kelsey said, ignoring Ron.

Kelsey kissed her father goodbye and hugged Mr. Wilder. Richard tried to kiss Kelsey as he was leaving, but she turned her head, and his kiss landed on her cheek.

Colonel Barrett quietly guided Richard out toward the sheriff's car, giving Jason and Kelsey a moment alone to share their reactions to everything they had just heard. Jason's father followed the two security consultants out of the house.

"I'm going to try to locate and contact the families of the men we lost that night," Jason said. "If they're still in North Carolina, and I can find them. If they're willing, do you want to go with me to see them?"

"Of course. Just let me know when. That's a good thing you're doing, Jason."

"It's nothing more than what they deserve. I'd like to give Burton what *he* deserves—and a good beating would only be the start."

"I'm with you on that one, Wildman." Kelsey rose up on her toes to kiss his cheek. Jason turned his head, and her kiss fell on his lips.

Kelsey blinked in surprise. It was just a brief touch on her mouth, but a jolt went through her. The odd tingle she always felt whenever Jason touched her ran up her spine. True, their shared experiences had created a natural bond between them. They were bound by fire and trauma. But that didn't account for the odd sensation Kelsey felt each time he touched her.

Jason smiled at Kelsey's surprised look as he drew back. "Never miss your opportunities! I'll let you know when I locate the families." He touched her arm, then turned and followed the others outside.

Kelsey followed Jason out onto the porch and watched him cross the yard. The rain had arrived and was beginning to come down heavily. Jason hurried to join the other men in the patrol car. She waved goodbye, then raised her hand to touch her lips.

What's happening? she wondered.

She had been over Lucas for years now, but for a long time after she caught him cheating on her, she had been afraid to trust anyone with her heart. Now, Kelsey was no longer afraid of love, but could it actually have found her in a little town in North Carolina? And with Jason, her army buddy?

Was that what was happening to her? The deep yearning in her core replied, *Army buddy or not, Jason Wilder affects you like no man before.*

Kelsey's eyes followed the patrol car as it backed down the driveway and drove off. She let her mind wander back to that night on the hill overlooking the hut in Afghanistan. *Barrett, don't lie to yourself. You were ready to roll in the grass with him that night, and now you're calling him your 'army buddy'?*

She tried to argue with herself. *But that was just because you were deeply lonely on a dark and dangerous night.* At the time, she was still smarting from Lucas's betrayal and traumatized by her mother's death.

Three years ago, she had not been interested in romance with anyone. She hadn't seen Jason as anything other than a fellow soldier. But now, there was nothing about Jason Wilder—civilian and local sheriff—that she didn't like and admire.

Kelsey pulled her runaway thoughts back from where they were heading and tried to put things in perspective. Jason got a kick out of teasing her and throwing her off her game. He never indicated that his interest was more than the pleasure he got from rattling her. Plus, there was his relationship with Stephanie to consider.

But didn't she feel a special connection with Jason?

Stop it, she ordered herself. She had been wrong before, so could she really trust her ability to differentiate between what was real and what she imagined or longed for? Of course, she was older now and not the young, inexperienced, and extremely naïve twenty-one-year-old she had been when she fell for Lucas. At that age, she had been under the misguided impression that all men were like her father: a straight shooter, someone who would rather die than betray those he loved and who loved him.

Lucas ripped the rose-colored glasses right off my face, Kelsey thought as she pushed thoughts of love and romance to the back of her mind. She didn't need these distractions. There were other things that required all of her concentration. Coeburn was her number one priority. Thoughts about her future had to be left for later—when her job in Mason Valley was finished.

CHAPTER TEN

J ason dropped his father, Colonel Barrett, and Richard off near their cars in the sheriff's office parking lot, then drove out to Don Philips's farm on the outskirts of town. Don had called earlier that morning with a problem, and Jason had promised he would be there later in the day. It took him about fifteen minutes to wrap up the case.

When he got back to his office, Jason tossed his cap onto his desk and opened his laptop to write up a report detailing the call and the incident that prompted it. The incident was hardly worth the time and effort it would take to write up the report, but Jason's army experience had made him a notetaker.

Jason believed in documenting every action he took as sheriff. The town deserved to know all that he did on their behalf. They had been ripped off by the previous sheriff, and he didn't want there to be any questions about how he handled even the smallest of crimes—though 'crime' was a rather strong word for this incident.

Jason filled in the blanks on the official report and added his comments that explained the incident in detail. Tyson Anderson and Jimmy Bentley, two local teenage boys, had thought it was a great idea to steal one of Mr. Philips cows, then stake it out on the lawn of Bobby Roberts, one of their classmates.

Tyson had asked Maisy Johnson to the prom, but she turned him down, and instead went with Bobby. Tyson blamed Bobby—not Maisy. Tying the cow to the light pole in Bobby's front yard was Tyson's revenge. Jimmy was just along for the fun.

The two boys couldn't explain how a cow had anything to do with going—or not going—to the prom. Mr. Phillips was an innocent bystander, but he was the cow's owner, and his farm adjoined the Roberts' farm. That proximity is what sucked Phillips into the case.

Jason couldn't help but smile as he detailed his conversation with the two boys. "Tyson, Jimmy," he had asked, "how is it that you two boys, who were born and grew up in the digital age, didn't know that there are security cameras everywhere? You're clearly seen taking the cow and clearly recorded leaving it on Bobby's lawn." The two boys had stammered for a few minutes, then shrugged. They didn't have an answer.

After a consultation with their parents and Mr. Philips, it was decided that an appropriate punishment would be for the two boys to muck out Mr. Philips's barn for a month. But first, they had to remove the cow patties from Bobby's front lawn.

Jason had cleaned a few stalls himself as a teenager. The boys wouldn't forget this incident, in large part due to the smell of manure that would fill their nostrils for months afterward.

"Small-town sheriff stops crime wave dead in its tracks," Jason muttered as he finished his report and closed his laptop. He was reaching for a folder that one of his deputies had left on his desk for review when the door to the sheriff's office opened and Colonel Barrett stepped inside, followed by another man.

"Colonel Barrett, I thought you had left town," Jason said as he rose to greet his visitors.

"I sent Richard back to Atlanta to check on the camera issue. I knew Joe was coming up, so I waited for him. This is my son, Joe." He indicated the man behind him. Jason saw the man's resemblance to Kelsey. He carried himself like a soldier, and his facial features were very similar to hers.

"What can I do for you?" Jason asked.

"We want to ask you about Kelsey," Joe replied, immediately getting to the point. "We want to find out how she's handling this, uh, operation. That's why I'm here... and to visit with her and Dad, of course."

"Have a seat and ask away. What do you want to know?" *Is that scowl his normal look, or does he have something on his mind?* Jason wondered.

"Look, Sheriff, I'm concerned about my sister. She's been through a lot. I'm concerned about any danger she may be in with this job. I don't know all the details, but I do know it's covert, and that makes it dangerous. Is she up to the job? Are you giving her back-up? Adequate protection? Is the job about over?" Joe asked without stopping to take a breath.

"Joe," his father cautioned, "slow down. Sheriff Wilder's not the enemy, and Kelsey is on contract through the firm."

"I know, Dad, but I'm worried. It's her first time on a job like this. What if she can't handle it? What if things go wrong... like the last time?"

"Let me get this straight," Jason said slowly. He didn't like Joe's attitude. "I contracted with Barrett Security Consultants to hire someone to handle a job for me, and now, you're asking *me* if the agent they sent is up for the job? Isn't that the job of the firm to know?"

"Yes, but you worked with her before, and look how that turned out," Joe replied.

Anger simmered just below the surface in Jason's face. He was struggling to hold onto his temper and not take Joe's assertions personally.

"I apologize, Jason," Colonel Barrett said. "I told Joe it was a bad idea to come here, especially with his current attitude." Joe and Jason faced each other, both scowling. "When he gets an idea in his head, he's like the old saying about a ram that meets another ram on a narrow cliff. He won't give an inch. Age thirty-five, and he still won't take my advice."

"She got hurt under your command," Joe pointed out, ignoring his father. "It's your job to protect her, Sheriff. It was your job to protect her in Afghanistan. My father and I sat by her hospital bed in Germany day and night, wondering if she was going to make it. I can still see her head and legs wrapped in bandages. I can still hear the machines beeping as we waited to find out the extent of her injuries." Joe paused to take a breath. Some of the steam went out of him, and his shoulders sagged. "I don't want to see her get hurt trying to do something she's not ready for—not trained for."

Jason rose from his chair, came around the desk, leaned back against it, and faced Joe. *Easy*, he reminded himself. He let Joe's accusations roll off of him. He saw real fear in Kelsey's brother's eyes. He'd probably feel the same way if it were Cate involved.

"Yes, I did work with Kelsey before. And yes, I hate the fact that I couldn't keep her from getting hurt. It's something I think about all the time." Jason grimaced as he made the confession out loud. He paused, and his eyes focused on something over Joe's head. His mind flashed back to his team in Afghanistan and how well they had all worked together.

Kelsey, as his second-in-command, always took part in their planning sessions. She made good comments and suggestions. Her recommendations were always backed up with sound logic and analysis. She performed just like any other member of the team, and she expected to be treated that way. She didn't ask for special treatment, and none was given to her.

"I also know that Kelsey is intelligent," Jason said as he looked back at Joe and began to answer Joe's questions about his sister's abilities. "She makes good decisions, and she's a trained soldier. She's always the ultimate professional and takes her job seriously."

"But," Joe protested, "the debacle in Afghanistan must have changed her. What if she loses her nerve when it counts?"

"I've seen nothing since her arrival here that would indicate she isn't as strong and steady as always. I'd trust her with my life, and I also trust her to use her skills and training to do this job as well as anyone else in the security business."

"But she's never done anything like this," Joe persisted. "You can't be sure."

"I believe I know Kelsey well. I know how she thinks and reacts in battle situations—in most situations, for that matter." Jason looked Joe squarely in the face. "But here's the most important thing I can tell you about Kelsey—your soldier sister."

"What? You'll keep her out of danger?" Joe wasn't letting up.

"No," Jason said slowly. "Just this: if Kelsey knew you were here today, questioning her abilities and her fitness for this job, she'd kick your ass all the way back to Fort Bragg."

Colonel Barrett hid a smile. Joe looked taken aback.

Jason moved back behind his desk, sat down, leaned forward, and placed his hands on his desk. His dark eyes stared at Joe, daring him to dispute what he'd just said. "Any more questions?"

Joe blushed. He relaxed, then flashed a sheepish grin as the truth of Jason's words sank in. "No, I think you just nailed it, Sheriff. You do know my sister. You're definitely right about the ass-kicking." He nodded.

"He is," Colonel Barrett added, "and you'd deserve it."

"I apologize," Joe said. "I'm just worried about her, you know?" His voice trailed off.

"Yes, I do know," Jason replied. "I have a sister of my own. She's older than me. And Joe, another thing: you've not had a thrashing until you get one from your sister. They fight dirty."

"I was seven when she was born, so I've always looked out for her," Joe confessed. "She tagged after me everywhere. I was her hero. I was proud that she looked up to me and always wanted to be with me—until I started dating, that is."

Both men laughed and relaxed. Joe dropped his antagonistic attitude. Jason acknowledged that brotherly love and worry could make one say things they wouldn't normally.

"My sister, Cate, is two years older than me," Jason said, attempting to commiserate with Joe somewhat. "When we were about seven and nine, my mother's most repeated words were 'Take it outside, you two.'"

"I see I have something to look forward to." Joe smiled. "I have two children, ages four and six. My wife and I are already constantly settling disputes over one thing or another."

Colonel Barrett cut in, trying to get the conversation back on track. "Joe, Jason was at Landstuhl Hospital at the same time as Kelsey. I met his mother there," he said. "I didn't know she was Jason's mother until I saw her again today. We shared a ride in the elevator to get coffee one day and had a brief conversation. Kelsey was better by then—awake and on the mend—but Jason was still in a coma. He was in the trauma unit on the floor above Kelsey."

"I... uh... didn't know," Joe said meekly. He flushed under Jason gaze. Kelsey's brother was likely single-minded when it came to Kelsey and hadn't taken the time to wonder about her captain.

"Jason, I invited your mother to join me for coffee that day, but she said she had to get back to your room. The strain on her face and the worry in her eyes... I knew exactly what she was feeling that day. Always afraid to leave the bedside, afraid something bad would happen if you turn your back or stay away for more than a few minutes...." The colonel trailed off, as if not sure how to finish the thought.

"I'm deeply sorry, Jason," Joe said. He dropped his eyes and ran his hands through his hair. "I took off on a tangent without thinking. My sister means the world to me."

"It's alright." Jason waved away Joe's apology. "I understand. I try not to think about my time in the hospital if I can help it." He quickly directed his visitors away from discussions of that period in his life.

Joe asked several questions about Mason Valley and what it was like living there. Jason filled him in on the community and the tourist season that was just ramping up. Their conversation soon moved on to sports and a discussion that revolved around the Carolina Panthers and the Atlanta Falcons football teams. Joe and Jason made a friendly wager on which team would have the best season that fall.

"Another question, Jason, before I leave," Joe said as he stood. "I acted like a heel earlier, so I think one more question shouldn't make things much worse."

Jason braced himself.

Joe paused, pushed ahead with his question: "Just what are your intentions toward my sister? Dad says he can practically feel a buzz when you two are together."

"Joe!" an embarrassed Colonel Barrett exclaimed. "There's a good reason why you're not in Army Intelligence. You can't keep a confidence."

"But I'm a lawyer in the Judge Advocate General's office. It's my job to ask questions," Joe replied with a smile. Apparently, the sheriff wasn't the only one who could go on the attack.

Jason flushed and rubbed the back of his neck. "You're messing with me now, aren't you?" he asked. "Let's just say that I admire your sister and leave it at that."

"Joe, we need to leave... before you get us both locked up," the colonel said. "It's a four-hour drive back to Atlanta, so we need to visit with Kelsey for a bit and then get on the road."

"Jason, please don't mention this conversation to Kelsey. Alright?" Joe asked.

"I'll keep your secret," Jason replied. He smiled before continuing. "But only for my own personal reasons. I just don't have time right now to investigate an assault case against a lawyer. And I'd hate to arrest your sister."

"Fair enough," Joe said as he reached out to shake Jason's hand. Colonel Barrett stood, and both men prepared to leave to visit Kelsey before they headed back to Atlanta together. Joe had plans to spend a couple of days with his father before returning to his duty station at Fort Bragg.

Once his visitors had departed, Jason reached for his phone and began calling the numbers his father had texted him that morning. After a few wrong numbers and some additional research, he had some of the information he had been looking for.

It was early evening when Jason called Kelsey. He now had information on the men from their team who had been killed. One of the families that lived in Charlotte had moved to Florida, but the other still lived there. He had already spoken with an aunt of the soldier from Raleigh. She had told him that the father had died and that the mother was in a nursing home. She was very ill and would not be able to talk with them.

"Do you feel like taking a drive to Charlotte tomorrow?" Jason asked. "I think we can get there, visit, and be back in approximately four hours. Are you free in the morning?"

"Yes," Kelsey replied. "Ron and I are going up the mountain tomorrow afternoon. We thought we'd go in the afternoon and see if there's different activity at a different time. I can be ready whenever you want to leave."

CHAPTER ELEVEN

Jason picked Kelsey up the next morning at nine o'clock. He'd arrived at the office at six-thirty a.m. and finished up his official duties: phone calls, work assignments, and paperwork. He left his deputy in charge, so he was free for the next few hours.

As they drove toward Charlotte, they discussed what they would say to the parents of the team member killed in the Afghan attack. "I don't want to go into what went wrong with the operation," Jason said. "They don't need to know what a FUBAR it was."

"I agree," Kelsey said. She cleaned up the military acronym as it was used by most soldiers, and added, "If there was ever a Fouled-Up-Beyond-All-Reason mission, this was it. They don't need any more grief than what they've already felt. They just need to know they lost him while he was doing his duty: serving his country."

As Jason drove into a small neighborhood west of Charlotte, he slowed and peered at the street names. "Jackson's parents live on Live Oak Street."

"Wait, what?" Kelsey gasped. "Jackson? You mean the fresh-faced kid that used to tease me about the owl noise and called me Lieutenant Hoot Hoot?" Kelsey hadn't asked who they were going to see. In her mind, it didn't really matter. All the team members deserved this long-delayed recognition.

"Yes, that's the one." Jason reached over and squeezed her hand. "You up for this?"

"Yes." Kelsey felt a stab in her heart. Sergeant Jackson had been a wonderful individual, very personable, and a good and faithful soldier. He had also been the main instigator behind the running joke about her inability to whistle.

Kelsey could shoot a rifle, no problem, and she had qualified as an expert marksman on the shooting range. She could clear the obstacle course in record time and could finish the two-mile run well within the required time. Sergeant Jackson thought it was hilarious that with all her accomplishments, she couldn't whistle and mimic the calls of the birds indigenous to Afghanistan. The team had settled on a call that sounded more like a mourning dove, since Kelsey could do that.

Never mind that the Afghan owl didn't sound like an American hoot owl; whenever Kelsey walked into the briefing room, she'd hear the *hoot* sound coming from the back of the room. She'd point his way and say, "I see you, Jackson! You're not funny!" Eventually, he began calling her Lieutenant Hoot Hoot.

Having fun at her expense was okay with Kelsey so long as it kept the mood light and easy. The soldiers were under enormous pressure, so if poking a little fun at her helped them relax, it was alright with her.

Kelsey had a fondness for all the team members, but especially Sergeant Jackson. He was so earnest and sincere in his desire to serve his country that he wore it like a badge. Some soldiers complained about everything in army life—sometimes it was an act— but not Jackson. He happily accepted everything his commanders asked of him.

Kelsey took a deep breath. Meeting the parents of this brave young man was going to be hard.

As Jason pulled into the driveway of a small white framed house, a middle-aged couple came out onto the porch. "You must be Jason and Kelsey," the woman said as they exited the vehicle and approached the older couple.

"Yes, ma'am. Can we come in?" Jason asked.

"You can. We were just sitting down to an early lunch. We'd love for you to join us. Melvin caught some nice-looking catfish this morning, and it's frying as we speak. Come in." Mrs. Jackson held the door for them. They stepped into a neat living room and followed Mrs. Jackson into the kitchen.

"Catfish is best when it's cooked right after it comes out of the water," Mr. Jackson said as he took down two extra plates and set them on the table. "I told Corey that eleven was too early for lunch, but she's the cook around here."

"Yes, and I know how to fix fresh catfish," Mrs. Jackson laughed. She turned to the stove and began dishing up the fried fish and hush puppies. "I cooked a pot of greens this morning, too. Come! Sit!"

Kelsey agreed with Mr. Jackson that it was a little early for lunch, but she felt it would be easier to bring up a difficult subject while they were occupied. Plus, the food smelled delicious.

"You said on the phone that you wanted to talk about my baby?" Mrs. Jackson was the first to bring up her son.

"Yes, ma'am," Jason answered. "He was an excellent soldier, and we wanted to let you know how much we admired and respected him."

"Do you have other children?" Kelsey asked.

"We have a daughter and another son, Charles. He's in the army, too. But James was my baby. Do you have children?" Mrs. Jackson addressed both Kelsey and Jason in her question.

"We... uh, I..." Kelsey stammered. She wanted to explain that they weren't a couple, but with the rings on her finger, that would only generate more questions. Their personal lives were not why she and Jason had come to visit the Jacksons. Besides, she didn't have a husband that she *could* talk about. She settled on a quiet, "No, not yet."

"I tell you, Mrs. Wilder, sometimes, your children can break your heart. Other times, they're so sweet, they can make you hear angels sing. James had all these big plans. The army was going to help him go to college and give him a career. He was sure it was the right thing to do. I worried, but your children must choose their own paths. You just have to hope and pray that it's the right one."

"That's what my father told me when I decided to join the army," Kelsey said.

"But what did your momma have to say about that decision?" Mr. Jackson asked. "Corey here cried for days when James left."

"I... I..." Kelsey stammered. "My mom passed away from cancer just after I graduated from college. I couldn't stand to be around where we lived without her there. I decided to join the army, hoping to get as far away as I could. I needed something to challenge my mind and give me something to focus on." She took a shaky breath. At least now she could talk about losing her mother without breaking down in tears.

Jason reached out and gently rubbed her shoulders before turning back to his food.

"I'm sorry, honey," Mrs. Jackson said. "It's not easy to lose a parent or a child."

Kelsey's turmoil over all that had happened to her—with the exception of losing her mother—suddenly seemed petty and small in light of what had happened to this couple and their family. This kind, generous woman's grace and compassion, even when dealing with her own overwhelming loss, showed where her son had learned his kindness and generosity.

Once they had finished the main course, Mrs. Jackson brought out a freshly baked apple pie for dessert. As they ate, Jason and

Kelsey told funny stories about James. They described the brave things he had done for the team and how much his fellow soldiers had respected and admired him.

When they were finished eating, Jason and Kelsey rose. Jason said sincerely, "James was the kind of soldier any commander would be honored to have on his team. We are deeply sorry for your loss."

"Thank you, Captain," Mr. Jackson said. He stood and shook Jason's and Kelsey's hands. "That means a lot to us."

"Would you like to see James's room?" Mrs. Jackson asked. She wiped a tear off her cheek. "I want you to know the person he was before he became a soldier. Come."

Mr. and Mrs. Jackson led them out of the kitchen and toward James's bedroom. On the way, they stopped in the living room.

"That's the flag that was draped over James's casket at his burial," Mr. Jackson said, pointing to a wooden case displayed on a table under the living room window. The case contained a folded American flag, along with the various medals James had been awarded during his time in the army. "Every time we look at it, we feel proud of our boy. James gave his life in service of others. Service to others—that's the lesson we always taught him."

Kelsey wiped at the tears that blurred her eyes.

The Jacksons turned and motioned for Kelsey and Jason to follow them into James's bedroom.

Kelsey looked around the small space. A full, happy life was evident from the memorabilia that was still scattered about the room. It looked as if the Jacksons had left the room exactly as it had been when James left. Pictures of high-school friends and sporting events sat on shelves against the wall. One, a prom picture taken with a pretty girl, sat in a place of honor. Posters featuring James's favorite athletes and musicians hung on the walls. Jason paused before a trophy that indicated it was for a football championship five years earlier. "This must be from the Fighting

Bulldogs' big win. James told me about it," he said.

"Yes," Mr. Jackson replied. "James caught the winning touchdown, but he talked more about the pass he dropped." He laughed. "James always wanted to be perfect. It didn't matter how many times I told him that no one was perfect. He wouldn't cut himself any slack."

"He felt the same way about his army job, too. He wanted to be perfect," Kelsey said.

Kelsey and Jason turned to leave and say their goodbyes to the Jacksons.

"We have to be going but thank you so much for inviting us into your home and sharing James's story with us," Jason said at the door.

"Yes. Also, I haven't eaten such a good meal in years," Kelsey added, echoing his thanks.

"Thank you for coming to see us," Mr. Jackson said. "James died doing what he wanted to do. We're at peace with that, but it's nice to know others recognized him for the wonderful boy he was."

As Jason and Kelsey waved to the Jacksons and backed out of the driveway, Kelsey said, "For some reason, I feel like a burden has been lifted. I don't know who was helped more today: the Jacksons or me." There was a lightness in her heart left by the Jacksons' kindness.

"I know," Jason said. "I feel more at peace just by acknowledging the Jackson family's sacrifice. Just by talking about James and remembering the time we spent with him gives him special recognition. It's not nearly what he deserves. After meeting his wonderful family, I believe more strongly than ever that Major Burton should be in jail. At the very least, he should go down in history as the worthless human that he is."

"You've summed it up perfectly," she agreed. "Thanks for inviting me to come with you, Captain Wildman."

"I wouldn't have it any other way, Lieutenant Hoot Hoot," he replied.

Kelsey smiled at the nickname. It had never bothered her, but today, hearing herself addressed that way felt like a badge of honor.

As they came to an intersection leading from the Jacksons' neighborhood, Kelsey's phone pinged, notifying her that she had a text message from Ron. She read it aloud to Jason: "Bored. Going up the mountain now. No need to rush back. Ron."

"If you don't need to get back right away, would it be alright with you if we stopped by the FBI office in Charlotte?" Jason asked. "I need to check on something, and this will save me another trip."

"Sure," Kelsey agreed. "Apparently, Ron has it all under control in Mason Valley"

Kelsey mused over Ron's text message and claim of being "bored." Maybe that was true today, but he had a variety of hobbies and interests that kept him occupied. He could usually keep himself busy and entertained without much effort. Kelsey wondered if he had another motive: manipulating her into spending the day with Jason.

Ron had been dropping hints recently about how much she and Jason had in common and how they made such a beautiful couple. Ron likely thought his comments were subtle, but Kelsey saw right through him. Her protestations hadn't deterred him from whatever he was plotting, though.

Jason drove into downtown Charlotte and parked in a city lot not far from the FBI office. It was a beautiful day, and since they were not in a hurry, they strolled along at a leisurely pace, window shopping, laughing, and talking as they made their way toward the building.

The receptionist relayed Jason's request to meet with Agent Baker, and the agent soon appeared from his office to greet them. Kelsey opted to wait in the reception area while Jason completed his business with the agent. She took a seat in a quiet corner, pulled her iPad out of her bag, and began to search the internet data bases she had access to.

Kelsey needed to research the four names that Doug Peterson, the tour-guide director, had given her and Ron at their last meeting in his office. Ron was a master at getting people to divulge information without realizing they were doing it. Sometimes, he was just curious about people, but other times, he was fishing with a hidden motive. As she searched the online court records, Kelsey thought back on their conversation with Doug.

"You've been at this for a long time," Ron had commented once they were seated in Don Peterson's office. "You must have learned how to match people with the right tours for them. Do you ever try to guess what tour a person might be interested in when they walk in—even before they tell you what they're looking for?"

"Sometimes, I can," Doug had said with an element of pride. "But other times, I'm dead-wrong. Take these guys." He pointed to a list of names written on his notepad. "They appeared antsy and nervous. I thought they were trying to psyche themselves up for something they might consider dangerous—like a zip-line adventure or skydiving. I was wrong. They were just interested in going into the mountains."

"Rock climbing, trail hiking, or both?" Ron asked.

"Just trail hiking," the director replied. "They started out asking about Love Vine Mountain, but I convinced them that Love Vine was too much of a wilderness for amateurs to hike."

"Did they book a tour at one of your easier sites?" Ron asked.

"They seemed interested in less-strenuous hikes but said they would get back in touch with me later. They never did," Doug replied. "Sometimes, clients are like that: you never hear from them again."

At that point, Doug was summoned from the room by an

employee in the back with a question about a freight shipment
that had just arrived. When he disappeared into the back room,
Ron rose and quickly took a picture of the notebook page with
his phone. The only other information written on it was the word
"Virginia."

After Doug returned to the room, Kesey and Ron spent a few
more minutes asking about other tours he might be able to offer
to their retreat business. As clues go, the list wasn't much, but at
this point, Kelsey and Ron were looking for anything.

There could have been many reasons for the men's nervousness, and that definitely didn't mean they were up to no good, but
it was a stone to overturn and see if any cockroaches came scurry-
ing out.

If the men were the ones who had visited Coeburn and he was
running some kind of illegal operation, it would be reasonable
to assume that the men had criminal records elsewhere. Now, as
Kelsey waited for Jason, she began searching court documents,
starting with the Virginia counties adjacent to North Carolina
and going east-to-west. The men's names hadn't popped up by the
time she reached the western counties of Virginia that bordered
Tennessee. This region of Virginia was very mountainous and
similar to Mason Valley.

Kelsey first checked the city of Bristol, Virginia but didn't find
any information on the men. She moved on to search farther into
southwestern Virginia, toward the Kentucky line, and bingo! The
four names were all linked to the same case—a drug case.

From the court transcripts, the men all lived in Pound, Virginia. They had been prosecuted and convicted two years ago for
growing marijuana in the mountains near Big Stone Gap, Virginia,
which was a small town near where they lived.

Kelsey studied the pictures in the arrest report with disappointment. They were not the men that she and Ron had seen
visiting Coeburn's camp.

But were they part of Coeburn's operation? Kelsey read the file on their case and concluded that they probably weren't. Plus, they wouldn't have needed to ask for information about Love Vine Mountain if they were involved with Coeburn. Most likely, they had come to Mason Valley to scout out a new secluded location to resume their marijuana business. The mountains in Haygood County would provide the perfect spot for such a thing.

Kelsey shut down her iPad just as Jason finished his visit with Agent Baker. They said their goodbyes, exited the building, and began to walk back toward the city parking lot and Jason's truck.

"I'm sorry I left you sitting there alone for two hours," Jason apologized. "Agent Baker knew my father, and he wanted to tell me about a few cases they had worked together."

"Did he have any new information on the men you asked him to identify?" Kelsey asked.

"No," Jason said, shaking his head. "Part of the reason why I wanted to meet with him in person was to ask if he could speed up the facial-recognition process. He hasn't had my request very long, and there's always a backlog. Lots of perverts to identify, I guess. He said he'd see what he could do."

"I hit a dead end on my research, too. I was looking up the names the travel director gave us—or, more accurately, the ones Ron lifted from his notepad. I found their pictures, but they're not our guys." Kelsey detailed her findings on the four men. "It didn't take me very long to find information on them, since they were arrested and convicted."

"I'm glad we've eliminated them as part of Coeburn's operation, but if they're planning to set up business in my county, I'll need to be on the lookout for them, too," Jason said.

Jason and Kelsey stopped at an intersection and waited for the light to change before crossing.

"Oh, by the way," Jason added, "I asked Agent Baker if they could use drones to get an aerial view of the Coeburn compound.

He didn't think it would work. With the tree coverage and thick foliage, he didn't think we'd get a good view. So, we're back to ground-level surveillance."

"We'll come up with something," Kelsey assured him. "Even if we have to go back into the compound again."

"We need some kind of break, that's for sure."

They continued walking toward the car, but Kelsey paused in front of a sporting goods store. "If we have time, I'll like to go in here," she said. "The briars and bushes on Love Vine Mountain have snagged, ripped, or torn almost all the shirts I brought with me."

"Sure. We have time," Jason said. "I need to check in with Ferguson, so I'll wait for you out here." He indicated an iron bench on the sidewalk in front of the store.

Kelsey quickly made her purchases and rejoined Jason on the sidewalk.

"It's only four-thirty, but since we ate lunch so early, I'm ready for dinner. How about you?" Jason asked.

"After that meal with the Jacksons, I didn't think I'd need anything else today, but I could eat something, too," Kelsey confessed. "What did you have in mind?"

"I know a great pizza place about thirty minutes from here. I used to go there when I was in college at Chapel Hill. It looks like a dive, but the pizza is excellent. What it lacks in style, it makes up for in flavor."

As they drove northward toward the pizza place, Kelsey asked a question she had been wondering about ever since she had found Jason again—and found him working in law enforcement: "You got a degree in criminal justice in college. So, why did you join the military instead of working in your chosen field?"

"In hindsight, I don't really have a good reason. I think I felt like everyone expected me to follow in my father's footsteps and join the FBI. I got this wild idea that I wasn't going to be pushed into something by others' expectations. I wanted to strike out on my own. And yet, here I am—in law enforcement—working as a county sheriff."

"Your path was actually a circle," Kelsey pointed out.

"Yep! I chose my own path, and it led me right back to Dad's."

Kelsey laughed. "So, you had an aversion to others' advice, even good advice?"

"Something like that. Let's just say that I was young and stupid." Jason pulled off the road and parked in front of a nondescript wooden building with a flat roof. A flashing neon sign read 'Portofino's Pizza & Italian.' "We're here," Jason announced.

There were only two other couples in the restaurant, so Jason and Kelsey were seated quickly. After they had ordered their pizza, Jason walked over to the old-fashioned juke box in the corner. He dropped a few coins into the machine and made his selection. As he walked back toward the table, the song "This Magic Moment" by The Drifters filled the room.

"I hope you like Motown," Jason said as he sat down. "I think the music selections are the originals that came with the juke box."

"I like the oldies," Kelsey replied, swaying to the music in her seat. "Too bad they don't have a dance floor."

"You like to dance?" Jason asked. At Kelsey's nod, he said, "When our situation on Love Vine Mountain is over, I'll take you dancing."

"It's a date! I mean..." Kelsey stammered. "I mean, that would be nice. It's been a while since I've gone dancing."

At that moment, the waitress arrived at their table with their order, saving Kelsey from the awkwardness she felt creeping over her from her turning a friendly invitation to go dancing into a date. Kelsey and Jason pulled pieces of pizza onto their plates and busied themselves with eating.

"You were right. This is good," Kelsey said as she swallowed her first bite.

They ate in silence for a few minutes, but then, Jason paused and looked up. "Kelsey, I've been wanting to ask you something but haven't gotten the chance. Are you and Richard a thing? I mean, are you seeing each other?"

"No," Kelsey said slowly as her heart rate quickened. *First an invitation to go dancing and now this?* she thought. "Why do you ask?"

"Ron mentioned something about you and Richard being a couple."

Kelsey laughed. "You should know by now not to take Ron too seriously—unless, of course, it concerns business or Vickie. He likes to stir up things," she said. "I've gone out with Richard a few times, but there's no attraction between us—at least on my part. We're just coworkers. Richard is a nice guy and a smart guy, but he sometimes gets ahead of himself."

"I thought 'stuffed shirt' when I saw him," Jason said ungraciously. With a scowl, he pulled another piece of pizza onto his plate. "When he showed up yesterday in that business suit and tie, he looked like he was going to a meeting with the CEO of a Fortune 500 company. I thought maybe you had invited him to come up."

"No, he took that upon himself," Kelsey said. "I had no idea that my dad or Richard were coming to Mason Valley. Apparently, it was a last-minute decision. Dad left me a voice mail saying that he was on his way yesterday morning. I didn't see the message until after I got your call letting me know that they were here."

"I... ah, well, maybe I'm just envious of Richard—that aura of spit and polish and good looks that floats around him. And it irritates me." Jason looked down at his jeans and pullover knit shirt. "I'll bet he gets a manicure and has his hair done once a week," he added grumpily.

Jason, envious of Richard? Of anyone? Kelsey had never seen this side of him or even heard him criticize anyone openly.

Jason held up his hands for Kelsey's inspection. His nails were trimmed and neat, but not buffed and shiny, like Richard's. His hair could use a trim. Kelsey mentally compared Jason to Richard. It was easy to conclude who the winner was.

Richard was sleekly handsome and polished, but Jason's handsomeness and masculinity didn't need enhancement. His hair, longer than military regulation and a bit unruly at the moment, made Jason look "raffish"—another word from Kelsey's Grandmother Gilbert's repertoire.

"Spit and polish?" an incredulous Kelsey echoed. "Captain Wilder, have you forgotten? I've seen you in your mess dress uniform, with your shoes shined so bright, I could use them as a mirror. All the women on our post were gaga over you." Kelsey took a bite of her pizza, then asked, "You didn't know that?"

"Some people say," Jason replied as he picked up his glass of sweet tea and stared at it for a moment, "that it's the uniform that makes the man, not the other way around. Take you, for instance. You're beautiful in or out of your uniform." Jason took a sip of his tea and froze. Kelsey noticed a dawning realization on his face of what he had just said and how it could be misconstrued. His glass thumped on the table as he set it down quickly. His eyes met Kelsey's smiling ones across the table. He swallowed and attempted to apologize for the remark. "I... uh... I'm sorry. Please ignore what I just said. Not very professional."

"And how would you know what I look like when I take off my uniform?" Kelsey gave him a teasing smile. As a faux pas, this was minor—she'd heard much worse—but she decided to milk it for as long as she could. "Have you been peeking?"

"Only in my imagination," Jason said. He immediately realized that this could be misinterpreted, too. He rolled his eyes and looked up at the ceiling. "Scratch that comment, too."

"No way. Keep digging that hole." Kelsey waited for the "Sorry, not sorry" twinkle to return to Jason's eyes, but he stared intently down at his plate. Something was bothering him. "No offense taken. It's rare to see you flustered, Wildman—well worth being the object of your suggestive remarks."

Jason flushed as he apologized for the double entendre. "I didn't mean it." Flustered even more, he pushed his tea glass around, dispersing the water ring on the table. "Oh hell, I'm making it worse! I meant it, but not the way it came out. I was just trying to return the compliment. I meant that you are beautiful no matter how you're dressed," he finished lamely.

"Still digging? You'll reach China soon." Kelsey was trying hard not to cackle as Jason squirmed.

"'Captain Suave' is probably closer to what the women on the post called me, and they didn't mean it in a flattering way," Jason added with a rueful smile. "I think I just need to stop talking now."

"You're being irritatingly self-critical right now, but trust me, that's not what the female soldiers called you." In private conversations around their quarters, Kelsey's dormmates sometimes entertained themselves by rating the men assigned to the post. Captain Wilder was at or near the top of everyone's list. "'Captain Hunk' would be more accurate," she added. "But seriously, what's with your current mood?"

She was secretly happy to see the tables turned on Jason—to see him flustered, even if he was the one who had rattled himself. But this grumpy mood was unusual. He was always self-possessed, confident, and cool. This was a rare moment of vulnerability in a man whose strength and composure she had witnessed during extreme and dangerous wartime situations.

Was he actually jealous of Richard's looks, or was there something more eating at him? Could it be that the frustratingly slow progress on the Coeburn case was getting to him? Or—and this thought made her heart speed up—could it be that Jason's uncharitable comments about Richard were due to the fact that she had dated him?

"'Captain Hunk'? Humph!" Jason shook his head, dismissing the title. He ignored Kelsey's question about his mood and turned the conversation to her life as an army brat. Richard's name didn't come up again, and they slipped back into easy conversation. Jason returned to his normal, easygoing self, and the teasing light was back in his eyes as he bantered with Kelsey.

They finished their pizza and left the restaurant to start the drive back to Mason Valley. The conversation was light and companionable during the two-hour drive home.

They were almost back to Mason Valley when Kelsey reached over and touched Jason's arm that rested on the center console. "Feeling better, Captain Suave?"

"You're not going to let me forget that, are you?"

"Not a chance." Kelsey smiled. "I have a long memory and a lot of payback stored up."

"Take your best shot, Lieutenant Hoot Hoot." Jason's grin promised a challenge. "I don't know where that mood came from. I'm usually pretty even-keeled and don't let much get to me."

"Is something in particular worrying you?" Kelsey felt his arm tense up beneath her hand.

"Nah, nothing specific that I can put my finger on." He slowed the truck and turned onto the street that led through town and toward their neighborhood. He sighed. "It's just that, lately, I feel like my life is not under my own control. It's like I'm setting up dominoes: one thing has to fall before I can take the next step."

"We'll get the Coeburn situation resolved soon," Kelsey assured him. "I can feel it in my bones."

"That would help," Jason said. "But don't worry about it too much. We'll take as long as necessary."

It was approaching nine o'clock when Jason walked Kelsey to her door.

"I had fun today," Jason said. "It was therapeutic to visit the Jacksons, don't you think?"

"Yes. Meeting them and talking about their son gave me some closure. Do you think it helped them?"

"I think so. Or, at least I hope so," he replied. "What are your plans for tomorrow?"

"I don't know. I need to check with Ron on our agenda."

Kelsey longed to rise up onto her toes and kiss Jason on the cheek. She wanted to thank him for a day that had taken her away from the grueling daily climb up the mountain and from the constant worry about how they might force a break in the case. But Kelsey held herself back. There might be people driving by or looking out their windows. Besides, it's not like she and Jason had been on an official date, although it had seemed like one at times. Jason's eyes roamed over her face and settled on her lips. Was he thinking the same thing?

"Goodnight. And thanks again for taking me with you," Kelsey said, breaking their eye contact. She turned to open the door.

"Kelsey," Jason said softly.

She turned back and looked at him. The shadows on the porch hid most of his face, but his dark eyes held a special brightness. He made a move as if to step toward her, but then stopped.

"Never mind." He stepped back. "I'm sure I'll talk with you or Ron tomorrow. Goodnight."

"Goodnight." Kelsey pushed open the door and stepped inside. After she closed it, she leaned against it for a moment. She heard Jason's truck start. He backed up and then drove down the street toward his house.

"You're out late, young lady," Ron called from the sofa in the living room. "Am I going to have to ground you for staying out past curfew?"

"You're not the boss of me," Kelsey returned playfully. "Curfew? It's not even nine o'clock. Are you practicing being a daddy?" She placed her purse on the hall table and went to join Ron in the living room. He was watching a professional soccer game on TV.

She sat down beside him and reached for the bowl of popcorn on the coffee table.

"By the glow on your face, I take it you had a good day?" Ron asked.

"We did." Kelsey shared the details of their visit to the Jacksons' home and the FBI's Charlotte field office.

"But that's not what has you all in a tither, is it?" Ron persisted. He peered at Kelsey's face and smiled smugly when she blushed.

"I'm not, as you put it, in a tither," Kelsey protested, though she couldn't suppress a smile as she threw a handful of popcorn at him. "Shut up and tell me about your trip up Love Vine Mountain today."

CHAPTER TWELVE

Jason spotted Kelsey pass his house on her usual early-morning run. He quickly finished his coffee, grabbed his phone, and took off after her. If he ran quickly, he could catch up with her, and together, they could run the track around the park.

He gained ground on her and was close enough to see her ponytail swinging back and forth. The small pack strapped around her waist bobbed on her hips with each step. He called out, hoping to get her to slow down and wait for him, but either she was too far ahead to hear him or the wind muffled his voice. She didn't slow her pace. Kelsey was a fast jogger and was almost out of the neighborhood by now. She would soon be at the entrance to the park.

Jason picked up his pace. He was nearing the last row of houses in the neighborhood when a voice called out to him from across the street: "Yoo hoo! Sheriff! Can I talk with you?" He groaned but stopped and turned toward the voice. Mrs. Murphy was crossing the street and coming toward him. A photograph flapped in her hand. Damn! Kelsey was going around the bend and would soon be out of sight.

Jason's duty as sheriff had to come first. Mrs. Murphy was a citizen and deserved to speak with her sheriff whenever she felt the need, even if it was inconvenient for him. His approach to his job was to always make himself available to the citizens of Mason Valley. Mrs. Murphy felt comfortable in stopping him, and she expected her concerns to be taken seriously.

"Good morning, Mrs. Murphy!" Jason looked anxiously toward the end of the neighborhood. Kelsey had disappeared. "What's wrong?"

"I want to report a missing person," Mrs. Murphy said as she reached him. She held the photo out to him. "It's my cat, but she's like a person to me."

"Let's see," Jason said as he took the photo from Mrs. Murphy.

"This is Callie. Someone stole her, I just know it! She's gone, Sheriff. I haven't seen her for three days."

"Take a deep breath, Mrs. Murphy. Why do you think she's been stolen?"

"She never goes off on her own. I've had her for a year, and she's never left home before. I let her out, but this time, she didn't come back." The woman had tears in her eyes. "Please, Sheriff, can you help me?" Mrs. Murphy pleaded.

Jason glanced toward the park. Kelsey was long gone. He was impatient to get back to his run and hopefully catch up with her, but he spent several more minutes talking with Mrs. Murphy and getting the details of her missing cat. "Can I keep the photo? I'll have one of my deputies make some posters and put them up around town." The older woman nodded, and Jason turned to resume his jog down the street. "Let me know if she comes home," he yelled back at her. *Small-town sheriff, small-town problems*, he reminded himself before he remembered the not so small problem of the Coeburn compound up on Love Vine Mountain.

He finished one circuit around the park but didn't catch up with Kelsey. Perhaps she had already finished and gone home. But if that were the case, she would have had to pass him on her way out of the park. Maybe she had taken a different route?

It was probably nothing, but Jason was still unnerved. He called Ron to see if she had come back yet. She hadn't.

"She's never changed her routine as long as we've been here. She's not at home, and you don't see her in the park," Ron mused as he ticked off the facts. "I don't know where she is, but I'm sure she's fine."

"Do you think she went up the mountain without letting you know?" The thought struck Jason suddenly. And he didn't like it.

"That doesn't sound like her. But I'm confident that if she did, she can handle herself. Don't worry."

"Well, I am worried," Jason said. "We don't know where she is, and as you say, she keeps to a strict routine."

"She might have changed her routine. It's not set in stone."

"Well, there's two girls up on Love Vine Mountain whose parents say they were kidnapped," Jason insisted. He was no longer trying to hide the concern in his voice. "Kelsey not following her usual routine seems odd. And in my experience, when things diverge from a usual pattern, it means something."

"It's probably nothing." Ron sounded like he was trying to reassure Jason as much as himself.

"It may be nothing, but I'll feel better if we go up the mountain and take a look around. If she is up there, we don't know that she went voluntarily. You in?"

"Of course," Ron replied quickly.

"Meet me at my house as soon as you can." Jason started to jog toward his house.

Jason's cell phone rang just as he hung up with Ron. He was annoyed by the ring, but stopped and looked at the caller ID. It was the sheriff from Arkansas. Jason slowed to a walk and accepted the call. As they talked, a slow burn began in Jason's gut and worked its way upward. By the end of their call, anger and fear sped up his pulse.

Jason called Agent Baker as he ran toward his home. He didn't waste any time with a greeting when the FBI agent picked up. He immediately spat out what he had learned from the Arkansas sheriff: "Sheriff Radnor identified Coeburn from a picture I sent him. He used an alias during his time in Arkansas. That's why there's no information on him. He was 'Campbell' there. The sheriff was suspicious about the number of young women who lived with him, but Campbell was evicted from his property and left town before the sheriff had any reason to investigate. But there's more," Jason said, as he slowed to a walk and took a breath. "A witness finally came forward and admitted that one of Campbell's men forced her friend, another young girl, to join the group. He threatened to kill the witness if she talked. The parents think their daughter is with him here on Love Vine."

When Jason was finished, he added, "I now have probable cause, so I'm going in." *With or without you*, Jason thought. "How soon can you get here?"

"I agree it's time to act. We'll be in the air immediately," Agent Baker promised. "Our ETA should be less than thirty minutes."

Ron was sitting on the steps of Jason's home with his gear when Jason arrived.

"Be right back," Jason shouted at Ron as he raced into his house. He quickly returned in his uniform with his revolver strapped to his side, a backpack in his hand, and two rifles slung over his shoulder. He tossed one of the rifles to Ron as they hurried toward the patrol car and climbed in.

The patrol car's tires squealed as Jason backed out of the driveway. Before he put the car in drive, he took a deep breath, filled his lungs to settle his nerves. This new information from the Arkansas sheriff made him even more anxious to find Kelsey, but he didn't need to drive like a maniac. It would take the FBI another twenty-to-thirty minutes to muster the agents and helicopter over from Charlotte.

Now, Jason had a new problem. If Kelsey was indeed up on the mountain, whether voluntarily or not, she didn't know armed agents were coming. She needed to stay out of any crossfire that might erupt.

Slow down and think, Jason commanded himself. *Regain control and remain in control. Kelsey knows how to take care of herself.* If she had gone up to the Coeburn compound on the spur of the moment, he had to count on her ability to take care of herself. Jason forced himself to push his worry aside and focus on the job before him. "Hey, what's going on?" Ron was more than just nervous now. Jason's actions scared him.

Jason put the car in park and filled Ron in on his conversation with the sheriff. The sheriff had just returned to his office from attending his father's funeral and helping his mother settle their financial affairs. His words about Coeburn made chills run along Jason's spine.

"Sheriff Radnor said that Coeburn—or Campbell, as he was known there—was renting a place near Mountain Home, Arkansas. He was there for only a short time before he failed to pay the rent. He was served an eviction notice but took his group and suddenly left without keeping the court date to fight his eviction."

"But the sheriff was suspicious of the group?" Ron asked.

"A little. He thought it odd that the majority of the people with Coeburn were young women. He wondered if they might have been runaways or, worse, kidnap victims. But just like when I visited Allie and Maddie at the camp here, Radnor was led to believe they were there willingly. Coeburn never did anything to further suspicions or indicate that he was doing anything illegal, but he was only there for a short time."

"Runaways are prime targets for cult leaders. Did the sheriff have any idea as to what they were doing in his county?"

"No, but I have an idea. I could be wrong, but with a camp full of young women, it's not a stretch to think he's engaged in human trafficking," Jason said.

"The girls were probably frightened into not speaking up," Ron said.

"I agree," Jason said. "When the sheriff in Arkansas searched their abandoned camp, they found straps that could be used to restrain a person, though they couldn't tell whether the items had actually been used on anyone. With no leads on where Coeburn had gone, Radnor let it go. He was just happy they had left his county."

"Out of sight, out of mind," Ron said. "Coeburn's camp has all the classic signs of sex trafficking. He doesn't seem to have any obvious source of income, so that would explain how he supports himself and his group."

"Damn!" Jason said. He rubbed his hands over his face in frustration. "I wish I had taken him down before now, but like Sheriff Radnor, I couldn't do it legally. But now, after talking to him, I feel I have probable cause to enter his compound. But just to cover all bases, I asked Ferguson to send one of the deputies to get a search warrant from Judge Kline. With exigent circumstances, like the possible threat of harm to the girls at the compound, I don't need one, but I want to do this right."

"A sex-trafficking ring would explain some of the things Kelsey and I witnessed at the camp," Ron said. "That's probably why those male visitors were there. They acted like they were inspecting the goods."

Jason slapped the steering wheel angrily. "Sheriff Radnor said that Coeburn had told him that he moved there from Oregon. He was probably run out of there, too. And now he's here. He moves on whenever questions start to be asked. He got smarter and bought property here, which gives him a little more protection and privacy. But when a group like that moves on when the authorities start asking questions, it usually means something is not on the up-and-up. I need to make this his last stop."

At the sound of a helicopter approaching, Jason put the car in drive and headed toward the park. They pulled into the parking lot just as a helicopter touched down. Agent Baker, three other men, and two women, all wearing jackets that read "FBI," stepped down from the helicopter and ran toward Jason and Ron. After brief introductions, they all moved toward the track at the foot of the mountain.

"We plan to enter the southern edge of the compound," Agent Baker said. "We have another team of six coming in from the other side of the mountain. They'll secure the northern side while we secure the south. By my calculations, we should all reach our designated spots at about the same time." They planned to have Coeburn surrounded before he even knew they were in the vicinity.

Agent Baker nodded for Jason to show them the way, and the agents quickly fell into line behind him as they made their way up the trail. The agents, all experienced members of the Violent Crimes Against Children and Child Exploitation Division from Charlotte, had taken down similar operations before. They knew how to handle scum like Coeburn. It was just the location of this current operation that was challenging.

Jason and Ron took the lead up the trail. Jason relaxed for a moment and focused on the climb, happy to have something to distract his mind from worrying about Kelsey. The climb was strenuous, but that helped Jason burn off the energy and anger that had coursed through him immediately after his phone call with the Arkansas sheriff.

His thoughts returned to Kelsey. *Where could she be?* She hadn't returned home by the time they met the agents in the park. Ron had called her phone once more before they entered the woods. Like all of his calls that morning, it had gone straight to voice mail. *Please, Kelsey*, Jason silently begged, *if you are where I think you are, please stay out of the crossfire.*

CHAPTER THIRTEEN

Kelsey had completed her first trip around the park's jogging track when an idea came to her. She and Ron had been up to the compound at mid-morning, the afternoon, and late at night. What if there was more activity in the camp early in the morning? She and Ron planned to go up that afternoon, but she could make it up and back before then. She'd take a quick peek at what was going on inside the compound and check the reception on the phone Ron had hidden in the bushes at the edge of the property. She'd be back before Ron even knew she was gone.

Kelsey felt invigorated this morning. After their visit to the Jacksons yesterday, she felt a lightness in her soul that comes when a heavy burden is lifted. She hadn't felt this guilt-free in a long time. She deeply regretted the loss of life—and she didn't think she would ever lose her anger over Major Burton's bungling—but she was grateful to learn that Jackson's parents were coping with their loss.

The Jacksons supported their son's decision to serve his country. That didn't make what had happened to him right, but neither was it right for Kelsey to let her personal anger and grief tarnish his willingness to make the ultimate sacrifice. She owed it to Sergeant Jackson and his parents to honor their belief in the rightness of their son's decision, despite the outcome.

"You were a good and faithful soldier, Sergeant Jackson," Kelsey whispered into the still woods. She included the other team members in her tribute.

The time spent with Jason—away from their worries about Coeburn's compound—had been fun and carefree. Seeing Jason becoming flustered during dinner and tripping over his words was the highlight of the afternoon. Kelsey was usually on the receiving end of his teasing, so it was a pleasure to see the tables turned. She'd like to throw Jason off-balance again—and often—but she wasn't a pro, like he was. She just couldn't compete in that game.

Kelsey turned off the jogging track and onto one of the trails that led up the mountain. The trees and underbrush were wet. Dew clung to spiderwebs that crisscrossed her path, making them sparkle like diamonds in the morning light. It was quiet in the forest except for the songs of the birds that flew from treetop to treetop. Their music blending joyfully to welcome a new day. Somewhere above, Kelsey heard the cooing sound of the mourning dove—another reminder of Sergeant Jackson.

Kelsey loved early mornings like this when the earth was quiet. It's like the land had renewed itself overnight and was now ready for the approaching day. There was no better place to watch nature come alive than here on Love Vine Mountain. *That's a human way to look at it*, Kelsey mused. *There are plenty of animals on Love Vine Mountain that roam the hollows and valleys only at night.*

Kelsey plowed through the underbrush and veered to the right until she picked up the same way she and Ron had taken the night they hid the spy cameras. Thus far, their plan for the cameras had been a bust. They had felt certain their clandestine trip into the compound to plant the cameras would be a game changer. That thought was quickly squashed by the weak signal they got in valley. Plan B had been to hide one of the phones closer to the cameras in hopes that it would pick up a stronger signal, but that had not worked yet, either. The last time they checked, the data was still distorted.

Richard was working with the manufacturer of the devices to find any defects in the equipment. The lab techs hadn't yet identified the problem, but they leaned toward the possibility that it wasn't the devices themselves and instead the location where they were hidden. Kelsey and Ron had discussed a Plan C—make another trip into the compound and find a new location for the cameras—and even a Plan D—scrap the cameras altogether and come up with a whole new plan.

Kelsey and Ron were frustrated and disappointed by the slow pace of their investigation. Nothing seemed to be going smoothly or turning out as planned. Maybe today she'd find good results that she could report to Ron and Jason. They sorely needed an answer as to whether Allie and Maddie were at the camp voluntarily or were being held there against their will.

Kelsey was impatient. Waiting around for a lucky break or for Coeburn to slip up and hand them the answers felt inadequate. But just as when they started this surveillance, they needed evidence that would stand up in court. She couldn't will that to happen just because she wanted it. It might turn out that Coeburn was legit, but she didn't think so. There were too many signs that said otherwise. Patience was still the key, and sooner or later, they would be rewarded. She had to believe that and keep trying to find new ways to break the case.

Kelsey came to a pile of boulders that blocked the trail. They were bordered by a tangled thicket on both sides. She picked her way over the rocks carefully. It was much easier to climb in daylight than in the darkness of night.

She paused at the top of the rock formation to catch her breath. The day was heating up, even here under the shelter of the thick trees. The air was heavy with humidity and caused Kelsey's shirt to stick to her skin and sweat to bead on her brow. As familiar as she had become with the trails up the mountain, Love Vine never took it easy on her—or any hiker, for that matter.

The fertile mountain rejuvenated itself quickly and erased almost all man-made disturbances in no time. Only a trained tracker would notice that she and Ron had traveled this way not quite two weeks ago. An overturned rock or a broken tree limb were the only evidence that anyone had passed this way.

Kelsey continued her hike and didn't take a break until she came to a large, flat rock. There, she sat down, took a long drink from her water bottle, pulled a handkerchief from her waist pack, and wiped her sweaty forehead.

She looked around at the woods on either side of her. Rhododendrons and woodland ferns covered the hilly areas beneath the trees and were in full bloom. Swaths of pink and red blooms were dappled by slivers of sunshine that streamed through openings in the canopy above. An artist would be hard-pressed to capture the full beauty on canvas.

In a thicket near the trail, love vine wrapped tightly around the bushes. *Maybe they should call it 'clinging vine,'* Kelsey thought. It certainly kept a firm grip on anything that grew near it.

Judging by the terrain and her memories of the night they had come this way, Kelsey estimated that she was well past the midpoint in her climb and almost to the compound.

As she took a few more sips from her water bottle, Kelsey thought about the tree stump fountain Jason had shown them that first day when he had brought her and Ron up the mountain. The fountain was incredible, as was the meadow by the waterfall. Before she left the area, Kelsey vowed to visit that picturesque meadow one more time.

She had spent most of her life in the suburbs of Atlanta—she was a "flat-lander," the term for city folk like her—but Kelsey's appreciation for the natural beauty and challenging terrain of Love Vine Mountain increased each time she visited it. There were very few mountains that could rival the beauty of Love Vine.

Kelsey rose and continued her climb. Her mind turned to Jason—one of her favorite subjects lately. Did she have the beginnings of a relationship with him? She thought she saw a glimmer of more than friendship in his eyes, but that could just be his mind working to come up with a tease or something to make her blush. On the other hand, he had kissed her a couple of days ago when he left the meeting with their fathers.

Jason's kiss had been quick and friendly—*a very light kiss*, she reminded herself. It was not the kiss of a hot, budding romance. *But your reaction to it didn't seem like it was small or light.* Her fingers touched her lips where she could still feel the slight brush of Jason's kiss.

Jason was hard to read. They had settled into an easy friendship, in part due to their shared experiences in a warzone. Was she confusing camaraderie between soldiers with physical attraction? Was she wishing for more between them than there was? And if that was her wish, was she fooling herself again? She had been deceived before and was hesitant to trust her own judgement where romance was concerned. No, she would wait and not take anything Jason did seriously until he made a move or confirmed that his interest was more than just friendly.

Yes, that would be best. A heart can't be broken if you keep it locked away and don't share the key. *Oh, Barrett, you're so full of it.* Kelsey smiled at the ridiculousness of her thoughts. The heart usually had a mind of its own.

Kelsey's unanswered questions about her romantic life—or lack of a romantic life—was just another reason the Coeburn situation needed to end. A romance with anyone couldn't move forward until it was resolved.

As Kelsey neared the compound's property line, she heard

voices and paused to listen. The voices were soft at first, cajoling, but as she snuck closer and peaked through the bushes, the voices became louder—and angry. Two young men and two young women were in the clearing near the women's quarters. Kelsey pulled the limbs apart slightly to get a better view. Her breath caught. One of the young women was dark-haired, and the other was blonde. It was Allie and Maddie, the two girls at the center of her and Ron's investigation here in Mason Valley.

"You're a tease, Allie. Enough!" one of the young men yelled. His back was to Kelsey, but she saw him grab the young woman and pull her toward him. Her face was white with fear as she struggled against his grip.

The second man had Maddie by the hand as well, and he was pulling her toward the shack. She planted her feet on the ground and resisted him. He yanked her hard, and she cried out as she fell. She sprawled in the dirt, rocks, and leaves. The young man grabbed Maddie by the hair and dragged her back to her feet.

"Stop! You're hurting me," Maddie cried.

Her attacker ignored her and turned to the other young man. "Clint, I need some privacy. I'm going in here." He pointed toward the girls' quarters, then looked back at Maddie. "There's no use resisting me. Pop gave you to me, and I'm not waiting any longer to claim what's mine."

Maddie dug her heels into the soft turf and pulled away from his grasp. She fell backward, but he grabbed her hand and tugged her roughly toward the shack. Maddie fought against him, furiously kicking and struggling to get away.

The young man named Clint pushed Allie hard against the trunk of a tree. He started groping her and trying to kiss her. "Whatever. I don't need privacy," Clint said close to Allie's face. "I have all I need right here. You can even watch, if you want." Clint laughed. "I've waited a long time for this."

Like father, like son, Kelsey thought with disgust.

Allie pushed hard against Clint's chest. It surprised him, and he stumbled, but he quickly righted himself. He grabbed Allie by the shoulders and shook her hard. Her head bobbed back and forth like a doll's.

"Stop fighting me," he shouted. "I've had my eye on you since the first time I saw you in town. You're mine. Pop said so. And there's nothing you can do about it."

Allie ineffectively pushed against his chest again and tried to twist free from his grip. Clint raised her skirt to her waist, and Allie fought against him harder.

As he raised her skirt, Kelsey spotted a GPS tracking bracelet on Allie's ankle. *Of course!* she thought. *That's why they didn't try to run away. The GPS device was hidden by the long skirts they wear. All the girls in the camp are probably fitted with one.*

Allie's resistance angered Clint. He grabbed the bodice of her dress, pulled hard, and ripped the fabric down to her waist. The white flesh of her breasts was exposed. Her face twisted in terror.

Allie and Maddie were being assaulted. Kelsey made an instant decision. She moved quickly, crouching low as she approached Clint. Daryl was busy pulling Maddie toward the shack's door. His back was to Kelsey, and Maddie's furious resistance drew all his concentration. With Clint's attention on Allie and lust filling his mind, he was unaware that anyone was behind him. Kelsey picked up a large rock and, with all her strength, smashed it against the back of his head. Clint grunted once, released Allie, and slumped to the ground. He groaned quietly and then lay still.

Kelsey didn't have time to speak to Allie or look around for Maddie. She barely had time to take a deep breath before some- one caught her from behind. Daryl's bear-like arms grasped Kelsey around the waist. He squeezed her rib cage, choking off her breath. Kelsey brought up her elbow, put all her force behind it, and smashed him in the throat, just above his Adam's apple.

Daryl doubled over as he tried to suck air into his lungs, but he still managed to grab Kelsey by her ponytail. He yanked, lost his balance and went down, but he sent Kelsey flying backward over his head in the process. Tears stung Kelsey's eyes as she landed on the ground with a thud.

Kelsey sucked air into her lungs as her mind automatically went over all the skills learned in her self-defense training classes. Just as her instructor had taught her, Kelsey cleared her mind of all thoughts other than her attacker. She centered herself and zeroed in on Daryl. To handle someone like him, she needed to go on the offense.

She rolled to her feet, aware that she couldn't be caught help-less on the ground. From the corner of her eye, she saw Allie and Maddie holding each other, their eyes rounded with fright. Kelsey shouted at the girls, who stood frozen in place, "Run! That way!" She pointed toward the northwest corner of the property. Then, she quickly brought her attention back to her attacker and con-templated what his next move.

Kelsey shifted her weight to the balls of her feet, faced Daryl, and sized him up as he staggered toward her. He was more the type who relied on brute strength than a trained strategic fight-er—more brawn than brains. Her self-defense classes and army training had taught her the moves she needed to handle someone like him: strike hard and fast while your opponent is off-balance. Use his brawn against him. Kelsey was light on her feet and quick. Daryl was tall but overweight. He couldn't maneuver as quickly as she.

Kelsey bent low and barreled straight ahead toward her assail-ant. Her offensive strike surprised Daryl. She caught both of his legs just above the knees and flipped him onto his back. She heard a *whoosh* as her momentum carried her, and she landed hard on top of him. His fist came up and hit her cheek with a glancing blow. He again grabbed Kelsey by the hair, rolled her over, and held her down with his weight. He pulled back his fist to strike again, but paused for a second, out of breath.

Kelsey chose that moment to strike. She jabbed his nose hard with her free hand. He loosened his grip on her other hand. She shoved hard at his chest, then kneed his groin. It wasn't a perfect shot, but it was enough to make him double over in pain. Kelsey flipped him onto his back, straddled him, and pinned his arms to his sides with her knees.

A red-hot haze filled Kelsey's vision. Everything that had plagued her for the last few years rose up and filled her throat. It mixed with the bile that had pooled there when she saw the assault on Allie and Maddie. Anger mixed with latent anguish fueled the power behind her balled fists as she slammed them into Daryl's face again and again. He weakly tried to buck her off, but he was stunned from the power of her first punch.

Kelsey didn't see Daryl's face as she held her attacker down and drew back her fist. She saw the face of Lucas, her ex, and punched his lying, two-timing face. She saw the face of cancer that had cruelly taken her mother. She pounded it with all the force she could muster. She saw Major Burton's reckless, arrogant face. With all the strength from the depths of her body, she slammed his face with the knockout punch.

Kelsey was too angry to stop. There were other people she loved who had been wronged. She added a punch for each of the team members who had trusted Burton and had been injured—or worse—due to his greed and incompetence. She gave the major one more punch just because he was a worthless human being. Then, just so Daryl would remember why she was here, she added two more blows for Allie and Maddie.

Kelsey finally stopped. Her anger was spent, and her arm ached and trembled with pain. Her attacker lay on the ground, unmoving. His nose was bleeding, his eyes were already swelling, and his face was covered in blood.

Kelsey shook her head and came back to her surroundings. She needed to move. She took only a moment to gasp for air before she was up and running to catch up with Allie and Maddie. There wasn't time to look for the other girls in the camp. The authorities could do that later, after she shared details of the assault she had witnessed. She, Allie, and Maddie had to get away. The ankle bracelets the girls wore were almost certainly some kind of GPS tracking devices. And someone had surely heard the commotion as she fought off Daryl. Within minutes, someone would come after them.

Kelsey raced up the steep hill and followed the path Allie and Maddie had taken into the woods. The broken limbs and vines made their trail easy to follow. Kelsey pushed and tore through the tangled brush as she hurried to catch up with them. After a few minutes, she caught a glimpse of clothing through the dark underbrush. She hurried toward them and found them sitting on a log, scared, winded, and gasping for breath.

"We have to hurry," Kelsey told them. "They'll soon know that you're gone—if they don't already. Let's go this way." She directed the two girls to turn westward. The underbrush was just as thick this way, but they would not have to climb upward. This would require less energy, so they should be able to move faster.

Kelsey encouraged them to move as quickly as they could as she pushed them through the forest. Allie and Maddie were not as strong as she, even though they had spent the last few months laboring in the compound. They were scared, and that sapped a lot of their energy, but they had to do it. It was crucial that they put as much distance between themselves and the camp as possible.

They had traveled almost a mile when Kelsey spotted a large rock that jutted out from the mountain. It was covered with a blanket of kudzu vine. Orangey-yellowish love vine was wound firmly around and mixed with the thick green leaves of the kudzu. The vines twisted together and draped over the jutting rock, forming a thick curtain. *This might be the invasive plant's one opportunity to redeem itself from its reputation as an annoyance*, Kelsey thought.

She pulled aside some of the vines, took a tiny flashlight from her waist pack, and scanned the small space behind them. She didn't see any snakes, and the room was big enough for the three of them. *Good enough.* She pulled the girls under the jutting rock. "Let's hide back here and try to remove those ankle bracelets."

The space behind the curtain of vines was like a small, dark room. Kelsey's eyes adjusted to the darkness quickly, and she was able to make out the rock face hidden by the vines. Kelsey indicated that the girls should sit and rest. Then, she opened her waist pack and retrieved a pair of scissors. She grabbed Allie's foot and began ramming the scissors against the plate that covered the screws holding the bracelet together.

Kelsey knew that it was possible to remove the bracelets this way; she just hoped they had enough time to do it. Sweat beaded on her forehead as she worked. Finally, the plate loosened and fell away. She passed the scissors to Maddie and instructed her to start trying to remove the cover plate on her own bracelet.

Kelsey next pulled out a Swiss Army knife, found the small attached screwdriver, and began the delicate task of removing the screws that held the bracelet together around Allie's ankle. Several times, she had to take a deep breath to steady her hand as she worked. *Just like target practice*, she reminded herself. *Steady your hands first and control your breathing.*

Working smoothly and quickly, Kelsey soon had one screw out. Then, the second screw fell to the ground. She removed the bracelet and rubbed Allie's ankle. It was bruised, and scabs ringed her leg just above the ankle.

Kelsey handed Allie some antibacterial wipes to use on the sores before turning to Maddie, who had not yet managed to get the plate off her own bracelet. Kelsey took back the scissors, and after a couple more strikes, it fell to the ground. It wasn't long before she had removed the screws and Maddie was free as well. Kelsey also gave her some wipes to tend to her bruised and scabbed leg.

They had to get moving again, but Kelsey paused for a moment to rub some wipes across her bruised knuckles and cheek. The alcohol strung with each swipe across the cuts, but Kelsey felt a deep satisfaction over how she had obtained the cuts and bruises. It was a good feeling—confirmation that she was once again doing something worthwhile and making a difference. She felt a new determination and resolve. She would not fail these two young women who were counting on her. Somehow, she would get them off the mountain safely.

Kelsey picked up the ankle bracelets and slipped outside through the curtain that shielded their hiding place. She checked the forest around them but didn't see or hear anyone in the vicinity. Of course, if Coeburn and his men were experienced mountain men, they could be somewhere close, silently stalking their prey. Kelsey hoped they were actually just as incompetent as Clint and Daryl. *Don't get too cocky, Barrett*, she silently cautioned herself.

Kelsey took the ankle bracelets, swung them around her head, let go, and threw them down the hillside as far as she could. They flew several yards before landing in a tree. They clung to its branches and slowly swung back and forth. Oh well! Maybe chasing the GPS signal up a tree would make it even more challenging for Coeburn's men to locate the three women.

In an impulse, Kelsey grabbed a fistful of love vine from where it tangled with the kudzu on the rock. Would the legend work for luck as well as for love? Sometimes, luck and love went hand-in-hand. If they were lucky enough to successfully get off the mountain today, love would take care of itself. Kelsey balled up some of the vine and tossed it over her shoulder. It couldn't hurt, and they needed all the luck they could get.

Kelsey called the girls from their hiding place, and they started walking west again. They were somewhat rested now, excited to be liberated from their ankle bracelets, and wanted to talk. Kelsey had to caution them in a whisper, "Shush. We've got to get to safety, first. Then you can tell me what happened." They walked in silence after that.

Soon, Kelsey felt a familiarity in the landscape and their surroundings. With a start, she recognized where they were. The tree stump fountain was just ahead. *Good. The girls need water.* She steered them toward the spot where she thought the stump was located. It soon came into view.

Kelsey unclasped the empty water bottle from her waist pack, filled it, and passed it to Allie and Maddie. They took turns drinking. Kelsey let them rest on a fallen log for a moment, but she soon motioned for them to get up. They began walking again.

Kelsey now had an idea of where she could take them. If Coeburn's men were on their trail but couldn't actually find Kelsey or the girls, maybe they would become discouraged and give up the search. That thought held a lot of 'maybe's, but they needed a safe hiding place for the time being. Then, Kelsey could figure out the best way to get Allie and Maddie down the mountain and into town.

The hidden cave behind the waterfall was not far. She steered Allie and Maddie slightly northwest. It wasn't long before they heard the sound of falling water. Creeping along the slippery ledge toward the cave would be a challenge for the girls, but with all they had survived, Kelsey had confidence that they could do it. They had to; she was all out of other ideas at the moment.

Kelsey led them toward the meadow but circled around it at first. She hugged the tree line and avoided the open space of the meadow. She stopped and scanned the area. Nothing moved, and the only sounds were the rushing water and the calls of birds high in their perches. Satisfied that no one had seen them, Kelsey led the girls down the sloping bank toward the falls. She stopped near the ledge and explained what they had to do.

"I'm scared," Maddie said. "I don't know how to swim. What if I fall?" She gazed at the deep pool at their feet.

"Don't worry. I'll take Allie first and then come back for you," Kelsey said. *Brave words!* she chided herself. *You've only been across once, and you had help.* But there was no time for self-doubt. They had to get to a hiding place quickly, and this was the closest—and the best—one she knew. They were prime targets standing here at the edge of the waterfall.

Allie had been holding her torn dress together with her hands ever since they fled the compound, but at Kelsey's instructions, she released the fabric and took hold of Kelsey's hand. She balanced herself by dropping the other hand to her side and pressing against the rock face. Red marks from Clint's assault were still visible on her exposed white skin.

Kelsey's heart ached for Allie's humiliation. As she inched along holding Allie's hand, Kelsey silently thanked God, fate, or whatever that had brought her up the mountain that morning. If she hadn't, Allie would have suffered far more than a torn dress and some scratches.

Kelsey instructed Allie to take small side steps toward the waterfall. They moved along the ledge slowly until Kelsey reached the cave's opening. She helped Allie step down into the cave and then returned for Maddie.

Kelsey took Maddie's hand and gave it a gentle squeeze before guiding her along the ledge, just as she had Allie. "Relax, don't think about it," Kelsey instructed. "Press your back against the wall and just move one foot at a time. It's not far."

Maddie closed her eyes as she followed Kelsey's instructions, and she didn't open them until they were close to the opening. Then, Kelsey, with Allie's help, assisted Maddie into the cave. They were now enclosed behind the curtain of water. Allie and Maddie sagged to the floor in relief.

Kelsey sat down for few minutes to rest and let her nerves

settle. She had been wound tight as a top since she had peeked through the bushes and saw Clint and Daryl's attack on the young women. Kelsey rummaged through her waist pack for something for them to eat. The three of them had been running on adrenaline, but adrenaline wouldn't keep them going forever.

"How do you get so much in that little bag?" Maddie asked as Kelsey pulled out a protein bar, split it in thirds, and gave each girl a piece.

Kelsey hid a smile at Maddie's question. *This* was the most important thing on her mind right now? Ah, to be that young again. But the comment made Kelsey realize the resiliency of the two girls. She had told them not to worry, and they were taking her at her word. They were confident that she would keep them safe and get them home.

"It takes practice," Kelsey replied to Maddie's question. "Thank goodness I never go running without it. Here's a safety pin for the front of your dress, Allie." A flush rose on Allie's cheeks as she reached for the pin. The memory of how her dress had been torn was written on her face.

Kelsey decided to give the girls a little time before she asked how they came to be at the compound. They needed to breathe free for a few minutes—a short respite from the trauma they had endured—before they were asked to relive it. Keeping her voice upbeat and positive, Kelsey asked, "Isn't this a great hiding place? The water is like a window. We can see out, but our trackers can't see in." She paused, then added, "Oh, and I'm Kelsey, by the way." She extended her hand, and the two young women shook it.

"Do you think they'll find us?" Allie crossed her arms in front of her and clutched her forearms to stop them from shivering. "I don't want to go back there."

"We're going to get out of here safely," Kelsey promised. "We just have to be smart about when we leave here. We need to make sure that Coeburn's men aren't in the vicinity."

Both girls nodded. Judging by their expressions, they now appeared ready to talk. Pouring out their story might be a relief for them.

Kelsey definitely had questions, but she wouldn't press them if they didn't want to answer. She fell back on her training as an engagement team leader in Afghanistan, when she sought information from the women and children of the tribes. *Start with the basics*, she reminded herself. "How did you happen to be there—at the compound?"

Allie spoke first. "Maddie and I were walking home from the movies. Clint and Daryl came along in a truck. First, they just asked if we wanted a ride, but when we said no, Daryl jumped out, grabbed us, and forced us into the truck. We tried to get away, but they were too strong."

"When we screamed for help, they put these cloths over our noses and mouths. We passed out," Maddie added. "When we woke up, we were at the camp. We've been there ever since." She hung her head.

"They drove up the mountain?" Kelsey asked.

"Yes," Maddie said. "At least, they drove part of the way. There's an old logging road. The men use it when they go to town."

"They park where the logging road ends. They must have carried us the rest of the way," Allie added.

"Mr. Coeburn was angry with Clint and Daryl at first. He said he didn't want them 'bringing townsfolk into the mountain.' But then, he told them, 'At least you picked two beauties this time.' The way he looked at us was creepy." Maddie shuddered at the memory.

"No one saw you get taken?" Kelsey asked.

"It was dark. We didn't see anyone around, and there wasn't a streetlight on that section of the road," Maddie explained. "We should have been more careful."

"Don't blame yourself. It's not your fault. Why didn't you tell Sheriff Wilder that you had been kidnapped when he visited the camp?" Kelsey suspected that she already knew the answer, but she wanted to hear it from the girls.

"When Sheriff Wilder came to the camp, Mr. Coeburn threatened us before he let us speak with him." Maddie plucked at one of the tears in her dress. Then, in a shaky breath, she added, "He said that if we said anything to the sheriff, he'd kill our families."

"We were afraid he'd do it, too," Allie added. "Two girls tried to escape at one point, and the men caught them. Mr. Coeburn put them in a dark room he had dug into the mountainside. They were in there for more than two days." Allied gulped. "They wouldn't give them any food—just water. Mr. Coeburn said they needed to lose a few pounds, anyway."

"He made all of us watch him as he chained them up and locked the door," Maddie said. "After that, he threatened us with, 'Do you want to go into the hole?'"

Kelsey bit her lip and tried to control her rising anger. *Be cool*, she cautioned herself. What she really wanted to do was march back to the camp, free the other girls, and smash in the face of anyone who got in her way. But she knew that Jason would take care of that just as soon as they made it down the mountain and the girls told him their stories.

Maddie continued their story. "They made us work all the time. Mrs. Coeburn was in charge of us. We spent all day cooking, doing laundry, cleaning, planting, picking crops, canning vegetables…" Her voice trailed off. "They treated us like slaves."

"How many girls are still held in the camp?" Kelsey asked.

"Ten," Allie said. "With us, it was a total of twelve. Mr. Coeburn was always talking about his 'dirty dozen' being groomed for 'better things.' What do you think he meant by that, Kelsey?" A note in Allie's voice indicated that she already knew but hoped she was wrong.

Kelsey shook her head and didn't answer. Later, these young women would learn how depraved men got enjoyment out of inflicting cruelty and pain on others. Eventually, they would learn about the evil they had narrowly escaped. Now was not the time to burden them or confirm their fears.

Kelsey cursed under her breath. There wasn't a shortage of assholes in the world. She had seen similar practices in Afghanistan. Young girls were captured, sold to the highest bidder, and forced to marry elderly men—or, even worse, used up and then thrown out on the trash heap to survive on their own. Even here in the United States, there were assholes. Kelsey silently vowed that Coeburn would pay dearly for what he had done to all the girls in that camp. But for now, she tamped down her anger. She needed to focus on getting Allie and Maddie home. She began formulating plans for when and how she would do that.

The girls had fallen silent. Maddie curled into a ball on the cave floor. Her eyes were closed, and she was clearly exhausted. Allie stared at the curtain of water in front of her. Her eyes held a far-off look. Kelsey knew from personal experience that they would need therapy when this was over. They seemed to be alright physically, but mentally and emotionally... well, that was another matter.

"Look! Kelsey!" Allie pointed through the curtain of water. "There, up on the hill."

Kelsey got to her feet, walked closer to the falling water, and looked toward where Allie pointed. Three men with rifles were surveying the waterfall and the surrounding countryside. As Kelsey watched, one man sat down on the ground and leaned against his rifle. The others soon joined him. Kelsey drew in a sharp breath. *Crap! Are they going to set up camp here and pass an idyllic afternoon dozing in the sun?*

Coeburn's followers seemed to be the bottom of the barrel, so he ought to expect this kind of service from them. Kelsey felt certain that they had come this way to look for her, Allie, and Maddie. Apparently, they were not inclined to expend much energy doing so. Their incompetence would be to her and the girls' advantage. Now, if only they would leave the meadow.

From her daily observation of the guards, Kelsey had little confidence in the abilities of Coeburn's men, so it was unlikely that they would track them to their hiding place. She had been careful not to leave any tracks as they entered the meadow, and the men didn't appear to know the cave even existed. But as long as they sat there, she, Allie, and Maddie were trapped.

If the men didn't leave, it would mean a cold, damp night in the cave. Even if the men did eventually leave, if they lingered too long, it would complicate the trip down the mountain. Traveling through the darkness would be risky for two novice hikers like Allie and Maddie. They would also soon need food. Kelsey had one more protein bar that they could share later, but that wouldn't be enough if they were trapped overnight.

Kelsey refused to accept that she was stymied with no solution. Someway, somehow, they would get off the mountain. She just had to figure out how. If it came down to it, she would be a decoy. She wouldn't accept that it was impossible. Suddenly, Jason's motto, "Whatever it takes," took on new meaning.

At least we have plenty of water, she thought ironically as she stared through the curtain of water.

"That's Carl, Martin, and Spike," Allie said as she came to stand beside Kelsey. "They were mean to all of us. Please, Kelsey, don't let them find us!"

Kelsey quieted her and moved all three of them away from the edge of the waterfall and into the darkness of the cave. "Stay back," she said. "I don't think they know about the cave, but movement might draw their attention this way."

After a while, the men stood up, surveyed the waterfall, and walked to the edge of the pool. Kelsey hoped it was a sign that they were getting ready to leave. Her hope turned to disappointment when they started walking down the embankment toward the waterfall. They were now only yards away from the ledge leading into the cave. Kelsey tensed up and held her breath. She motioned for Allie and Maddie to be quiet. Maybe she was wrong, and they did know about the cave.

But the men didn't come any closer to the ledge. They placed their rifles on the ground and began taking off their clothes. The naked skin of their buttocks was stark white against their deeply tanned backs. They posed on the bank before diving into the rippling pool below the waterfall.

Probably the first bath they've had in months, Kelsey thought. She glanced over at Allie and Maddie. If they were embarrassed by the display of the men's naked bodies, they didn't let it show on their faces.

Kelsey placed her finger against her lips and pointed for the girls to move even farther into the cave. Kelsey moved to the side of the cave opening and stood in the shadows. From there, she could observe the men while remaining hidden behind the curtain of water.

As Kelsey watched and waited, she revised her list of options now that the men were occupied in the water. She could rush out to the embankment, grab their guns, and hold them at gunpoint. *And do what with them?* she wondered. There was no way she could force them down the mountain and clear the trail at the same time. Plus, the men might overpower her. What would happen to Allie and Maddie then?

She could just shoot them as they played in the waterfall's pool. It would be easy, like shooting fish in a barrel. But as much as these men might deserve such a fate, it would likely be too traumatic for the girls. Kelsey had no appetite for bloodshed, and she'd rather see these men tried and convicted by a court. They deserved to spend the rest of their lives in prison, locked up just as they had locked up the young women in the compound.

No, the best option was just to wait them out.

The men splashed and swam in the water for what felt like hours, though Kelsey knew it was no more than thirty or forty minutes. They eventually grew tired, left the pool, and picked up their clothes and rifles. They climbed back up to the meadow where they casually sprawled out on the grass, letting the sun dry their bodies. A couple of the men lit cigarettes and leaned back on their elbows to relax in the sunshine.

Kelsey started to reach for her phone to check the time, then remembered where it was: at home on her dresser in her bedroom. She normally carried it whenever she went for a run, but today, Ron had asked her a question and distracted her as she readied her waist pack for her run.

The words of one of her Officer Candidate School instructors suddenly came back to her: "Actions without foresight lead to unnecessary risks." Captain Daniels's words correctly fit her current situation. She had not adequately prepared for her impulsive trip up the mountain. But under the circumstances, she'd do it again. Her arrival had saved Allie and Maddie from sexual assault and a life haunted by it.

There was nothing Kelsey could do now about the phone. She wouldn't waste any effort lamenting the fact that she had left it at home. Instead, she began a mental calculation of the time. She estimated that she had arrived at the compound shortly after eight a.m. It had taken her about thirty minutes, more or less, to fight off Clint and Daryl and rescue Maddie and Allie. Then there was their stopping to remove the tracking bracelets, their walk to the waterfall, and the time they had spent hidden in the cave. Kelsey guessed that it was now approximately half past noon. The sun's position overhead confirmed that she was close, if not completely accurate, in her estimation.

By now, Ron and Jason were probably looking for her. Love

Vine Mountain was the most likely place they would start. She'd like to get moving and meet up with them before they came up the mountain and accidently stumbled into one of Coeburn's search parties. Of course, given that Jason and Ron were professionals and that Coeburn's followers apparently were not, that scenario seemed unlikely. Jason and Ron would be aware of anyone close to their vicinity. Still, she needed to get the girls to safety and back to their families.

Another half hour went by before the men stood up, got dressed, picked up their rifles, and strolled back the way they had come: east, and presumably toward the compound. *Goodbye and good riddance*, Kelsey thought. *But I'll see you again soon. Count on it.*

Kelsey felt the tension leave her shoulders. Now she had a new problem, though: how long should they wait to leave the safety of the cave? Before taking the girls from their hiding place, she needed to make sure that the men had completely left the area and were not hiding in the woods nearby.

CHAPTER FOURTEEN

I'm going up to the meadow for a quick look. I need to make sure those men have left and aren't still lurking around," Kelsey told the girls. It had been about thirty or forty minutes since the men had left the meadow. She hadn't seen any activity from where she stood in the cave, but she'd be able to get a better look if she went higher.

"Don't leave us," Maddie begged.

"I won't leave you, sweetheart." Kelsey reached down and brushed a stray hair off Maddie's face. Her forehead felt warm, but that could have been from the excitement and exertion of the last few hours.

"Be careful," Allie said. "They're cruel, evil men." She sat back down on the ground beside Maddie. "Maddie, we're going home. Can you believe it? You're strong, and I know you can do this." Allie took Maddie's hand and held it between hers.

"I know." Maddie sat up and hugged Allie. "I'll be fine. I'm ready. I was just resting. I want Kelsey to be careful."

"I will," Kelsey assured her. "It's not me they're looking for." Well, that wasn't exactly true, since she had coldcocked one of their men, bludgeoned another—possibly breaking his nose—and helped their prisoners escape. "I'll be back soon." She stepped toward the curtain of water. "And don't open the door to any strangers while I'm gone." Her comment elicited a smile from both girls.

Kelsey eased out onto the ledge and inched her way toward the bank. She scanned the hill above her. Nothing moved, so she slowly climbed up the embankment toward the meadow. When she reached the top of the hill, she dashed from the exposed meadow into the tree line. She paused in the shadow of a group of pine trees and checked all directions. Nothing moved, and she didn't see any signs that a person or animal lurked nearby. She did see where the two-legged animals had wallowed around in the grass and wildflowers. The impressions of their naked butts showed in a patch of trampled grass and flowers. Bird calls were the only sounds in the air.

Kelsey decided it was time to leave. Darkness came early up here in the thick forest, and she didn't think it was wise to wait any longer. She didn't think Maddie was sick, but if there was even the slightest chance that she was, they needed to reach town sooner rather than later. They would have to stay off the normal trails used by people like the Coeburn group. Allie and Maddie were novices at negotiating the tangled underbrush, so forging a new trail would slow them down. Kelsey longingly thought of her gear bag sitting near her phone back at the house. Her revolver, as well as her phone, would have come in handy. Instead, they would just have to make it down the mountain using their wits and without any firepower for protection. Kelsey returned to the cave. Both girls looked up expectantly as she entered. "We need to leave now. The men appear to be gone, and we don't want to wait around and have them come back." She used her knife to sketch out a simple map on the floor of the cave to show the girls the general direction they would travel down the mountain.

Allie and Maddie eased across the ledge of the waterfall, this time without Kelsey's help. They were braver now. Maybe the realization that they were going home gave them extra courage.

Kelsey led them up to the meadow and once again pulled them into the shadow of the tree line. They would start their descent further west of the hunting trail Jason had shown her and Ron. Was that really only three-and-a-half weeks ago? In many ways, it felt like a lifetime ago.

This route would be a little longer, but they were less likely to run into a search party from the Coeburn compound. Kelsey cautioned the girls to move as silently as they could. They were not dressed for hiking in the mountains. Their long dresses caught on the briars and bushes, which only added to the long tears in the fabric from their flight from the compound.

Kelsey found a thick tangle of wild blackberry vines, kudzu, and love vine a little west of the waterfall. She pulled back the vines and brush and cleared a path into the forest. Then, she led the young women through the opening she had created. "It'll get better once we're deeper inside the forest," Kelsey whispered as she helped the girls disentangle their dresses from the blackberry thorns.

She kept an eye on Maddie and felt her forehead whenever they paused to rest. So far, it remained cool. Their rest stop in the cave had been exactly what both girls needed to regain their strength.

Kelsey had filled her water bottle before leaving the falls and frequently gave the girls sips of water, rarely taking any for herself. Kelsey had gone for long periods without water during army training exercises. She'd be alright with just an occasional sip so long as she had estimated how long it would take to get down the mountain correctly and everything went smoothly.

The sun sank lower behind the mountains. Although it was only about three p.m., it was becoming darker under the trees. Allie and Maddie determinedly pushed aside vines and brush, keeping up with Kelsey as they worked their way through the thick underbrush. Scratches and bruises covered their arms, and their hands were dirty and sticky with sap from the bushes. Their dresses hung in tatters in places. Kelsey had a long tear in the sleeve of her shirt—it was one of the new ones she had purchased on the trip to Charlotte. A long scratch on her face from a tree branch rose in a red welt next to the bruise left by Daryl's fist.

They had been on the trail for a little over an hour when Kelsey's ear caught a distinctive sound. She held up her hands for the girls to stop and remain quiet. Kelsey heard it again: the cooing call of a mourning dove. But there was something different about it. The lilt at the end of the sound was not what one usually heard from the mourning dove's call.

The cooing call came again from the east. Kelsey turned her head in that direction. She placed her hands to her mouth and sent out an answering call. Maddie started to speak—there was a question in her eyes—but Kelsey held up a hand to quiet her. More cooing came back from the same direction. Kelsey had heard this particular sound before.

It was Jason. Kelsey was sure of it. That lilting sound was an inflection that she had only heard from him in Afghanistan. The girls needed a rest anyway, and if it was Jason coming to find them, the best thing to do was stay where they were.

Kelsey pulled Allie and Maddie farther into the shadows of the trees and found a large rock to sit on while they rested and waited. She didn't tell them that she thought rescue was on the way. They would be crushed if she was wrong, and she didn't want to have their hopes dashed while still facing the prospect of another mile of hiking down the mountain.

Kelsey sent out another dove call. An answer came back quickly. The sound was getting closer. Over the course of the next fifteen minutes, she sent out the signal a few more times. Each time, an answering call came back. She was increasingly confident that it was Jason. She silently prayed that it was him. As Allie and Maddie watched her strange behavior, excitement built in their eyes. They realized that a possible rescuer was close.

"Girls," she finally whispered. "I think we're about to be rescued, but if it turns out to be Coeburn's people coming this way, you start running down the mountain as fast as you can. Going straight down from here will take you into Mason Valley Park."

"But what about you Kelsey?" Maddie asked. "We can't leave you."

"Don't worry, sweetheart. I'll be right behind you," Kelsey replied with a laugh.

At that moment, she heard a thrashing sound in the underbrush above them. Jason and Ron, followed by one of Jason's deputies and a man wearing an FBI jacket, broke through the thicket a few yards up the hill from where they sat.

"Hello there! What took you so long?" a giddy Kelsey asked as the group came nearer. She stood up and faced the rescuers.

"Kelsey!" Jason yelled as he slid down the trail toward her, dirt and rock streaming down with him. He pulled her into a fierce hug, and Kelsey hugged him back. She remained cool, though she wanted to kiss him fiercely and never let go.

Jason pulled back and scanned her face. His mouth tightened as his eyes fell on the bruise on her check and the vivid red scratch.

"Saved by the "owl call"! Where's the joke now?" Kelsey laughed. She couldn't hide her excitement and relief at seeing Jason and the other rescuers.

"I was wrong," Jason replied with an answering smile. He squeezed her arm, reluctantly released her, and stepped away. Kelsey nodded. Jason was there in his official capacity as sheriff, and everyone around them except Ron thought she was Ron's wife. Jason, as always, was conscious of ethical boundaries.

Ron smiled happily and stepped to Kelsey's side. He gave her a tight, brotherly squeeze. "Can't you stay out of trouble, my darling? You're going to be the death of me yet."

Jason began questioning her about what had happened at the camp while the deputy and FBI agent attended to Maddie and Allie. Kelsey briefly explained the day's events but left out the details of the assault on Allie and Maddie. She didn't want to embarrass them in front of strangers. Kelsey finished with, "Coeburn needs to be arrested. He's running a human trafficking ring."

"Not anymore," Jason replied. "I got a call from the sheriff in Arkansas this morning, and he filled me in on what he suspected had been going on there. I called in Agent Baker for help. The reason we didn't find you sooner is that we went up with the FBI to close his camp. Coeburn's been arrested, along with the rest of his men." Jason's eyes sparked with anger as he finished speaking. He ran his hand over the back of his neck and rolled his shoulders, releasing tension that had likely been there all day. "I thought we'd find you at the camp. I don't know whether I was relived or worried when you weren't among the people in the camp."

"We escaped and hid at the waterfall. Three men came after us, but they apparently didn't know about the cave," Kelsey explained.

"Coeburn and his men gave up without a fight when they realized they were surrounded," Ron said. He laughed and added, "I wish you could have been there, Kels. This one guy kept yelling over and over, 'Some bitch broke my freaking nose!'" Ron picked up Kelsey's hand and examined her skinned knuckles. "I wonder who that could have been? Hmmm? You fight like a girl, Mrs. Moore. Well done." Ron kissed her injured knuckles.

Jason, Ron, the FBI agent, and the deputy cleared a path for the remainder of the way down the mountain. Kelsey, Allie, and Maddie were exhausted, and they were happy to just follow along. It didn't take the four men long to clear the rest of the way down, and the group soon exited the woods near the park.

Allie's and Maddie's parents were waiting for them. Deputy

Ferguson, at Jason's instruction, had called their parents to let them know that their daughters had been found safe and were coming home. The news had spread through town quickly, and there were quite a few people waiting for them on the jogging tack. A cheer went up as the girls and their rescuers stepped out of the woods. The girls ran to their parents, who embraced them with tears of relief. The town's Ladies Auxiliary had brought water and coffee for the rescued and the rescuers.

"I love small-town people," Kelsey remarked to Ron as they accepted bottles of water. "They care about you whether they know you or not." None of the citizens present seemed to question why Kelsey and Ron were part of the effort to shut down Coeburn and rescue Allie and Maddie. The couple had become such a part of the landscape that the townspeople simply accepted their presence without question.

Jason intercepted the media and kept them away from Allie and Maddie with a promise to hold a press conference later once he had all the details. Kelsey agreed with this decision. This was not the time for the two girls to be pummeled with questions, many of which they might not be able to answer. Allie and Maddie needed some time to recover, decompress, and rest from their experience.

Kelsey spoke briefly with the female FBI agent as she loaded the girls and their parents into a van to take them to the local hospital for a medical exam. It wouldn't be long before the agents began grilling the girls about their capture and days at the camp. "The girls are in a delicate and fragile state," Kelsey said to the agent. "Go easy on them."

"I got this," the agent assured Kelsey. "I've interviewed many captives upon release. I always let them set the pace and decide what they want to share. We do need to get to the facts eventually, though, and put these perverts behind bars for good. What you did today was a good thing." The agent touched Kelsey's arm, then climbed into the van behind the girls.

Yes, she thought. *It's a pretty good feeling when things work out well.* Maybe, just maybe, having saved these girls from abuse and torture would remove some of the bad taste left by the deaths in Afghanistan.

Kelsey and Ron climbed into Jason's patrol car to ride to the sheriff's office. Jason needed to take Kelsey's statement regarding her involvement in the rescue. Before he started the car, he pulled some medicated swabs from a first aid kit in the glove compartment. He reached over, placed his fingers beneath Kelsey's chin, turned her to face him, and gently dabbed her injuries. The gentleness of his touch contrasted with the anger in his eyes as he treated the bruise on her cheek.

"I'm alright," Kelsey assured him. She reached up and touched his hand, stopping his motion. "I gave as much as I got."

"More," Jason replied with a short laugh. "I think Daryl will be drinking his meals through a straw for some time." He closed the first aid kit, put it back in the glove compartment, and started the car.

As they drove to the sheriff's office, Jason and Ron filled Kelsey in on the arrest at the Coeburn compound that morning. The FBI agents had quietly taken out the perimeter guards and surrounded Coeburn and his men before they even knew anyone was near the compound. Coeburn had been enjoying his morning coffee and holding court with his men at the table under the trees when the agents swarmed over them. They were under arrest and handcuffed before they knew what hit them.

"They're all brave men when faced with defenseless women," Ron remarked, "but with armed agents? Not so much."

When they arrived at the sheriff's office, Jason gave Kelsey a pad of paper to write out her statement. Once she had detailed her part in the morning's rescue of Allie and Maddie, she signed the document and handed it to Jason.

He read Kelsey's description of the assault and their flight through the woods. He rose from the table and began pacing around the room. Ron excused himself with vague comments about needing to call Vickie and the office back in Atlanta.

"I shouldn't have let this go on so long," Jason castigated himself. "I should have gone in there and cleaned out that viper's nest as soon as Coeburn set up shop. I knew he was up to no good." He slammed his fist into his hand. "I shouldn't have let legalities stop me. It was clear from the start that Coeburn was nothing but trouble."

"That's not how you do your job—by doing something illegal," Kelsey said gently. "And we've got hard evidence now. According to Allie and Maddie, there were another ten girls being held against their will on the compound."

"We found them all, and if there's any justice, Coeburn and his cohorts will be behind bars for a long, long time," Jason said. "And, I might add, anyone who did business with him." He didn't look comforted by his own prediction.

"Jason," Kelsey said, "you're blaming yourself for not acting sooner, but if you had run Coeburn off Love Vine Mountain, he would have just moved on and set up shop someplace else." She rose from the table, went to his side, and placed her hand on his arm. He covered her hand with his own. "You now have the evidence—lots of it—that will put him out of business for good."

"I know you're right," he sighed, "but it still makes me ill to think that such a sick man was operating in my own backyard. He hurt those girls, and his sons hurt you."

"Let it go. Stop beating yourself up," Kelsey repeated. "And never mind about me. I'm not hurt." She raised her hand and rubbed her thumb across the scar on Jason's chin. It was white against the stubble of his day-old beard.

Kelsey had wanted to touch that scar ever since she noticed it when she saw him for the first time in this very office. That moment now seemed like a lifetime ago. She wanted to ask whether the scar was from an injury in the Afghan ambush but felt it would have been out of place tonight. Maybe later. Jason's eyes darkened as he looked down at her.

"You did good today, Wildman." Kelsey reluctantly pulled away from Jason and returned to her chair; she needed to sit down. She felt a little lightheaded as the adrenaline of the day began to wear off. She had come close to being one of Coeburn's captives today. "And truthfully?" she added with a grin. "I enjoyed punching Clint and Daryl."

Ron came back into the office as Kelsey finished speaking. "My little wifey is bloodthirsty," he joked.

"No," Kelsey said, turning toward Ron, "but if ever anyone needed a beating, they did. I just want Jason to stop blaming himself for the evil of others. Without him, that camp would still be up there."

"What we did today was good. Nothing more needs to be said. In the end, you handled it in the best possible way," Ron said. He stepped behind Kelsey, placed his hands on her shoulders, and began massaging the tension that ran across her back. "And Slugger here will be immortalized by a new legend about Love Vine Mountain: 'Killer Kelsey takes on the mountain and wins!'"

Kelsey ignored Ron's comment. The massage on her tired shoulders felt so good that she couldn't even think of a comeback. Instead, she focused on buoying up Jason's spirits. "Face it, Sheriff: you're a hero!" Before he could refute her statement, she asked, "So, is the FBI sure they captured all of Coeburn's men? There were three over near the waterfall."

"They're pretty sure," Jason said. "Coeburn kept a list of his employees—and I use the term 'employees' loosely—so they should be able to verify the arrests against his records."

"Three men wandered back into camp from the direction of the waterfall while we were still there," Ron said. "They were immediately arrested. They weren't even aware that a raid was going on!"

"And two more were caught running down the logging road. Cockroaches always run when they're disturbed." Jason smiled at the men's ineptitude. "The moral of this story is that it doesn't take brains to be a criminal."

"You took down a human trafficking ring today, Sheriff," Kelsey said. "No second-guessing or lamenting what might have been. Accept your kudos. It's been a rewarding day."

Soon after, Jason dropped Kelsey and Ron off at their house. He declined her invitation to join them for dinner, citing a large stack of paperwork. Before he left, he instructed them to call if they needed anything.

What Kelsey needed at the moment was a hot shower, some food, a glass of wine, and to sit down and talk with Jason for the rest of the evening, but she knew that his duty to the people he served came first. Any woman who loved him would have to accept that

Love? Getting ahead of yourself, aren't you, Barrett? The mental word choice must have been due to having survived a horrifying day. But she quietly admitted to herself, she would like to explore the look she saw in Jason's eyes today.

Ron and Kelsey sat down in the living room with a bottle of wine. A neighbor, having heard of the raid and their part in Allie and Maddie's rescue, brought them a casserole for dinner. Kelsey thanked the neighbor profusely. She didn't think she could move from the sofa to cook anything herself. Showering away the mountain grime had zapped what energy she had left.

The fresh, clean clothes, the lasagna, and the glass of red wine should have relaxed Kelsey, but the scenes of the day continued to replay themselves in her mind: the red-hot fury that had consumed her when she witnessed the assault on Allie and Maddie; the escape through the wilderness; hiding in the cave as the men appeared on the hillside meadow; the hurried trip down the mountain while always on alert for the sound or sight of the Coeburn men. Kelsey felt lucky to have escaped. Any one of those things could have gone horribly wrong.

Kelsey had been on point, focused and zeroed in on handling each incident as it arose and not living beyond the moment. She had fallen back on her military training without consciously thinking about it. Now that she, Allie, and Maddie were safe, the realization of the danger they had been in finally hit her. She began to shake, and her wine splashed over the edge of her glass.

"Hey, it's alright," Ron said as he sat down beside her and put his arm around her. "You did a great job today, kiddo."

"It's just delayed reaction. Don't worry. I'm good." Kelsey leaned forward and shakily placed her wine glass on the table. "I was just thinking about what could've happened if I hadn't gone up to the compound this morning. Isn't it strange how we sometimes know things without knowing we know?"

"I know," Ron said with a laugh. He squeezed her shoulders. "You probably saved their lives, Kels. I'm proud of you. As for knowing things when we don't know we know, I will never question a woman's intuition again." He paused, then turned to look at her with a question in his eyes. He asked softly, "But now we'll be going home in a few days—as soon as Jason and the FBI are done with us. Are you ready for that?"

"Yes. I'm ready to get back to sleeping in my own bed and to my regular, if boring, job."

"Your bed and your job aren't what I'm referring to," Ron said.

"Oh! You mean Jason?" Kelsey didn't even try to pretend that she didn't know what Ron was talking about. He had been her best friend for many years, and if anyone knew her well, it was him. "These things have a way of working out. A long-distance relationship is difficult, but if Jason and I are to become more than friends, we'll make it work. Love happens in its own time."

"More intuition?" Ron asked. His smile turned playful. "You and Jason? Really? I had no idea there was anything between you two! What will Richard say?" Ron laughed as Kelsey slapped him on the arm.

Only then did Kelsey remember her sore arm and skinned knuckles.

CHAPTER FIFTEEN

The morning following the raid on the Coeburn compound, Kelsey met with the investigators assigned to the Violent Crimes against Children and Human Trafficking task force. The task force was a partnership between various local, state, and federal law enforcement agencies to fight crimes against children and human trafficking. The agents from Charlotte, who had made the arrests yesterday, had set up a temporary headquarters in Mason Valley's city hall.

Coeburn had committed a long list of crimes that fell under many jurisdictions—kidnapping, human trafficking, and prostitution being the most obvious. Several divisions of the FBI were anxious to get a piece of him. Agent Baker was the lead agent on the case, and he revealed that FBI investigators were busy piecing together the details of all his crimes. As part of that effort, Agent Baker requested an interview with Kelsey.

Kelsey gave Agent Baker a detailed account of what she had witnessed when she arrived at the camp. She described her confrontation with Clint and Daryl and the subsequent flight through the woods.

When Kelsey finished telling her story, Agent Baker nodded and said, "Some of our most important evidence is coming from the cameras you and you husband were able to plant in the camp. He gave them to us yesterday, and we've already been over them. Vivid evidence of this type of crime is not always available, Mrs. Blackledge."

"Please," Kelsey interrupted Agent Baker, "my name is Kelsey Barrett. Ron and I work together, but we aren't husband and wife. That was just part of our cover story when we were setting up the surveillance."

"I see," the agent said. "Sheriff Wilder told me about the surveillance team he had hired. Forgive me. I just assumed that you were actually a married couple. Apparently, your cover worked, even with me."

Kelsey waved the misunderstanding away. "Ron and I were disappointed that the cameras didn't work as planned. We never saw or heard anything from the girls' quarters through them, so I'm curious as to what evidence you saw."

"The camera in the building didn't have much," Agent Baker said. "Coeburn had the girls convinced that he was watching everything they did inside their quarters. They were afraid to say or do anything. We don't actually believe Coeburn had a camera hidden inside their quarters, but it's possible we just haven't found it yet. Either way, his threats worked. And the perp did have a camera planted in their bathing area. He watched them as they bathed—dressed and undressed—and shared the recordings with his clients. He saved the videos on his computer, and we have those, too."

"I don't understand," Kelsey said. "If there's nothing on the camera we planted in their quarters..."

"It was the camera you planted outside. It picked up the women's conversations when they were outside the building, where they figured Coeburn wouldn't hear. We got comments from and videos of some of the guards, too."

"Oh? The camera outside?" Kelsey said in surprise. "I had forgotten about that one." She had planted it under the rock near their quarters when she needed to get out of the compound quickly. As it turned out, it was the perfect place since the girls felt safe enough to talk outside the building. Sometimes, the best breaks in a case came by accident.

"The sound and pictures from outside are of poor quality," Agent Baker said. "Coeburn apparently installed a jammer on the property. That's what distorted the data. He didn't trust anyone, not even the clients he invited in. We haven't found the jammer yet, but two of our agents are up on the mountain this morning looking for it. The property is twenty acres in size, but we can narrow down the location." Agent Baker paused. "And we will find it. I can promise you that."

"But I don't understand. If there's a jammer, how do you have any recordings at all?"

"Our digital forensic specialists worked their magic. They were able to enhance the recordings, and we got enough off the videos and recordings to support our case against Coeburn." The agent paused, then leaned back in his chair and laughed. "Miss Barrett, that was quite a "whoopin'" you gave those two guys yesterday. I think we need you on our team."

"Yes, well…" Kelsey couldn't keep from returning Agent Baker's smile. "As I said, it was purely by accident that I was there at the right time."

"It's good you were," Agent Baker said. "You saved those two girls. The video of the assault on Allie and Maddie is leverage we can use against Clint and Daryl to get as much information from them as we can. But they're not getting off easy. They'll face extensive time in prison, regardless of how much they tell us."

Agent Baker explained that Clint and Daryl Coeburn, young and frightened by the prospect of life sentences, were becoming increasingly eager to share most, if not all, of they knew. The FBI still needed to verify what they and other members of the Coeburn group had told them in their initial interviews, but it only helped strengthen the FBI's case.

Agent Baker also let Kelsey know that she and Ron were the major reason why they had such a great trove of information. "You should know that the two of you helped disband a major operation," he said.

"In that case, would you mind telling me at least some of what you've learned?" Kelsey asked, curious about the bigger picture of the case they had been hired to help with.

"Of course," Agent Baker said, launching into his story. "Coeburn is an evil man. He's part-cult leader, part-militia leader. He also believes he's a sovereign citizen, bound only by his own laws, not those of the United States." Agent Baker leaned back in his chair, grimaced, and said, "He had a cache of weapons and was willing to use them against the US government—or anyone else that threatened his kingdom. Unfortunately for Coeburn, many of his men were not as passionate about his cause as he was."

"Ron and I thought they were pretty reckless and inept," Kelsey said, nodding. "What makes someone join a man like Coeburn if they don't share his ideology?"

"We frequently see this," Agent Baker explained. "They hook up with him because he feeds their voyeurism through the cruelty and pain he inflicts on others—most notably defenseless young women. His followers fit the pattern: weak, shiftless men who admire someone they perceive as possessing the strength they don't have themselves."

"A father figure," Kelsey suggested.

"Something like that," Agent Baker said. "But they weren't ready to die for someone else's beliefs. Yesterday, they gave up quickly when we surrounded the camp. Coeburn's ideology wasn't in their minds when they faced armed agents of the US government."

"Thankfully, they didn't try to defend Coeburn and cause bloodshed." Kelsey gazed out the window behind Agent Baker's head. She could see Love Vine Mountain in the distance. The brush, vines, and trees would overtake Coeburn's compound in a few months. Any signs of the horrors that had gone on there would be wiped clean. It would be a fitting ending to the campsite.

"Coeburn's followers were cowards, but they had as few scruples as Coeburn," Agent Baker said. "They were willing to inflict mental and physical abuse whenever and against whomever Coeburn directed them to."

"What about the women?" Kelsey asked. "Why would they join in?"

"Some of the women were married to Coeburn's men. Coeburn demanded they follow his rules, and he used his own interpretation of the Bible to brainwash them. If they questioned his authority, they were intimidated, punished, and coerced through beatings. Some had no other place to go."

Kelsey's training and experience as a community engagement officer in Afghanistan had exposed her to similar situations. Local leaders, sometimes similar to cult leaders like Coeburn, used religion to set rules for life in the villages or camps. Women were chattel—something to be owned—and were forced to obey the males in the camp. Coeburn set the rules for his clan and demanded their complete loyalty.

"The young women there were nothing more than source of income to him." Agent Baker shifted in his chair and clasped his hands on his desk. The knuckles on his fingers were tense and white as he gazed at Kelsey. He was a seasoned agent, but Kelsey could tell he was angered by this story. He shook his head sadly and added, "But in a way, that's what saved them from rape—and worse. Coeburn needed them 'pure,' as was demanded by his clients. That status brought the highest price."

According to the story Clint and Daryl had told the agents, the Coeburn group left Arkansas with six girls they had obtained through a variety of measures. They picked up another five on their way to North Carolina. Some were runaways, a couple were immigrants, and all were scared, vulnerable, and down on their luck. Most wouldn't be missed by anyone. They were promised jobs and money and had no idea of the future Coeburn planned for them.

"Clint and Daryl were the recruiters and kidnappers," Agent Baker continued. "Coeburn sent them into the towns they passed through with instructions to bring back young women by any means necessary. Coeburn's 'inventory' had been depleted by the scrutiny of the sheriff in Arkansas, so he needed more. However, he kept his inventory low, with only a dozen or so young women in captivity at a time. He felt this would prevent the notice of the local authorities.

"But Daryl and Clint messed up when they set their sights on Allie and Maddie." Agent Baker slapped his palm on the table and leaned forward with fire in his eyes. "They let their lust lure them into kidnapping two girls from loving families, in a town with a dogged sheriff that didn't give up on trying to rescue them. I have a twelve-year-old daughter, Miss Barrett, and stories like this just make me sick to my stomach."

"I know," Kelsey agreed. Her hands were clenched in her lap. "I wish I could do more. We need to exorcise this cancer from our society."

"Taking down Coeburn and convicting him is a start. We here at the task force are grateful to Sheriff Wilder—and to you and your partner—for doing this the right way. The evidence you gathered will make the prosecutors' cases airtight."

Agent Baker had still more to say about Coeburn. "One young woman was traded for the parcel of land on Love Vine Mountain, home of his current operation. He also paid a small sum to make the sale appear legal on the deed records. But by recording the deed, that didn't mean Coeburn was suddenly complying with county law. It was only meant to help him avoid a repeat of what had happened in Arkansas: scrutiny and eviction."

"Judging by the amount of information you have on Coeburn, he clearly didn't hide his trail as well as he thought," Kelsey said with a rueful laugh.

"As usual, once you find a thread and start pulling, the whole story unravels quickly," Agent Baker replied. "The man who sold Coeburn the property was an absentee owner and lived in Tennessee. He's now in custody. The young woman, a runaway, has been reunited with her parents. Hopefully, this experience will make her rethink running away again."

"And did Coeburn actually promise Clint and Daryl their pick of the girls, as they said?" Kelsey asked. "And they chose Allie and Maddie?"

"Yes, but Coeburn kept dangling the prize in front of them to keep them in line," Agent Baker said. "Coeburn's greed and the joy he received from teasing his sons with empty promises saved Allie and Maddie from a forced marriage to Clint and Daryl."

"Pure scum," Kelsey spat. She was more and more thankful for her spur-of-the-moment decision to visit the compound yesterday morning. But there was another thing she was curious about: "But how did Coeburn fund his operation?"

"Coeburn has been at this game for a long time," Agent Baker said. "He has an illegal gun-smuggling operation, in addition to his human-trafficking ring. He sold guns. He sold some young women and pimped out others to wealthy men around the country. Some women were sold, not for sex, but into slavery. He was basically a slave trader."

Kelsey shivered at the description. "I can't believe his own wife helped him with his operation." She paused, then asked, "I presume you're searching for other victims throughout the US?"

Agent Baker nodded. "I promise you, Miss Barrett, we will find his accomplices, and they will join Coeburn in prison. We won't stop until we put him—and all involved—away for good."

Kelsey brought up her own observations from the weeks they had surveilled the compound. "Did you identify the four men who visited the camp? The ones Jason gave you the pictures of?"

"Yes, we've identified them," Agent Baker assured her, "and our agents either have them in custody or will soon."

It was late morning by the time Kelsey left the FBI's field office. She was drained just from listening to all the details of Coeburn's operation. She felt cold to her bones, even though she stepped out into a warm, sunny day. All she wanted to do was go home and take a shower, but she doubted that any amount of water could wash away the vileness she had just heard from Agent Baker.

Kelsey had just started down the city hall's concrete steps when she heard someone call her name. She stopped, turned, and waited for Stephanie Landry to catch up with her.

"Kelsey!" Stephanie called out. "Do y'all have time to stop at Rita's for lunch?"

For a moment, Kelsey couldn't answer; she was too distracted by Stephanie's exaggerated Southern drawl. But Stephanie's fresh face was so beautiful that Kelsey's mood lightened. There was still beauty and sweetness in the world—even if it was wrapped up in a sugary Southern drawl.

How much of that accent is real, and how much is an act? Kelsey wondered. Most young people had homogenized their language in the twenty-first century, and only the much older generations still spoke with the drawn-out sounds of a Southern plantation owner. Even Kelsey's grandparents didn't have much of an accent. Perhaps sounding like a fragile Southern belle helped Stephanie in her career—and her love life. Kelsey was immediately ashamed of her thoughts. *That's not very kind, Barrett,*" she scolded herself. *"You wouldn't be jealous of her, would you?"*

Kelsey's stomach rumbled. "Sure. Lunch sounds good," she replied after returning Stephanie's hug. Maybe Stephanie's constant chatter would take her mind off her morning's visit with Agent Baker, and the visions of evil that still lingered in her mind.

As they walked down the sidewalk toward Rita's Café. Stephanie kept up a steady conversation along the way. "I just left Daddy's office. I'm taking a break from modeling later this summer—after my current contracts are done. I wanted to tell him that I will be coming home for an extended stay this fall. I'm tired of traveling."

Kelsey looked at the girl beside her. There were tired lines across her beautiful face. A glamourous life must not be as easy as it looked.

"I'd like to settle down in one place," Stephanie added wistfully. "I'm tired of never spending more than a few days in one place."

"I'm sure your parents will be glad to have you home," Kelsey said. What would a world traveler like Stephanie do in placid Mason Valley?

Kelsey and Stephanie entered the café, were seated, and were awaiting their lunch orders before Jason's name came up. "Daddy wants Jason to run for sheriff this fall," Stephanie said. "He said he'll put his machine behind Jason. He's sure he'll be elected." She paused to sip her tea. "Shoot, after what y'all did this week, Jason wouldn't have a problem even without Daddy's machine."

Kelsey didn't comment. Jason had not mentioned any of this to her—but why should he? Friends didn't always tell each other everything that was going on in their lives. Plus, Jason had been quite busy these last few days.

Their food was delivered, and Stephanie took a bite before she asked, "Has Jason told you whether he's going to run for sheriff?"

"To be honest, this is the first I've heard of the offer," Kelsey said. She did remember the animated conversation she had witnessed between the mayor and Jason at the mayor's Spring Fling.

Maybe that was when Mayor Landry had made the offer.

As they ate, Stephanie got around to the real reason for the invitation to lunch: "Are you and Jason seeing each other—dating, I mean?" Her green eyes tried to look indifferent, but Kelsey saw suspicion in their depths. "I wasn't worried at first, but it's all over town that you and Ron are just coworkers and aren't really married. I've worried, you know, that there's something more between you and Jason." Stephanie quickly cut her eyes toward Kelsey. Obviously, she hadn't meant to admit that she was worried.

"We aren't dating," Kelsey answered honestly. "I've known Jason a long time. We're good friends, but we've never been on an official date."

Stephanie visibly relaxed at Kelsey's assurance and began entertaining her with stories of her modeling jobs and all the places they had taken her.

"It's exciting," Stephanie said after a few tales of fun and hilarity. "More so at the beginning, to be honest. Now, I'm tired of traveling and being away from my family."

Kelsey heard the longing in Stephanie's voice and could relate. She recalled that last night in Afghanistan, when the yearning for a more normal life where she was surrounded by people she loved, had taken over her thoughts and momentarily blotted out everything else.

"I'm burned out," Stephanie confessed. "I'm ready for a break—to do nothing for a while." *Burned out at twenty-five?* Kelsey wondered. *It's a good thing her family is wealthy.* Kelsey mentally kicked herself again. *Where's your compassion, Barrett? The constant pressure to stay on top as a model or to look a certain way had to be difficult.* She looked at Stephanie with sympathy and respected her honesty. "What will you do instead?" she asked.

"I really don't know," Stephanie admitted. "Maybe try to get into television in Charlotte if nothing else comes up."

Like marriage? Kelsey wondered. She didn't let herself dwell on why the idea of Stephanie marrying Jason kept popping into her mind... or why it bothered her so much.

They soon finished their lunch and said goodbye on the sidewalk.

"Good luck. I know you'll be successful in whatever you try." Despite her earlier catty thoughts, Kelsey did mean it. "Come see me if you're ever in Atlanta."

"Thanks, Kelsey. That means a lot to me, coming from you," Stephanie replied as she hugged Kelsey.

As Kelsey walked toward her car, she again wondered why Jason had not mentioned the mayor's offer. Well, it wasn't really any of her business.

She paused in front of a store window to read the "Lost Cat" posters the sheriff's department had hung there. Included was the sheriff's department phone number and a small reward for any information. That was Wildman "Whatever It Takes" Wilder. No issue was too small for his attention if a constituent felt it was important. He had proven himself to the people of Mason Valley. If he chose to run for sheriff, he'd have no problem getting elected.

Kelsey had a couple of other stops to make before she and Ron left town. She drove to the neighborhood where Allie and Maddie lived. They were next-door neighbors and best friends. When Kelsey arrived, they were sitting together on the wide front steps that led into Maddie's house. Kelsey climbed the steps and sat down beside them.

"How are you feeling?" She would probe slowly, letting them set the pace and share the parts of their story that they wanted to talk about. *Don't push too hard*, her therapist had told her during her own recovery.

Allie and Maddie both looked down, embarrassed, and would not meet Kelsey's eyes. Finally, Maddie raised her head and looked off into the distance. "We... uh, I... I couldn't sleep last night." She looked over at Allie. Allie nodded in agreement. "I kept seeing the ugly faces of the men in the camp. Their shadows were outside my window. I was afraid to close my eyes."

"Me, too," Allie agreed. "I was afraid that if I went to sleep, they'd come back and use that stick on us. It shocked us with electricity..." Allie's voice trailed off.

An electric cattle prod, Kelsey assumed. Those bastards had used an electric cattle prod! Of course! That was the stick Mrs. Coeburn carried around. A trial was too good for them.

Kelsey talked with the girls for a bit, but they soon clammed up, unwilling or unable to relive any more of the details of their captivity. She left them with the advice to talk with someone, whether their parents, each other, or—if possible—a professional psychologist. The closest mental health clinic was in Asheville, and a broader spectrum of services would be found in Charlotte. It was a long drive, but it would be worth it in the end. Kelsey also gave them her business card and phone number. She invited them to call if they ever needed to talk and to stop by for a visit if they happened to be in Atlanta.

The next morning, she and Ron packed up their things, tidied the house, and prepared to leave Mason Valley. They were loading their bags into the car when Jason stopped by. He shook Ron's hand and thanked him for his assistance. Ron then turned and went back into the house to make one last sweep before they left.

Jason turned toward Kelsey. "Well, Lieutenant Barrett, it's been exciting, what you've brought to our little community over such a short period of time," he said as he stepped closer to her. He reached out, placed both hands on her shoulders, bent his head, and then paused for a second. "What the hell," he muttered, then nodded as if he had just remembered something. "No need to worry about the neighbors now."

He bent his head again and brushed a soft kiss across Kelsey's lips. He let his lips linger for a few seconds, then straightened. There was a pleased twinkle in his eyes as they tracked the blush that spread over Kelsey's face.

"I'll be in Atlanta soon—well, as soon as we wrap up the Coeburn investigation. I don't know how long that will take, but when I am in town, I'd like to stop by and see you, if that's okay." His hands were still on her shoulders, and the tingling warmth from his touch traveled down her arms. "We could have dinner together—maybe?" he asked.

"That sounds like a plan, Wildman." Kelsey's heart sped up at the thought of seeing him again—and soon. "Will you call me with the details?"

"I will. I want to speak with your dad, too, while I'm in town. I'll see you at the office, and we can decide on dinner then." With that, Jason stepped back. He held the SUV's passenger door for Kelsey as she climbed in. Ron appeared behind them, closed the door to the house, came down the steps, and climbed into the driver's side. He waved to Jason as he started the engine.

With a final wave and a "Tell your folks thanks for welcoming me into their home" from Kelsey, they backed down the driveway and began their return trip to Atlanta.

As they wound their way toward Atlanta, Kelsey thought over the roughly four weeks she had spent in Mason Valley. So much had happened over such a short time. Finding Jason alive was the highlight, of course, but she was also satisfied by having gotten out into the field and accomplished something meaningful.

The assignment had turned out to be a tough one, but she had helped bring down an evil empire. Perhaps 'empire' wasn't the correct word for Coeburn's crude operation, but 'evil' certainly was. He preyed on the weak and used human misery and cruelty to feed his black soul, as well as the souls of his followers.

As they approached Atlanta, Kelsey busied herself with an imagined conversation with her father and an "I told you so" moment in which he congratulated her and Ron on their successful completion of the operation.

They drove directly to the office. After accepting his congratulations, Kelsey cajoled her father into admitting out loud that
she had managed to do the job as well as any other agent on staff
could.

"I never doubted your ability," Colonel Barrett said. "I worried
about your safety. And, I might add, I was right about the dangers. But you handled yourself well. I'm proud of you; I'm proud
of you *both*," he corrected himself. "It took brains and courage to
save those two girls, bring them home safely, and shut down that
operation. A boss—and a father—couldn't ask for more from his
agents."

Over the next few days, Kelsey settled back into work at
Barrett Security Consultants. Having proven to herself and to her
father that she could handle difficult assignments, she was now
content to work in-house for the time being. She had saved Allie
and Maddie from a terrible ordeal, and she needed a few calm days
to decompress from that.

The successful completion of the Coeburn operation helped
wash away any lingering self-doubt. She had answered a question
that had plagued her in recent years: whether she could coura-
geously make the right decisions when it counted.

The period of Kelsey's contentment with in-house work was
short lived, however. As she relived and reflected on what she and
Ron had accomplished, she began to realize that her current job
wouldn't satisfy her for very long. She coerced a promise from her
father that he would periodically send her out on other covert
projects—if she chose to accept them.

In addition, larger plans began to take shape in her mind.
Within days of returning to work in the office, Kelsey was re-
searching and compiling facts and figures. Her time in North Carolina had shown her the need for agents that concentrated exclu-
sively on the crime of child exploitation and human trafficking.

Kelsey put together a passionate presentation and convinced

her father that her idea was a good—and much-needed—one.
He agreed to add a new division to the company, which would be
devoted to online tracking of child pornography and the predators
who used the internet to exploit young people. Colonel Barrett
put Kelsey in charge of the new division, and another agent was
promoted into the position she had held before her assignment in
North Carolina.

The problem of human trafficking had become so prevalent—
or maybe it had always been that way, just in another form—that
law enforcement now viewed it as an epidemic. The digital age
had given new tools to vile people who had no compunction about
using any and all means to entrap the young and unsuspecting.

Kelsey's plan was to contract with local, state, and federal government agencies and provide assistance in the search to identify,
track, and connect the dots between missing children and predators. She called Agent Baker to brainstorm ideas. If done properly
and legally, they could disband groups before they managed to set
up an operation similar to Coeburn's.

Kelsey developed organizational plans for the new division and
determined how many agents they would need. She wrote up job
descriptions for the positions. She planned to start interviewing
candidates to fill those positions as soon as possible.

A couple of weeks after her return to Atlanta, Kelsey had a
much-needed and long-delayed conversation with Richard about
their relationship. He asked her to go out to dinner with him.

She declined, took a deep breath, and decided that now was
the time to tell Richard the truth. "You're a nice guy," she said as
they faced each other across the desk in his office. "I'm sorry, but
I don't see us having a future together as anything other than
friends." She reached across the desk and touched his hand. She
wanted to let him down as gently as she could. To her surprise, he
took the news in stride.

"I know," he said, "but I had hoped our friendship would

develop into something more. But I'm good with friends." He squeezed her hand and then turned back to his computer. He was quickly immersed in the data on his screen.

Huh! So much for "Richard the Romantic."

"He thinks it's your loss. He loves himself most of all," Ron teased when she told him of her conversation with Richard. "Plus, I think the colonel had a little talk with him about intercepting calls from people who ask to speak with him directly. Richard knows he needs to tread lightly at the moment. He'll never jeopardize his job—not even for a romance with the boss's daughter."

Kelsey missed seeing Jason. Granted, she hadn't seen much of him when she lived in Mason Valley, but she did see him occasionally. They had spoken on the phone a few times since she and Ron had returned to Atlanta. He was very busy and still involved in the Coeburn investigation, and he updated her on its progress. She and Ron would be called to testify once the trial began, but he still didn't know the date.

Jason and the FBI agents had been back to the Coeburn compound several times to scour the area for additional evidence. That part of the investigation would be wrapping up soon, freeing Jason to spend more time on his routine sheriff duties. The FBI agents had spread the word to their counterparts across the country to look for anyone who had assisted Coeburn in his schemes.

Just as Agent Baker had predicted, they found the jammer. It was no bigger than a remote control and was hidden in the hollow of a tree between the cooking and eating area and the girls' quarters. Apparently, Coeburn feared being infiltrated by law enforcement or being blackmailed by one of his followers or clients. He jammed all cellular devices brought into camp.

Coeburn was apparently ignorant of the ever-increasing abilities of digital forensic experts to salvage distorted recordings. More likely, he simply thought he was smarter than the authorities and never expected to be arrested. The jammer's range didn't extend to the bath house, so Coeburn's sordid spy game had gone on there, uninterrupted.

Kelsey frequently dropped hints to Jason, hoping he would share his future plans, but he never took the bait. He still hadn't told her about the mayor's efforts to get him to run for sheriff. Kelsey was certain that, should he decide to run, he'd win. Naturally, the county commissioners would give him as many deputies and resources as he asked for.

The thought that Jason could build a life that didn't include her left a heaviness in Kelsey's heart. The yearning she had experienced in Afghanistan—to be surrounded by her family in Atlanta—suddenly didn't seem like enough.

Her family was not all Kelsey longed for.

CHAPTER SIXTEEN

The gray SUV hummed along the winding highway. Kelsey was driving her personal vehicle this time, but she was traveling the same road she and Ron had taken almost a month ago on their return trip to Atlanta. It was mid-June, and except for a few hangers-on, the spring blossoms along the highway to Mason Valley were gone. The trees on the mountains had sunk into the summer doldrums to await the colder months when autumn would turn their leaves into a fiery blaze of red, orange, and gold.

Kelsey noted the kudzu vines growing along the hillside beside the road as she passed. It wrapped around the tree trunks, and grew thick in places where the trees were absent. Deeper into the trees, she spotted patches of the orangey-yellow love vine.

The vines reminded Kelsey of her hikes on Love Vine Mountain. She had developed a soft spot for the invasive vines after they had given her, Allie, and Maddie shelter as they ran for their lives from the Coeburn compound.

As she drove past a larger stand of love vine, Kelsey thought back to her first trip up Love Vine Mountain and Jason's story about the legend of the love vine. She didn't believe in the vine's magical powers, but her wish that day on the mountain with Jason and Ron had come true—in a sense. She had wished for happiness, contentment, and love.

She was basically happy. Her job was expanding and fulfilling her passion to make a difference in the world. After finding Jason alive, learning the truth about the Afghan mission's failure, and paying a visit to the Jacksons, she was more content than she had been in a long time. Most of her questions had been answered, and any guilt or misgivings about her part in the failure were purged from her thoughts. And as for love? Well, she didn't have a personal relationship with anyone, but she was surrounded by a loving family and many caring friends.

Kelsey turned her thoughts back to why she was traveling to Mason Valley today. She had several appointments on her schedule. Her first stop would be at the local realtor's office, followed by a visit with John Wilder, Jason's grandfather. He and Barbara were still in Mason Valley, having decided to spend the summer in North Carolina. They would stay until cold weather returned to the mountains and drove them back to sunny Florida. Kelsey smiled as she thought back on their conversation when she had called John to ask if she could come by and speak with him.

"Hi, Mr. Wilder," she had said when he came on the phone. "This is Kelsey Barrett."

"Who?" he'd asked.

"Kelsey Barrett." She spoke louder, thinking he might have a hearing problem. "You remember? Ron and I were there a few weeks ago. I'm from Atlanta. We worked on the Coeburn situation."

"Oh, yes, Kelsey," John said. "I remember you. You're Jason's girl."

Kelsey had almost dropped the phone. A warmth settled over her at the mention of Jason's name. "Yes, I'm Jason's friend from Atlanta." She explained the reason for her call, and he invited her to come by the house whenever she got into town. He would give her the help she was looking for.

As she topped a rise and saw the city of Mason Valley laid out before her, with Love Vine Mountain rising in the distance, Kelsey had a momentary feeling of returning home. She had come to love this mountain community and its people.

Kelsey mulled over the real reason she was returning. She hadn't been able to forget her discussion with Mrs. Bridges even after she'd returned to Atlanta. Her and Ron's deceit about their presence in Mason Valley had been necessary, but she'd still felt like a fraud for disappointing the woman.

But then, another new plan had formed in her mind. She feared that it might be difficult to get her father's blessing on her newest endeavor just days after she had persuaded him to add a new division to his company. He had given in to her first idea without much argument. But now, she was asking him to support a new and very different plan.

Once she had finished the preliminary work on putting together the new division, she approached her father about her newest plan. She was prepared to put everything into selling him on her new idea. She had time for another project. For this project, she would make time.

Standing before her father's desk in his office, she explained her thoughts.

"What? Another project? My dear daughter, your mind has been busy!" her father said. "Don't you ever rest?"

"I feel terrible about leaving Allie and Maddie on their own—to get over their ordeal alone. They don't have the care and counseling they're going to need." She took a deep breath and plunged in. "I think we should set up a charitable foundation and fund a mental health clinic in Mason Valley."

"Aren't you overloading yourself?" her father asked. Kelsey had been working tirelessly since she returned from Mason Valley.

"Can't they get help in Charlotte?"

"Sure, but that's a long drive. And who helps them in the middle of the night when the nightmares come?" she asked. "They need someone nearby who can see them routinely." Kelsey paced the floor in front of her father's desk. This new plan was grounded in a deeply personal cause—one that touched her heart. She knew what she was talking about. She had firsthand experience.

Colonel Barrett's eyes scanned her face closely. Kelsey knew what he was looking for: evidence that she was covering up problems that she might still have.

"This isn't about me, Dad. I'm better now." Kelsey answered the question in his eyes. "I want to help Allie and Maddie recover, too. Mason Valley needs a clinic."

"Do you know how to set up a charitable foundation?"

"Not really, but I'm smart enough to know when I need to ask for help from people who do know," she replied. "I plan to call John Wilder and ask for his help."

Without further argument, her father gave his approval. "Just let me know what you need. Money won't be a problem," were his only instructions.

The only thing she'd had scheduled in Atlanta today was a meeting with the designer of the office space where the new digital division would be housed. She'd asked Ron for his help, and he'd agreed to fill in for her.

Now, Kelsey drove toward the realtor's office that was located just down the street from the sheriff's office. She waved to several pedestrians who recognized her as she parked in front of Roy Benson's office. Roy had called that morning to let her know that he had the papers ready for her to sign.

Mr. and Mrs. Bridges waited inside the realtor's office. Mr. Bridges was still unable to walk without a cane, but he stood up as Kelsey entered. He reached out to shake her hand. Kelsey noted signs of relief on both of their faces. The money from the sale of a portion of their property would help them get through this summer and the coming winter. It would keep them afloat until they could get back to their usual occupation: farming. Kelsey signed the papers and handed over the cashier's check that closed the deal. It was a good feeling.

Kelsey knew very little about what she was doing. Learning as one goes along may not work for everyone, but she recognized when she needed professional advice and willingly accepted it when it was offered. Roy gave her the names of two local building contractors who were waiting for her call. "They promise they can have the building done in two months," he said as Kelsey thanked him and took her leave.

Next, she walked toward the sheriff's office, hoping Jason was in. The pieces of her plan had fallen together at the last minute, so she hadn't been able to let him know she was coming in advance. After Roy's call, she had finished up what she was working on, spoke with her father and Ron, and left for North Carolina immediately. She had called Jason from the road, but her call went to voice mail. He hadn't yet called her back.

Deputy Ferguson was sitting behind the desk when she walked in. "Is Jason here?" she asked after they greeted each other.

"No, he's gone to Charlotte. He said he wouldn't be back until late."

Charlotte? Stephanie was based in Charlotte for the summer while she completed all of her contracted modeling job. Kelsey gave herself a mental slap. She didn't even know if Stephanie was in North Carolina or New York or Europe. Jealousy was not a feeling Kelsey normally dealt with.

Kelsey's attention came back to Ferguson when he added, "Some preliminary court proceedings against Coeburn's group were scheduled for today. The sheriff had to attend. I'll tell him you stopped by. I know he'll be disappointed that he missed you. Are you staying overnight?"

"No, I have to drive back to Atlanta this afternoon. Just tell him I stopped by." She didn't have time to dwell on her disappointment. She had another appointment to keep.

Kelsey said goodbye to Ferguson and drove to the Wilder farm. Ben, Carolyn, John, and Barbara greeted her from the front porch as she got out of her car and walked toward them. They hugged her and welcomed her into the house, happy to see her again in Mason Valley.

They all gathered around the table in the dining room, and John spread out the paperwork he had assembled for Kelsey. "This should be everything you need to set up a public charity foundation for a mental health clinic in Mason Valley: articles of incorporation, bylaws, and forms to apply for a federal identification number and tax-exempt status," he said as he handed each document to Kelsey.

Kelsey felt her eyes tear up when she saw her mother's name across the top of the first page: The Elizabeth Barrett Mental Health Clinic, Mason Valley, North Carolina.

"You can take care of the filings and other organizing functions while you wait for the building to go up," John added. "You'll need a board of directors when you file your paperwork for incorporation."

Kelsey turned to Ben. "I was wondering if you would accept a position on the board of directors. I've spoken with a local retired doctor that Roy Benson recommended—Doctor Harper. He's agreed to serve as the expert on the board. He lives here in town, so he's close. He said he knows all of you and is willing to accept the position since he needed something to occupy his time. Said he was driving his wife crazy being around the house so much."

Ben nodded and smiled. "I know Doctor Harper. He's a good choice. We golf together occasionally. I keep telling him it's a requirement for retirement: driving your wife crazy." Ben reached out and touched Carolyn's hand. She smiled and clasped his hand in hers, undermining the truth of his statement. Ben added, "I would be honored serve on the board."

"And I'd be happy to volunteer in the office," Carolyn said. More of Kelsey's plans fell into place.

"My dad agreed to be on the board, too. I'll be the interim CEO until I can find someone experienced to take the job," Kelsey said. She turned to John and asked, "Would you mind being our legal counsel?"

"Yes, and pro bono, of course," he agreed. "Nothing would make me happier than to dabble in the legal profession again, especially for such a worthy cause."

Barbara spoke up next, adding, "I know lots of people in Palm Beach through the organizations I've volunteered with over the years. I can start fundraising any time."

"I don't know what to say." Kelsey clasped her hands to her heart. "You have all made my day. Thank you, Barbara. Thank all of you."

"Think nothing of it," Barbara replied. "My friends have roped me into many, *many* fundraising campaigns over the years. It's time they returned the favor."

Kelsey explained more of her plans to the Wilders. The services at the clinic would be free of charge to all who need them. "I plan to set up a network of services in the Mason Valley area that would best fit the needs of the community. I've spoken with the director of the horse-therapy farm, and she's agreed to create a program that could help wounded service members," Kelsey explained.

The idea for the horse-therapy program was based on what Jason had shared about his experience after coming home from the army. The director promised to find spots for anyone that the clinic's psychiatrists felt would benefit from the program.

Kelsey's next chore would be to find the professionals she needed to staff the clinic. She had a call in to her therapist at Walter Reed Hospital, asking for recommendations on the best way to find therapists that would fit the clinic's needs.

By the time the clinic was ready to open, Kelsey hoped to have therapists on staff that could work at least a few hours each week. A rotating group would suffice if, together, they could cover the hours the clinic was open. If she ended up finding someone who was willing to move to Mason Valley for a full-time job, that would be ideal.

Kelsey also planned to incorporate the region's amenities, which she and Ron had explored during their time undercover. As with the horse-therapy program, they could put together programs that would combine fishing, rafting, and hiking with clinical sessions. Using the beauty and healing power of nature would serve the needs of some of their clients.

Kelsey would also involve Stephanie, if she were willing. After all, what better way was there to promote the clinic than commercials featuring a beautiful international model, who also happened to be a local girl?

It would take a lot of coordination, but Kelsey was ready to tackle it and do whatever it took to make it a success. Jason's creed, "Whatever it takes," popped into her head again, as it frequently did, of late. It seemed to apply to her new endeavor—or, endeavors.

Kelsey bid the Wilders goodbye and began the drive back to Atlanta. She checked her phone, but Jason had not returned her call. The Coeburn case was very complicated, with many twists and turns. It involved many people and would take some time to sort out. She was disappointed that she hadn't seen Jason, but she didn't let it deflate her excitement over her new undertaking and how successful the day had been.

It was late and Kelsey was home by the time Jason called. At the sound of his voice, a warm glow filled her heart, and it began to speed up. *Don't faint, Barrett*, she lectured herself. Grandma

Gilbert would say she was having a severe case of "the vapors."

"I'm leaving Charlotte now, on my way home," Jason explained. "I'm sorry I missed you. The meeting with the prosecutors lasted until just a few minutes ago. They're working hard to nail down every piece of evidence they can find."

"Are they close to finishing up the investigation?" Kelsey asked.

"They're still searching for anyone who may have been involved with Coeburn. A few that have been arrested have flipped and will testify against Coeburn. It seems like the investigation just keeps expanding. The prosecutor has assured me, though, that he won't cut any deals with Coeburn himself to lessen his punishment."

Jason asked about Kelsey's day in Mason Valley. She told him about her plans for a mental health clinic and how his parents and grandparents had agreed to help her make it possible.

"That's wonderful," Jason said, sounding as excited for Kelsey's plans as she was. "I know how much this means to you."

"Yes," she agreed, "I had to do something. I saw how lost Allie and Maddie looked when I said goodbye to them just after they were rescued. They endured unimaginable mental stress, and now, they need help to recover and learn skills to help them cope with what happened to them and live happy lives. You and I both know about that." Kelsey paused and took an audible breath.

"You're an angel, Lieutenant Hoot Hoot. Of course, Clint and Daryl Coeburn might say you're an avenging angel, but an angel none the less," Jason said with a smile in his voice.

"Whatever it takes, Wildman." Kelsey smiled into the phone. "I've had good role models in my life."

Jason hung up the phone with a promise that he would be coming down to Atlanta in a couple days and would meet her at Barrett Security.

CHAPTER SEVENTEEN

Kelsey was excited—more excited than she would admit, even to herself. Jason was driving into Atlanta today, and he would be arriving at the office sometime in the afternoon.

She had dressed in her best office attire that morning and had spent extra time on her hair and makeup. "Look at you!" Tina had exclaimed when Kelsey strode by her friend's desk, which was located just outside Kelsey's office. She came around from behind her desk and inspected Kelsey's face. "I believe someone has contoured her makeup today! And your hair! It's never looked so bouncy! My, oh, my. I wonder why?"

"Okay, Tina," Kelsey had said. "I do dress up now and then. I have an important meeting today with a client." In truth, she was interviewing a candidate for a position in the new division, but that didn't account for the extra hour she had spent on her makeup and hair that morning.

"Humph! Sure, honey! Keep telling yourself that," Tina had said as Kelsey stepped into her office. Not much escaped Tina's eagle eyes.

It was almost quitting time when Kelsey looked up from her

desk and saw Jason standing in her doorway quietly eyeing her. Her heart leapt. He was dressed in a suit and tie. Tina stood behind him outside the glass wall of Kelsey's office. She was mouthing, "Oh wow! Oh wow!"

"Oh wow!" was right! Jason made a handsome picture with his tall body leaning casually against the open doorframe. The smile on his face and the sparkle in his dark eyes left her short of breath.

"Hi," was all she could think to say as heat rose in her checks.

"Hi back, Lieutenant Barrett. Are you ready to get some dinner?" Jason asked. He didn't move away from the doorway. His eyes roved over her before coming to rest on her face. His eyes locked with hers. Kelsey recognized the twinkle in their depth. She saw it every time he caused her to blush. Now, Jason knew he was the cause of her blush, and that made her blush even more.

"Have you finished your business with my father?" Kelsey asked in an effort to break eye contact before her face became an unattractive blood-red.

"I have. I'll fill you in, but first, let's get out of here. Where do you want to go?" he asked as he finally moved from the doorframe and straightened his posture.

"I'm preparing dinner at my house, actually. That way, we won't have to shout to be heard, as we would in a crowded restaurant," Kelsey said. "Unless you'd rather go out, that is," she added.

"Home cooking sounds good to me. Lead the way," Jason said as Kelsey picked up her purse and approached him.

Jason still blocked the door. When she got close, he reached out and pulled her into his arms. He kissed her gently, and Kelsey leaned into him, returning his kiss. Jason kissed her once more before reluctantly pulling away. "I couldn't wait any longer to do that. I hope I haven't embarrassed your coworkers."

Kelsey looked over his shoulder and saw Tina through the glass wall. Tina stood at her desk, her eyes round with laughter as she wrapped her arms around her body and hugged herself. She made kissy faces at Kelsey. She was taunting and mocking Kelsey's earlier denial that Jason's expected arrival was nothing special.

Kelsey had been friends with Tina for a long time—even before she came to work at Barrett Security. Tina never let the obvious go unnoticed, especially when Kelsey denied it. "You couldn't embarrass my coworkers if you tired," she replied. "I am about to fire one, though," she added as she led Jason through the door and stopped at Tina's desk to introduce him.

Tina dropped her mime performance long enough to greet Jason, but as Kelsey and Jason turned down the hall leading to the elevators, Kelsey caught Tina's wide smile and her thumbs-up gesture.

They left the building and walked to the adjoining parking lot. Jason followed Kelsey in his pickup and pulled in behind her as she parked in the driveway of a large, white, clapboard house with four small Greek columns that held up the front porch roof. Two magnificent oak trees shrouded in Spanish moss cast shade over a swing at one end of the porch. The swing moved back and forth in the late afternoon breeze.

"This is your grandparents' house, isn't it?" Jason asked as he closed the truck door and came to stand beside Kelsey in the driveway.

"Yes, it is. But how did you know?"

"I heard you mention it in Afghanistan," he said. "See? I paid attention when you talked."

"Oh? But you never said much of anything to me unless it was official business."

"I was afraid. You kept sticking that diamond ring in my face. I didn't want whoever put it on your finger to come gunning for me," Jason replied with a smile.

"Oh!" Kelsey gasped. She paused, then explained, "That was just a shield."

"I know. Ron told me. And Kelsey, truthfully, we weren't in a place where one should get distracted by personal relationships. We needed to concentrate on army business and on surviving. That was our main goal."

Kelsey nodded and turned back to the house. In an effort to change the subject, she pointed to the top floor. "That front room up there with the dormer window was my bedroom when I visited my grandparents as a kid. I used to pretend that I was Rapunzel and that my room was a castle. Other times, I'd play Scarlett O'Hara. I was the belle of the ball in my grandmother's long dresses and pearls. I'd stare out the window, waiting for Rhett to come sweep me off my feet. My grandmother was a big fan of Scarlett and Rhett."

"And did Rhett ever come by?"

"Umm, not yet. Still waiting."

"What happened to them? Your grandparents, I mean," Jason asked, then added with a laugh, "I know what happened to Scarlett and Rhett."

"My grandparents are fine. This house just became too much for them to maintain. They live in an assisted-living community in Decatur, not far from here. Truthfully, this is more house than I need, but I couldn't bear to see them sell it. So, I bought it. Of course, they gave me an excellent deal."

"And your other grandparents? Where do they live?" Jason asked. He was clearly trying to fill in all the blanks spots in her life.

"They're alive and well, too. They live in Savannah." Kelsey knew that Jason's maternal grandparents had both passed, so she was aware of how lucky she was to have both sets of grandparents still with her. "We don't get to see each other as often as I would like, but I try to get down there every two or three months—at least, since I got out of the army. I'll take you down there sometime."

"I'd like to meet them."

"Grandma Gilbert was an English professor at the College of

Savanah, and Grandpa was the City of Savannah's historian—a keeper of the long and notable history of Savannah—before he retired. It was his passion, but now, as he tells it, he's an expert deep-sea fisherman. He loves to take anyone who will go with him out on his fishing boat."

"I love fishing of any type. I can't wait to meet all of them," Jason said as he followed her into the house's cool interior. Kelsey went to her bedroom and changed into shorts and a T-shirt. When she returned, Jason had removed his jacket and tie, rolled up his shirt sleeves, and was sitting on the sofa.

"How about a glass of wine? I also have beer," Kelsey offered. "Then, you can tell me about your business with my father." Jason said either was fine, so she went into the kitchen and opened a bottle of wine that she had been saving for a special occasion. Tonight, with Jason here in her home, seemed like a very special occasion.

She handed Jason a glass of wine, settled herself on the sofa, and turned to him. "So, tell me, what was it you wanted to see my father about?"

"He offered me a job, and I wanted to talk with him about it."

"Really? He never mentioned it to me. Are you taking it?"

"No, I turned him down, but I wanted to tell him face-to-face," Jason said.

"Oh," she said again. "So, you're staying in North Carolina?" Kelsey asked slowly. She couldn't hide the disappointment in her voice. "Stephanie told me about the mayor wanting you to run for sheriff. And it is you home."

"True, I was raised there—or on the coast at least. But, Kelsey, I was just hiding out in the mountains and running away from the stuff that happened in Afghanistan. When I first took a job there, I didn't want to decide anything more complicated than what to have for breakfast. And that was usually whatever I found in the fridge or cupboard." Jason's eyes drifted around the room before coming back to rest on her face. "I think I'm ready for something more involved than looking for stolen cats—although, I do think that's important, just in case you're a cat person. Stopping small crimes stops larger crimes, you know." He repeated his often-used slogan and grinned. "I suggested to the mayor that he have Commissioner Bryant appoint Ferguson to finish my term after I get through with the Coeburn case. And," he added, "I suggested they find money in the budget for a part-time animal control officer."

"Did you find the cat?" Kelsey asked.

"Yes. 'She' turned out to be a 'he,' and 'he' had taken up residence where a 'she' lived. He came back home once his promiscuous adventure was over. Callie is now called Calvin."

Kelsey laughed, then waited for Jason to tell her the rest of his news.

"Actually, let's start dinner now, and then, I'll finish telling you." Jason suddenly appeared nervous. Kelsey didn't push him; maybe she wouldn't like his decision, either. In that case, later would be better.

"I know I said *I* would cook, but how are you with a grill?" Kelsey asked as she stood up and motioned for Jason to follow her into the kitchen. He sat down on a barstool at the counter as Kelsey pulled two steaks from the refrigerator and starting prepping them.

"I think that when I was laid up with my injuries, I watched every cooking show on TV. I can handle a grill."

Kelsey prepared the salad and potatoes while Jason took the steaks and asparagus spears out to the grill on the deck. From the kitchen window, Kelsey watched him as he waited for the grill to heat up. A slight breeze ruffled his hair. He was deep in thought as he leaned on the deck railing and looked across the ravine that ran along the back of the yard. *Jason, Jason*, she silently pleaded. *Please don't break my heart. I don't want to lose you again.*

She had known Jason for almost four years now, but only in

the last few weeks had she confirmed what she'd suspected when they served together in Afghanistan. By working with him in North Carolina and getting to know him better, she had come to see the full depth and breadth of his character. She would trust him with her life. She just hoped she could trust him with her heart as well.

Kelsey took place settings and napkins out to the deck and set up the table near the firepit. The sun had gone down, and the stars were beginning to dot the night sky. A sliver of moon was rising behind the line of trees on the far side of the shallow ravine. Fireflies flashed at the edge of the yard. It was a lovely evening.

Jason lit the kindling in the firepit, and warmth from the glowing embers soon spread toward the eating area. In a couple more weeks, the nights would be too warm for a fire, but tonight, it warmed the cool breeze that blew through the gathering twilight.

Kelsey turned on the music system. The playlist she selected was an eclectic mix of slow and fast tunes, but all were from what Grandma Barrett called the "Golden Age of Music." Soothing, nostalgic sounds floated through the night air.

Much of Kelsey's life, including her taste in music, books, and movies, had been influenced by her grandmothers. One can't go wrong with the tried-and-true. "I want love songs where I can understand the words and feel the emotions," Grandma Barrett always said. There were times when more modern recordings fit her mood, but tonight, this playlist seemed perfect.

It wasn't long before they had the food plated, and they sat down at the table. As they ate, Kelsey updated Jason on her progress with setting up the new division of Barrett Security, organizing the charitable foundation, and searching for clinic staff. Jason watched Kelsey's animated face as she explained that if the clinic in Mason Valley was a success, she planned to expand and set up a second location in Atlanta.

Her father had given her his full support. He had wiped tears from his eyes when he saw that the foundation was named after his late wife and Kelsey's mother.

"My father has given me permission to devote as much time as I need to make both my projects a reality. Being the boss's daughter certainly has its advantages," Kelsey added with a laugh.

"Are you sure you aren't spreading yourself too thin—taking on too much for one person?" Jason asked. His current job as a sheriff with a short staff and a major federal investigation that began in his backyard had showed him what 'stretched too thin' really meant.

"I can handle it," Kelsey assured him. "The new division is coming together smoothly, and I'm hiring people would will carry most of the daily workload. They'll only need minimum supervision. I can also set up the clinic without sacrificing the attention both organizations need. It all centers around the people I hire. And, if I do become overwhelmed, I won't be shy about asking for assistance."

Kelsey paused. She needed—earnestly needed—to make Jason understand how important she felt the mental health services were. "Jason, both of my projects are important, but a mental health clinic is badly needed in Mason Valley. You and I had top-tier psychiatric help after our injuries, and we still struggled to get back to where we were before the ambush."

"The army's secrecy was partially to blame for that," Jason said, "but I know what you mean. An unbiased person to help you understand the aftermath of trauma is important."

"I don't want others, especially young people like Allie and Maddie, to try to get over their nightmares alone. And there are veterans out there who might not be getting the help they need for a variety of reasons: cost, location, or even the fact that their problems may not appear until long after they leave military service."

"You're doing a great thing," Jason said. "You know I'll help you and support you in any way I can."

Finally, Kelsey couldn't stand the suspense regarding Jason's decision about his future any longer. "That's enough about me and my pet projects. I'm dying over here, Wildman. Spill. What are your plans after you resign from the sheriff's position?"

Jason leaned back in his chair, took a sip of his wine, and said, "After a small-town sheriff took down a major sex-trafficking operation—with the help of two hotshot investigators from Atlanta—it seems the small-town sheriff is a hot commodity." He pushed back his chair a little and crossed his legs. He swirled his wine in his glass. "I've had a *plethora* of job offers." He smiled at her.

"That's good, right?" Kelsey asked.

"Well, yes, it is. I turned your father down because I don't think I should mix business with pleasure." He cast a glance at her. "And I was afraid that, one day, I'd rip that tie right off of Richard and stuff it down his throat." He smiled, belying the threat.

Jason placed his wine glass on the table and rose from his chair. He came around the table to stand in front of Kelsey. He reached for her hand and pulled her up from her seat. "I turned the mayor down because, well, there's this girl—no, there's this woman—who lives in Atlanta and..." He paused and ran his hands up and down her arms.

Kelsey felt the familiar tingling at his touch. "It's always a woman with you, Wilder. Is this woman wise like the Indian woman?" Kelsey teased. She liked where this was headed.

The soft sounds of music mixed with the chirping of crickets floated across the deck. Jason put his arms around Kelsey and led her into slowly swaying with the music.

"As I was saying, there's this *wise*, beautiful, compassionate woman in Atlanta, and I want her to help me decide which of my other two offers I should accept."

"What does this woman have to do with your career choice? Why would she care?"

"That's why I'm nervous. I don't know if she cares or, if she does care, how much." Kelsey started to say something, but Jason placed a finger on her lips. "Let me explain. I have an offer from the FBI's Joint Terrorism Task Force here in Atlanta. My father may have something to do with that offer, although he denies it. I also have an offer from the Criminal Investigations Division of the Atlanta Police department. I interviewed with both today."

"And what did you decide?"

"I was thinking that this woman—if she cares, that is—should have some input on the job I choose. I was wondering which job she thinks she could live with."

"Jason," Kelsey whispered, "I think this woman would be crazy not to care for you, regardless of what job you have." She wrapped her arms around his neck and leaned back to look into his face. "You should choose whatever will make you the happiest."

"Happiest?" Jason paused, as if thinking. "What will make me the happiest, you say? Well, if this woman would tell me that she's interested in me...as more than friends, I mean... interested in a relationship with me, I mean..." Jason paused again.

"What would happen then?" Kelsey prompted.

Jason's mouth twisted in a self-deprecating smile. "God, I told you I was Captain Suave! I'm stammering like a twelve-year-old. A friend once told me, 'Opportunities, man! Never miss your opportunities!'" Jason mimicked Ron's voice, then added. "Good advice."

Kelsey smiled, and waited for Jason to finish. He was aggravatingly, slowly attempting to say something. But she wasn't going to help him by putting words in his mouth. He was all on his own. It gave her immense pleasure to see cool Jason Wilder flustered around her for a second time. Turn-about was fair play, according to the old saying.

Jason twirled Kelsey around, keeping time with the music, then pulled her back into his arms. "I would be happy—no, I'd be ecstatic—if this woman felt the same way about me."

Jason stopped moving, placed his finger under her chin, and tilted her face up to his. "As the sheriff, I have to ask whether the person who witnessed said sheriff fall in love with this woman is willing to make a statement about a future with him. Will the witness please answer the question?"

"The truth is..." Kelsey paused. She felt Jason flinch. Did he think she might reject him or put conditions on her answer? "Said sheriff must be blind if he can't see that this woman has fallen madly in love, too—with Jason "Wildman" Wilder, world-famous small-town sheriff. To put a fine point on her testimony, this woman wants to get to know everything about him: his annoying little habits, what makes him sad, what makes him happy. She will swear to the truth of this under oath."

Jason's shoulders relaxed. "What annoying habits?" he asked with a smile. The teasing sparkle was back in his eyes.

"Will you quit stalling and kiss me?"

"Yes, ma'am. I always follow orders." Jason pulled her close, looked into her eyes, and whispered, "I guess the legend is true."

"What do you mean?" Kelsey pulled back and looked up at him. "You wished for love when we hiked up Love Vine Mountain?"

"Not exactly," Jason said. "I wished not just for love, but for love between you and me. It was playful—and wishful thinking. At the time, I thought you and Ron were a couple. Then, when I found out that wasn't the case, there was Richard to consider. And yet, my wish seems to be coming true. And what was your wish?"

"My wish was broader." Kelsey smiled and laced both arms around his neck. She ruffled the hair on the back of his head. "At the time, I was still in shock. Finding you alive knocked me for a loop, and then there was my meltdown. I was embarrassed. I wished for love, happiness, and contentment. Jason, you fill all three of my wishes."

"You pushed the legend and asked for more than one wish? Greedy!"

"Yes—greedy for you." Kelsey pulled his head down and softly brushed her lips across his, barely touching him. She pulled away and then came back and brushed her lips across his again. "How does it feel to be teased like that?" She moved to brush his lips again, but he brought his hands up to both sides of her face, holding her still.

"Wonderful! But now it's my turn," Jason whispered as his mouth moved closer to hers, yet hovered just out of reach. Kelsey strained to reach his lips, but he shook his head. "Don't rush," he whispered, then moved his lips a little closer. An electric spark pulsed between them. Jason's lips finally touched hers—but just barely. He pulled back ever so slightly, letting his breath tease her lips before his mouth closed over hers.

Jason charted the course, and Kelsey willingly followed and gave herself up to the deeply moving kiss. He began to sway them in time with the music while never breaking contact with her lips.

Kelsey's last conscious thought before totally losing herself in the magic of this kiss and the wonder of her love was, "No one can kiss like Jason 'Wildman' Wilder."

Etta James's soulful voice wrapped around them and enclosed them in a private world of mutual happiness. It was a fitting song, but it was just a backdrop to the two people who, at the moment, were not aware of anything except each other.

They had faced more challenges in their young years than most couples would face in a lifetime. A tiny ember of longing that had started in a warzone had flamed into love coupled with deep respect in the peaceful shadows of Love Vine Mountain. Regardless of what problems came their way in the future, they would face them together, just as they had searched for the truth of what happened to them in Afghanistan and fought to take down a cult led by a monster.

They would never forget what happened in Afghanistan or on Love Vine Mountain, but the healing love they had found in each other would temper the memories and become the strongest pillar of their lives.

EPILOGUE

The late October day in Mason Valley, North Carolina, was going to be a beautiful one. Cool, but not cold. Warm, but not hot. In a word, perfect. A weak sun valiantly broke through the clouds around the top of Love Vine Mountain, bringing with it the promise of bright, sunny weather. The autumn leaves warmed in the rising sun and celebrated a new day in colors of red, gold, and orange. A gentle breeze rustled the dry grasses around the city park and across the dormant farmland.

The blaze of color on the mountain signaled that another summer was gone. The hot sweltering days were now replaced by cooler weather. Activity in the city was slowing down as tourists left and life returned to normal. The citizens could take a short respite until the holiday crowds descended to enjoy a country Christmas in the valley. In January, they would again return to calm and quiet until spring arrived. And then, they'd start the whole routine all over again.

It was the perfect day for a wedding. Located at the foot of picturesque Love Vine Mountain, Mason Valley city park had been turned into a wedding venue. The park was festooned with decorative arches. A bandstand and dance floor were strategically placed away from the carpeted path that led to the altar. Long tables were set up near the soccer field, just waiting for Rita's Café to fill them with food.

The wedding ceremony was by invitation only for close friends and relatives, but all the residents of Mason Valley were invited to attend the reception for the marriage of Kelsey Elizabeth Barrett, the person responsible for the Elizabeth Barrett Mental Health Clinic located just outside of town, and Jason Benjamin Wilder, Mason Valley's former sheriff.

What had initially seemed like an impossible task—planning a large wedding in four months—came together surprisingly quickly and smoothly. Neither Kelsey nor Jason wanted a long engagement. They had firsthand experience with how life could change in an instant. Neither wanted to wait very long to join their lives together.

When Kelsey and Jason informed their families that they were planning to get married soon—at city hall, if necessary—Jason's mother, Carolyn, had said, "City hall won't be necessary. We can do this. We have a whole town that will help."

Kelsey asked Stephanie to be one of her bridesmaids. Stephanie was now dating an ad executive she had met in Charlotte and had moved on from thoughts of a romance with Jason. Stephanie had immediately accepted Kelsey's request and added, "Let me know your color scheme, and I'll take care of the bridesmaids' attire."

"Are you sure?" Kelsey asked, hardly believing what she had heard. That was the one part of wedding planning—outfitting a diverse group of women with different tastes and styles while doing her job in Atlanta and setting up a mental health clinic in North Carolina—that Kelsey hadn't been sure how to pull off.

"Fashion is what I do," Stephanie replied simply. She ended up taking the bridesmaids on a shopping trip to New York. Using her contacts at several fashion houses and under her guidance, the bridesmaids had all found the perfect dresses in the perfect colors.

Barbara and Carolyn arranged for the Ladies Sewing Circle to nip, tuck, and do any needed alterations. Grandmothers Barrett and Gilbert supervised the alteration of Kelsey's mother's wedding dress until it fit as if it had been made for Kelsey.

All it took was a quick phone call to Mayor Landry to book the city park as the wedding venue. The Wilders' minister would perform the ceremony. A band made up of Jason's college friends who had a good following in the area was hired to provide the music. The remaining piece fell into place when Rita volunteered to cater the affair.

Coordinating the wedding was handed off to Jen, Kelsey's sister-in-law and Joe's wife. Jen was an experienced organizer and managed a volunteer group at Fort Bragg that assisted military families when their loved ones were deployed. Coordinating a wedding was a simple task compared to the situations Jen usually managed. She kept everything moving along on schedule and handled any problems that arose with ease.

With Kelsey free from having to coordinate the wedding plans, she could concentrate on her projects. The mental health clinic had opened in early August, as promised by the general contractor. Kelsey hired a psychiatrist with exceptional credentials that had been recommended by Dr. Watson, Kelsey's prior therapist at Walter Reed Hospital. Dr. Blankenship, a divorced mother of two from Alexandria, Virginia, was willing to move permanently to Mason Valley. She was an empty nester, with both of her children now in college at Duke University in Durham. It didn't take much persuasion to get her to agree to a move that would bring her closer to her children.

Kelsey also found two other psychiatrists—a husband-and-wife team willing to drive into Mason Valley from Asheville—who would cover the clinic two days per week when the patient load demanded it. A retired nurse ran the office, with Carolyn Wilder volunteering whenever extra help was needed.

True to her word, Barbara Wilder had started a charitable fundraising effort called Saving Minds and had pressured her Palm Beach society friends into donating time and money. Grandma Gilbert, not to be outdone, roused Savannah's society ladies to the cause under the same name, Saving Minds.

The clinic had been open for just over two months, but already, the number of patients was growing. Kelsey had convinced Allie and Maddie to visit with Dr. Blankenship at least once per week. They had yet to miss an appointment. Their youthful resilience was helping them move ahead as they tried to put their experience with Coeburn behind them.

The clinic's current patients also included a fourteen-year-old girl whose parents had brought her there after she had run away from home during summer break. There were four wounded veterans, one of whom had lost his leg in an IED attack. Another was homeless, unable to keep a job outside the structured military life. The director of the horse-therapy farm gave him a job taking care of the horses, and he had recently moved into a small apartment above the local drug store on Main Street. Two other veterans had PTSD, flashbacks, and nightmares after losing their fellow soldiers in battle. They had not been physically injured but needed someone to talk to, to explain the unexplainable to them. It was a valuable exercise in healing, as Kelsey well knew. She checked on them all weekly, and thus far, the reports indicated that they were improving, with a few setbacks now and then. Kelsey was glad that they were progressing in their recovery and taking back their lives.

Stephanie starred in commercials for the clinic on local TV. They were spreading the word and encouraging others to take advantage of the clinic's services.

Jason ultimately decided to take the job with the Atlanta Police Department in the Criminal Investigations Division. The FBI's Terrorism Task Force would have required him to travel. Perhaps he would be open to a job like that in the future, but right now, he didn't want to travel and be away from Kelsey. He'd had enough of life among strangers and away from the people he loved.

Jason frequently travelled to Charlotte as the prosecutors continued to build their case against Coeburn, his followers, and his clients. The trial would be held the following spring, and according to the prosecutors, conviction was a certainty.

Jason had located the five soldiers who had survived the ambush in Afghanistan. They were all still in the army and stationed together in Alabama. The night of the raid, they had fallen behind the forward group of five while getting into position. They were in the right place at the right time to save themselves but arrived just in time to see the carnage left behind by the attack. Most of them had sustained burns as they tried to pull their fellow soldiers from the fire.

The soldiers were all invited to the wedding and had arrived in town a couple days ago. Jason still owned his house on Willow street—it was a place to stay when he and Kelsey made their frequent trips to Mason Valley—and the soldiers were staying there now. Jason and Kelsey had spent the previous evening with them recounting stories of when they served together.

Reconnecting had been therapeutic for all of them. Of course, the evening could not go by without someone bringing up the nickname, Lieutenant Hoot Hoot. Kelsey quieted the teasing by sharing the story of how she and Jason had used that same call signal to help him locate her, Allie, and Maddie on Love Vine Mountain.

Jason and Kelsey chose not to share the full story of Major Burton's betrayal, adhering to the request of the major who had given them the truth about the failed mission. And, they reasoned, why cause the soldiers to relive the nightmare? The five men appeared to have moved on with their lives and their military careers.

Jason still reveled in his ability to rattle Kelsey whenever he

was presented with the opportunity. He'd kiss her unexpectedly—
as usual, a light kiss, barely touching her lips—just to see the blush
rise in her cheeks. Kelsey admitted that it annoyed her sometimes,
especially when she was in deep concentration on a project and he
diverted her attention. She knew that he knew it annoyed her, and
that's why he did it. Kelsey was more annoyed with herself. Each
time she felt the tingling heat caused by his touch run over her,
she couldn't control the blush that spread over her fair skin. Yes,
she did get annoyed with him at times, but not enough to ask him
to stop.

Kelsey, painfully, missed her mother during the planning of
her wedding. The support and guidance of Kelsey's grandmothers
during the most important event in her life eased some of her feelings of loss, but not all. Her father missed her mother, too. Kelsey
saw a wistfulness in his eyes each time the wedding was brought
up.

It was four o'clock and the sun was starting its descent behind
Love Vine Mountain when the wedding procession began. Joe,
acting as an usher, escorted three sets of grandparents, Jason's parents, and Mr. and Mrs. Jackson from Charlotte to a place of honor
in the front row. There had been an extended explanation to the
Jacksons to clear up why Kelsey and Jason were just now getting
married.

Jason had asked Ron to be his best man. The two men entered,
took their places on the dais under the arch, and turned to face
their guests. Missy and KJ came down the aisle first, followed by
Joe's children, Lizzy and Joe, Junior. They dropped handfuls of
petals from native wildflowers along the carpet leading to the dais.
Five bridesmaids—Cate, Allie, Maddie, Stephanie, and Victoria—
followed next. Their dresses of burnished orange and tawny beige,
along with their bouquets of bronze-colored mums and Queen
Anne's lace, rivaled the colors of the leaves on Love Vine Mountain.

The bridesmaids were escorted by five soldiers—the surviving team members from the mission in Afghanistan—who stood straight and tall in their uniforms. The soldiers and bridesmaids took their places beside the minister, Jason, and Ron. Next came Tina as the maid of honor, followed by Kelsey on Colonel Barrett's arm. As they began their march toward the alter, the colonel whispered, "She's with you today, you know."

Kelsey swallowed back tears and squeezed his arm. "I know," she replied.

Jason came down from the dais and took Kelsey's hand from her father. Before they turned to face the minister, Jason whispered, "I love you," then bent his head and brushed his lips against hers—his signature kiss. Kelsey blushed as his kiss set off the familiar tingle throughout her body.

Kelsey handed her bouquet to Tina, an arrangement in shades of red, orange, and gold mixed with foliage of dark green and sprigs of lime green. In place of ribbon, entwined throughout the bouquet was the orangey-yellow vine from Love Vine Mountain.

Once Jason and Kelsey had exchanged rings and pledged to love each other forever, the park was opened to all citizens of the town. The celebration could begin.

Stephanie snagged the wedding bouquet from Tina's outstretched hand during the bouquet toss. Toasts were made. Jason and Kelsey took to the dance floor for their first dance. They moved as one as the female singer in the cover band did a beautiful rendition of Adele's "Love Song." Jason sang quietly in Kelsey's ear as they danced. Kelsey's love for Jason shone in her eyes as she acknowledged the truth of the words in the song.

Congratulations and handshakes followed as the newly married couple was celebrated by the boisterous crowd. Everyone helped themselves to the tables laden with food. The sounds of fun and laughter floated up Love Vine Mountain, partially erasing the horrendous events that had happened there only a few months before.

The sun had gone down and the stars filled the night skies when Jason went in search of Kelsey. He found her surrounded by citizens of Mason Valley, chatting and laughing as they told stories of their own wedding days. Kelsey gave them her undivided attention as she listened to each of them. She loved the people of this town, and it was clear that they felt the same about her. But Jason was ready to have his wife all to himself.

"Are you ready to get out of here, Mrs. Wilder?" Jason asked as Kelsey left the group and came to stand beside him.

"I am, Mr. Wilder."

Jason bent and kissed her. This time, it was more than just a teasing brush. Kelsey responded in kind.

It was fate, more than a dubious superstition, that had brought them back together in Mason Valley and given them the chance to love each other. Their kiss on this cool October night sealed a pact and a promise to protect that love and each other for the rest of their lives.

Whatever it takes.

Made in United States
North Haven, CT
08 February 2023

32202823R00171